THE GLASS MAGICIAN

THE TANESH EMPIRE TRILOGY: BOOK 1

LEAH CUTTER

KNOTTED ROAD PRESS

The Glass Magician
The Tanesh Empire Trilogy: Book One
Copyright © 2018 Leah Cutter
All rights reserved
Published by Knotted Road Press
www.KnottedRoadPress.com

ISBN: 978-1-943663-75-0

Interior design copyright © 2018 Knotted Road Press http://www.KnottedRoadPress.com

Cover design copyright © 2018 Humbert Glaffo
https://99designs.com/profiles/1756599

Never miss a release!
If you'd like to be notified of new releases, sign up for my newsletter.

I only send out newsletters once a quarter, will never spam you, or use your email for nefarious purposes. You can also unsubscribe at any time.

http://www.LeahCutter.com/newsletter/

The Shadow Wars Trilogy

The Raven and the Dancing Tiger

The Guardian Hound

War Among the Crocodiles

The Clockwork Fairy Kingdom Trilogy

The Clockwork Fairy Kingdom

The Maker, the Teacher, and the Monster

The Dwarven Wars

Seattle Trolls Trilogy

The Changeling Troll

The Princess Troll

The Fairy-Bridge Troll

Tanish Empire Trilogy

The Glass Magician

The Desert Heart

The Ghost Dog

The Cassie Stories

Poisoned Pearls

Tainted Waters

Spoiled Harvest

Bloodies Ice

MAP

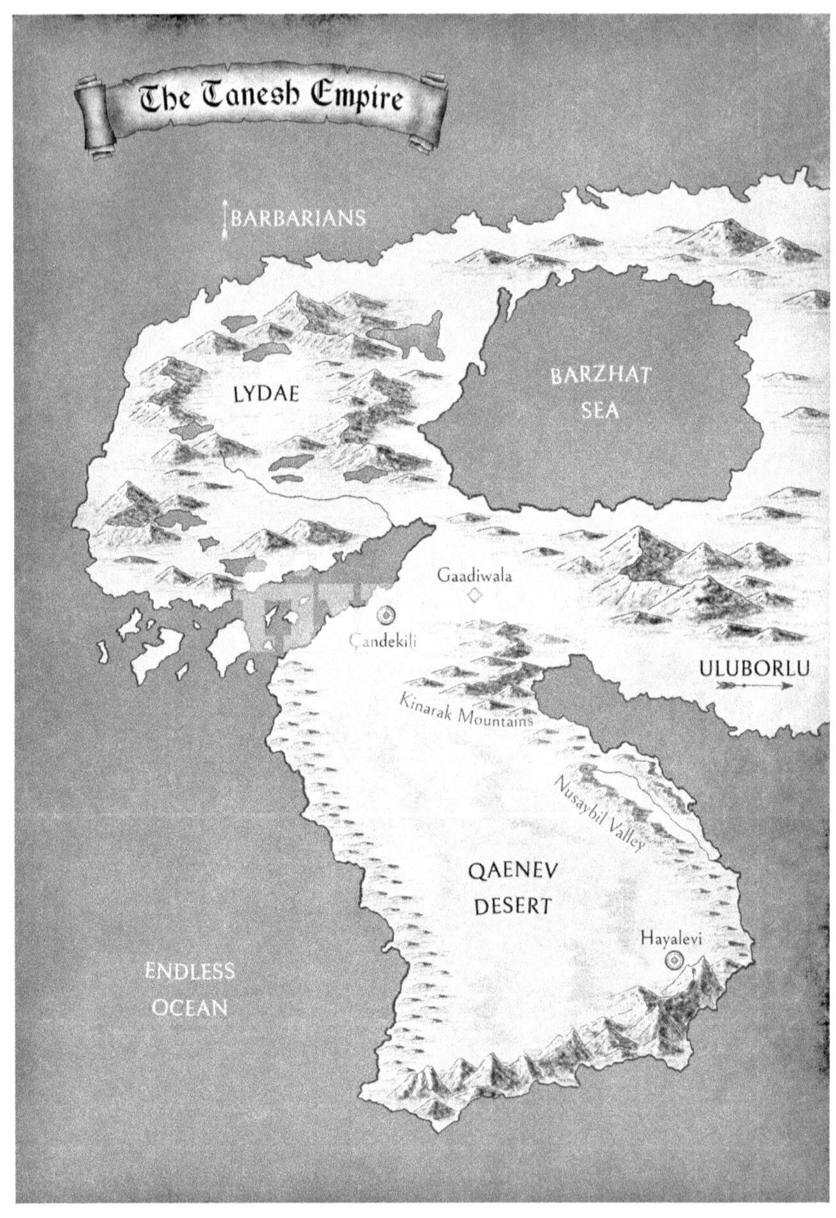
The Tanesh Empire
BARBARIANS
LYDAE
BARZHAT
SEA
Gaadiwala
Çandekili
ULUBORLU
Kinarak Mountains
Nusaybil Valley
QAENEV
DESERT
Hayalevi
ENDLESS
OCEAN

PRONUNCIATION GUIDE

Ç—pronounced as the S in "Sea." TRU-llis (Trulliç)

Zh—pronounced as the S in "Measure." MEER-i-zhah (Myrizhah)

ş—Pronounced as SH. KAR-desh (Kardeş)

ğ—Pronounced with a hard, guttural sound. AH-gkhree-khat (*ağrikat*)

CHAPTER ONE

TRULLIÇ

TRULLIÇ FIRST WALKED THE DESERT when he was twelve.

He woke with the dawn, throwing back the heavy sheepskin that had kept him warm during the cold desert night, and eagerly looked around.

The horizon blazed orange and purple, as though it was on fire. No clouds covered the sun's face, of course. Even during the rainy season, this side of the Kinarak mountains rarely saw storms. Streams of sunlight—like fingers—stole across the horizon, tickling the sparse brush on the hill.

Trulliç shook his head. His cousins would tease him mercilessly if they heard him talking like that, mimicking the poetry that Atça, Trulliç's mentor, had insisted that Trulliç memorize.

Below the foothills where Trulliç had camped stretched the Qaenev desert. Trulliç stared hard at it, willing for it to show itself to him.

The sand glittered on the places the early light first touched it, then settled into a pale gold color. It stretched to the far horizon, where Trulliç had been taught grew a foreboding mountain range that dropped abruptly into the endless ocean.

Much closer, but still out a good distance on the flat sands, stood a dark jut of rock. It sheltered an altar to Serril, the god of deserts and desolate places.

The first place Trulliç would officially visit on this, his manhood journey.

Thorn bushes struggled to grow in the border between the true desert and the foothills. A tiny yellow lizard skittered across the sand, popping up out of its hole then racing across to a second hiding place where it would escape the heat of the day. To his left, birds lazily circled the sky, welcoming the dawn.

Nothing else moved. No brown and white sheep grazed for sparse feed. No tiny mice hopped across the quickly heating sand. No caravans made their way along the trade route to the Kinarak mountains, then up the Ladikah pass and to the first town of Gaadiwala.

Trulliç had seen the endless ocean as a small boy. It was one of his first memories. His mother, Myrizhah, still talked of the journey with awe, all that they'd seen, how afraid he'd been of the waves.

He'd never told her what he remembered: How alive the ocean had been, the waves constantly talking to themselves. It had been too loud, too active, too overwhelming. He hadn't been afraid, not exactly. But he hadn't liked it. In fact, it had been the opposite of everything he liked.

Quiet ruled the Qaenev desert. Peace settled into Trulliç's bones. He took a deep breath, breathing in the smell of the dry foothills, the lighter scent of the sand, the air tinged with the precious spices he carried in his pack, of cinnamon and cardamom, of thyme and rosemary, of mint and sage. He'd use the spices either in trade (if he met anyone), or as offerings.

As part of his manhood journey, Trulliç would start his search for his home, to find where he truly belonged, where his magic would be the most powerful.

Magic tied a male magician to a piece of land, whether it was a forest, a lake, a collection of boulders in the foothills, the slope of a mountain, or even an oasis in the desert. While a strong enough magician might be able to affect all trees anywhere, he could only do truly special work with trees growing in his own grove.

Trulliç hoped to find his place, his part of the desert, with his first manhood journey. Atça, his mentor, had warned him that it frequently took several tries, particularly with an area as large as the Qaenev desert. Plus, Trulliç had never dreamed of the desert, something Atça told him was very odd. Normally a magician dreamed often of his home, letting his feet guide him on his manhood journey.

No matter. Trulliç was determined to prove his mentor wrong. His feet would lead him to his home. He just had to watch where they went.

Trulliç quickly gathered up the blanket he'd slept on and his sheepskin, rolling them up and tying them to the bottom of his pack. He shivered in the cool morning air, having slept in just a shirt and unbelted pants. Before he reached for warmer clothes, he patiently rolled up the sleeves on his plain, unbleached muslin shirt, uncovering his hands. Then he rolled his gray pants up around his waist, belting it with a rope. He pulled out his heavy wool tunic, sleeveless and dyed a dull red. When he put it on over the shirt, it hung to the middle of his thighs, too big for him, like all of the hand-me-down clothes he'd inherited from his cousins.

Though this was Trulliç's manhood journey, Myrizhah wasn't rich enough to buy him all new clothes. Mended and recently-cleaned clothes would have to do.

As the heat grew over the course of the day, Trulliç would change out of his wool tunic into a much lighter one that *was* new, a gift from his mentor, made from a stiff linen and striped in gold and green—the pale gold of the desert at first light, and the light green of the hills at the start of the rainy season.

Gold and green were also the colors of the old kings who'd ruled before the *Padisha-i-Ghazi*, the great emperor. Because of Trulliç's studies, he knew that the emperor had ruled for approximately two hundred years (many records had been lost, and scholars argued over the exact date the emperor had come to power). Most of the villagers believed the emperor was immortal, that he'd always been the emperor. They knew very little of the old kings. They easily complied with the latest decree that the emperor be publically thanked at every feast, like he was one of the gods.

Trulliç knew better. He also knew better than to try to say anything to his cousins.

However, Trulliç also had more reason to learn about the old kings than most.

While Myrizhah had been pregnant with Trulliç, she'd bought a tin horseshoe, intending for Trulliç's magical power to be bound to the northern mountains that his father had come from.

Like all women pregnant with a babe of power, a magical blood hound had followed Myrizhah everywhere, intent on protecting her and the child. When Trulliç's birth had started to go wrong, the blood hound had transformed the tin horseshoe into glass.

Myrizhah insisted that meant that Trulliç was a desert magician. Glass was made from sand blasted with such heat that it melted. It was also very expensive, and took a lot of precision and skill to make.

Did the horseshoe mean that Trulliç would be a powerful magician?

His mother certainly hoped so. She'd insisted that the tavern her family owned have a horseshoe mortared into the stones above the doorway.

Atça couldn't confirm if Myrizhah was correct or not. Atça, in addition to being the town of Gaadiwala's only magician, also read dreams for the local people. He claimed that no one had ever had any dreams that foretold of Trulliç becoming a great magician. Plus, there were no stories of glass magicians who'd performed heroic deeds, though there was usually at least one magician who lived out in an oasis in the desert.

As no other magicians lived in the Qaenev desert at the current time, it was up to Trulliç to find his home on his own.

The first morning that Trulliç would walk the desert, he planned to travel for a few hours, then wait out the heat of the day in the shade next to Serril's altar. Only the desperate trekked across the sands during the day; most traveled in the early morning and the late afternoon and into the night.

Trulliç broke his fast with one of the travel rolls that Myrizhah had baked for him, made out of cracked wheat, hazelnut pieces, and slivers of dried figs, spiced with mint and nutmeg, all held together with *meslit* syrup, made from the boiled bark of the *meslit* thorn trees that grew everywhere.

Atça had once traded for some honey so Trulliç could taste how similar the two were.

Trulliç understood the comparison but preferred *meslit* and the smoky flavor that came from the wood fires that refined the syrup to the pure honey that his mentor waxed lyrically about. Many poems from the olden days, before the emperor, had been written about milk and honey, two foods that Trulliç really didn't like.

He'd dutifully learned the poems along with the other students. However, Trulliç didn't believe that his tastes would change as he grew older, that he would grow to like the sweeter honey and the softer rugs that Atça sat on.

While Atça was very wise, he was wrong about a few things. For example, how the wolf star traveled across the sky during the rainy season. Not that Trulliç would ever try to correct his mentor. Myrizhah had taught him better than to question his elders.

Finally, Trulliç was ready to start his manhood journey. He put on his wide leather belt, checking his knife, the two bronze coins hidden in a secret pocket, and his horseshoe.

Trulliç, now looking out at Qaenev's endless sands, seeing the boundless desert for the first time, knew that he'd finally come home. This was his place, where he belonged. He felt it in his bones, the sand already singing underneath his skin.

Now, he just had to find which part of it was his home.

Trulliç paused at the edge of the true desert, where the hard stones gave way to open sand. Hot winds blew across the gulf at him, carrying the dry scent of the land. Twisted thorn bushes grew on this side, barely reaching mid-calf, with thin, leafless branches that only the most hungry of goats would eat. Up ahead, still further out than Trulliç had first thought, stood the first station of his manhood journey: the small rock building that held Serril's altar.

This area of the desert wouldn't support a full temple. No water lay under the sands. So what he saw was just a lone, rough building, containing a simple altar, with no priest in full-time attendance of it.

Trulliç would still make the journey to the altar first, then travel to the south and east, to one of the minor caravan routes through the Qaenev desert. He wasn't lazy, like the stories he'd learned about Atyla the scribe who'd tricked his way out of his chores and only pretended to visit the altars of the gods, and instead, kept the offerings himself. Atyla had been punished for his laziness eventually, though Trulliç had still admired his cleverness.

The major caravan routes skirted the desert completely and stayed closer to the mountains that ran along the east and west coasts. Minor routes would follow an oasis trail that only sometimes held water, depending on the season. As Trulliç was making his journey just after the rainy months, water should await him once he found a trail.

Trulliç assumed that his home would be somewhere along one of the caravan routes. He anticipated that he'd always have travelers going through it, kind of like the tavern that his family owned back in Gaadiwala.

He just had to take that first step onto the sands.

Atça, as well as Trulliç's oldest cousin Bekbel who'd also been to the desert, had told him that where the foothills ended and the desert truly began was unclear. The lands overlapped and the border shifted depending on how much rain had come that season, how strong the winds were, and from which direction they blew.

To Trulliç, the difference was as bright as the oil lamps Atça burned in his house during the rainy season, lights encased in glass that no one else in town could afford.

Still, Trulliç paused. This was the start of his manhood journey, right here. Not the visit to the altar just a few hours' walk away. Not leaving Gaadiwala and traveling by himself through the Ladikah pass, making it to the other side of the Kinarak mountains on his own.

Stepping onto the sands for the very first time. That was truly the start of his journey, the start of the rest of his life.

Trulliç reached down for the glass horseshoe held securely against his belt with special leather straps that Atça had given him. Even in the heat of the morning, the horseshoe felt cool and smooth against his fingertips.

Trulliç took one last deep breath, holding in the air of the foothills, the ground behind him.

And stepped forward to find his destiny.

The world exploded into being around him.

Trulliç felt as though he'd already walked the length of the desert more than once, his feet knowing how long it would take him to go from the Kinarak mountains to the far coast. He felt the rocky mountains that made up the southern border, the less desolate foothills to the west and east. He tasted the salt in the air beyond them, harsh and hateful to the desert heat.

Trails went through the desert, springs of water that the desert suffered to live. Men, too, traveled across its sands, carrying the precious metals found down along the coast along with spices and exotic birds.

Trulliç felt as though he could find every single caravan, as if he could draw a map of every trail with his eyes closed.

The smell of baked sand suddenly carried many other scents as well, like the sweet palms that grew in the oasis, the secret salt caves that lay buried under the nearby rock, and the musty scent of lizard burrows. Ground-nesting birds cawed sweetly to their young, well hidden by their dusty color. Sand shifted in the wind, a sliding sound as it brushed over the tops of dunes.

Trulliç blinked, surprised. If he felt this much just stepping onto the desert, how much more would he feel when he found his home? His heart would surely burst with the joy of it.

Suddenly, Trulliç understood why the heroes of old broke into song when they made a great discovery, won a colossal battle, or even found their love.

Trulliç wouldn't sing himself, not loudly, not now. The desert left him quiet.

Besides, if his cousins ever found out about it, he'd never live it down.

He still hummed mightily as he took his next step, and his next, and his next, swinging his arms open and free.

***

Trulliç looked up with dismay.

Damn it! Why were the rocks sheltering Serril's altar so far to his left again!

Walking to the altar should have been easy. He could *see* the rocks that held the altar shimmering up ahead.

However, it was as though his feet had a mind of their own. Despite the heat of the sand, the desert enticed him and made him wander without thought.

Trulliç sighed, lined himself up with the rocks, then took a step toward them. Then another.

He looked away on his third step, only to find he'd taken another half dozen or so over the sands without meaning to, not going anywhere near his goal.

Why was he having such problems? It wasn't because he thought that his true home lay in that direction. It didn't lay in *any* direction, as far as he could tell.

Trulliç gritted his teeth and focused on walking toward the rocks again. He was *not* about to fail the first part of his manhood journey. How could he get lost on the way to Serril's altar? It was visible from the foothills!

His cousins would laugh themselves silly if Trulliç had to admit a failure like that.

It took all of Trulliç's concentration, as well as most of the morning, to reach his destination.

The building holding Serril's altar was shoddily constructed. The rocks hadn't been shaved or formed to match. They looked randomly stuck together, as though each came from the bottom of the builder's barrel.

The mortar between them looked just as poor, flaking away with every wind.

The temple (though Trulliç wasn't convinced it deserved that name) had three walls connected one to another, like a square U. The fourth wall wasn't connected. Instead, it stood just inside the open doorframe, as if to suggest a door, with a wide opening on either side.

Trulliç bowed his head and stepped inside. At least it was cooler in there. However, he already knew he didn't want to spend much time in the temple. His skin crawled, as if ants covered it, making him twitchy.

Light streamed in from holes in the rock walls. The roof slanted from one side to the other, leaving Trulliç with barely enough room to stand up straight. When he reached his full height in a couple of years, he'd have to duck his head.

Inside the tiny square room a horizontal slate slab took up one entire wall. Nothing indicated that it was the altar, but Trulliç didn't see where else it could be. Sand had blown across the slab, piling up in the far right corner.

With a sigh, Trulliç carefully knelt, then started brushing the sand from the altar.

Underneath the sand, he unearthed two camels that had been left there, made out of twisted branches. Probably someone's offering, asking for a safe journey for their caravan across the desert. They were about as long as Trulliç's forearm and were cleverly made, the ends near the feet tied off with red thread, as well as around the noses. The male had a black stripe down the center of his back, and the other, presumably female, had a similar white stripe.

Trulliç carefully placed the camels back down on the now clean altar, then he closed his eyes, folded his hands in front of him, and prayed to Serril, asking for the cleverness to find his home, for the courage to defend it from all others, and for the patience to let it grow and become all that he'd ever imagined.

When he finished, he dug out his own offerings from his pack. He'd chosen a flat stone about the size of his palm. Then he'd carved a six-sided star on both sides, the symbol of Serril. It had taken him a lot of time and skill to get the stars perfect (and a few nicked fingers when his knife or his concentration had slipped). He'd followed the traditional form and made each star out of two interlocking triangles.

He'd then rubbed a red dye into the lines of the stars to make them stand out. Once the dye had set, he'd painted one side of the stone white and the other side black.

Serril/Serrat was a two-faced god, both male and female.

Serril, the male god, had brought magic to men in the ancient times and been banished to the desert (and other desolate places) by the other gods because of it. Many stories told of how he tricked liars or cheaters into revealing their bad deeds.

As a magician, Trulliç had always worshiped Serril, learned the prayers dedicated to him and celebrated his feast days. But here, in the god's lands, it wouldn't do to forget the other side, the goddess Serrat, who'd birthed the star sisters, the female magicians.

When a babe was born in Gaadiwala who had power, if the child was female, the mother generally walked to the desert and left the babe there, for the star sisters to come and claim as their own.

Sometimes boys were left as well, though generally other magicians didn't take them on. Atça barely tolerated Trulliç living in Gaadiwala, the place of Atça's power.

Male magicians were bound to a piece of land and could do great magic there. Atça claimed that he could always feel Trulliç, like an irritation in his side or an itch he couldn't quite scratch. Still, he had still volunteered to help train Trulliç in all the magical arts.

Female magicians had no such land bond, but their magic was also illusionary. They could trick a caravan into stopping for the night at an oasis when there was none, then steal all their goods. Or fool a man into sleeping with her, so that she might break his vows.

Trulliç had met more than one star sister in the tavern his family ran. He'd rarely talked to one, though. They tended to sneer at him, what they called his paltry magic.

And it was, compared to theirs. He was also just a boy, not a man with his own lands—yet.

His mother or his aunt dealt with the sisters at the tavern. They were less likely to cheat a woman and to pay with coins that changed into stones after they'd left.

But now Trulliç didn't know what to do.

Did he place the white, male side up on the altar when he gave it to the god? Or the black, female side? Which would bring more luck to him? Which would please Serril more?

If Trulliç had only thought! He would have shaved off one side of the stone so it was no longer round. That way, he could place it on its edge and he wouldn't have to decide.

Though Trulliç was tempted to just toss the stone in the air and let it fall on whatever side the fates decreed, he knew that wasn't actually a choice. Atça had chided him more than once for not being more firm or making a decision.

What if Trulliç made the wrong choice? What if he offended Serril/Serrat instead?

Trulliç was a desert magician, after all. He needed to stay on the good side of the trickster god. If that was possible.

In the end, Trulliç placed the male side down, reasoning that Trulliç himself was the representation of male in the desert for now.

He needed the help of the female side, of Serrat the goddess, to keep his eyes clear of deception and illusion and lead him clear along the path to his true home.

Trulliç changed out of his warmer wool tunic into his cooler one. He had already sweated through his shirt. The sun blazed outside the rough rock structure holding Serril's altar. The smell of baked sand filled his nose.

He took another sip of the sweet water from Atça's well.

For a moment, he thought it had a milky taste to it before it cleared up to just water again.

Huh. He'd thought that only his feet were being fooled out here.

Then he shivered. Damn it! The sensation of ants crawling all over his skin increased. Chicken flesh raised up along his arms. How could he just sit there and look out on the sands? The desert was there. Just beyond the door. Calling him.

No, he needed to stay here. In the shade. Out of the direct sunlight. At least until the afternoon.

Was it that dangerous out there, in the desert? It didn't look that dangerous. It looked beautiful. The sands invited him to walk on them. The softer winds encouraged him to try. The occasional skitter of a tiny mouse or lizard sounded intriguing, not threatening.

Why should he wait?

He was a desert magician, after all. Surely, if anyone could survive out there, he could.

Trulliç rocked back and forth, trying to recall one of the hymns to Serril, but all that kept running through his head was that he had to go, and go *now*.

He should wait. That would be sensible. His mother would tell him to wait. So would Atça.

But the siren song of the sand kept calling…

Finally, Trulliç couldn't stand it any longer. He shouldered his pack and took another sip of water before firmly attaching the flagon back to his belt. He shouldn't be drinking so much water. He only had three flagons with him. If he wasn't careful, he wouldn't have any water left. He needed to find the oasis and soon.

That was why he was leaving the shelter. So he could go find the oasis. So he wasn't being reckless, despite it being the heat of the day. He was being sensible. Yes. That was how he'd explain it.

Trulliç felt great relief when he stepped on the sands again. His itching skin soothed. He took a deep breath, breathing in the wonderful scents of the desert again.

He'd made the right decision. Despite the sun beating down on him, how the horizon glared.

He could do this.

Trulliç directed his feet to the east. The oasis lay that direction.

But which one? There were so many!

Stop being fanciful. Atça had told Trulliç that again and again. He couldn't really see magic, couldn't really feel it when Atça performed it. Certainly couldn't tell how Atça's power diminished every time he left Gaadiwala.

The nearest oasis stood to the east. All Trulliç had to do was walk that direction.

How hard could it be?

By the time the sun reached its zenith, Trulliç couldn't *wait* to find his true home.

Trudging across the desert sands was *hard*.

Trulliç's cousins had always teased him about how easy his life was. He sat in the hall of his mentor and wrote out poems, learning not just how to read their own Tanesh tongue, but Lydean, the language of the kingdom to the north, as well. He knew his numbers and his fractions.

He knew the stars and all the stories of the heroes. (Though if he was honest, he'd learned more about the stars from the goat and sheep herders he'd waited on at the tavern, as well as watching them on his own.)

Trulliç knew that his life was easier than his cousins'. He still carried water from the neighborhood well to the shack he shared with his mother on the edge of Gaadiwala, and on days when he didn't have classes with Atça, Trulliç hauled barrels of beer and ale, and refilled the clay oil lamps, as well as swept and cleaned the tavern. However, the next day, Trulliç went to his lessons, leaving his cousins the hard work again.

Atça had pointed out more than once that Trulliç's life would change dramatically once he came into his powers and found his home. Atça was a town magician, the only one living in Gaadiwala. He lived in a three-story brick house, with real wooden floors imported from Lydae. Thick rugs covered them, soft and comfortable to sit on. He didn't have the regular clay lamps filled with oil and burning a small wick. No, he had expensive glass lamps that burned brightly, making the inside as clear as day.

For now, though, Trulliç kept walking. His feet wanted to lead him all over the place, first to the left, then the right. Was it Serrat's trickery that kept leading him astray? He'd assumed that he should have found the oasis trail by now. He couldn't see anything, though, just sand and more sand.

The sun beat down mercilessly on Trulliç. He'd finally remembered to put on his *chafiyek*, a square scarf folded around his head and tugged slightly over his eyes to shade them. He'd already run out of the sweet water he'd carried from Atça's well. He had to find the oasis trail. He couldn't live without water.

Black spots formed before Trulliç's eyes. Suddenly, he found it hard to breathe. Sweat poured from him, instantly soaking through his shirt and pants.

Trulliç found himself sitting on the ground. He wasn't sure how he'd gotten there. Had he fallen? He pulled his knees up, put his arms across them, then put his head down, struggling to draw in the burning air.

He couldn't remember the prayer to Serril to help guide him. He had difficulty forming words in his head.

It finally occurred to him that he had heat stroke. He'd had it once before, working in the tavern the previous summer.

He needed to get out of the sun, to someplace shady and cool.

But where?

Trullıç struggled to his feet. He swayed, willing the black spots before his eyes to go away. His pack weighed more than a barrel full of ale. He stubbornly adjusted it on his back. He couldn't lose it. To drop it here would mean death, particularly once night came and the temperature plummeted. Bile filled his mouth.

Where could he go? Trullıç scanned the horizon. He didn't see anything but endless mounds of sand. The sun shone down from directly above him. He didn't even know which way was north. He couldn't feel the desert anymore. Looking around, the wind had already blown away his footprints.

Should he go back to town? He didn't want to be a failure.

He also didn't want to die.

His brain cleared a little as he took more deep breaths. He just needed to find shelter. He closed his eyes and tried listening to the desert. Where did the oasis stand? Where was the closest water?

That way.

Trullıç followed his feet. He knew he must be hallucinating because instead of trudging through the sand, he now glided over it, like a gnat skirting across a bowl of water.

Quicker than he expected, a dark outcrop of rocks appeared. Trullıç headed that direction, effortlessly skimming across the sand. His clothes had dried from the wind, or more likely the water had baked out of them by the sun.

The outcrop shimmered in the heat. Was it real? Or was this an illusionary place, a trap set by the star sisters?

Roughly hewn rocks formed an arch in the middle of nowhere. Beyond that stood another cluster. Like the building holding the altar to Serril, the rocks looked as though they'd been haphazardly placed, one on top of another.

But this wasn't a man made place. The rocks were huge, each taller than Trullıç. Instead of being the gold and brown of the desert, they were an orangeish-red, like the color of the sunset during the rainy season.

Once Trullıç drew closer, he realized they weren't individual rocks but a series of pillars, each oddly carved by the elements. They stood close together, as if they'd sprouted from a single seed.

Darkness beckoned from between them. Trullıç could smell the water they hid.

He made himself walk all the way around the outcrop. It was bigger than the shack he lived in with his mother. The shape was roughly square, with only one opening.

Harsh sand blew against the rocks, as if hoping to wear them down. But the rocks stood stubbornly proud, unwilling to bend or break.

Trulliç walked back to the entrance. The ground sloped down and in beyond the arch. Rough stones filled the path. Coolness breathed out from shadows within.

Could he just sit outside, in the shade of the rocks? Rest until nightfall, then travel again?

Except he needed water. And there was water inside.

Trulliç hit the edge of the arch with his hand. *Ouch*. If this was an illusion, it sure was a realistic one.

Cautiously, Trulliç took a step inside. He instantly felt better out of the sun. The thick stone of the outcrop kept the interior cool.

Like the building around Serril's altar, another tall stone stood just beyond the entrance. Looking back, Trulliç realized that the door faced the west. The stone standing in the doorway protected the interior not just from sand but from the afternoon sun as well.

He stepped around the stone carefully, then paused, letting his eyes adjust. It was darker inside than he'd expected.

Could he raise a light here? Atça had taught him how to create his own mage light, to set a magical yellow fire that floated above his palm.

It had never been much of a light. And it certainly hadn't been useful. It wasn't as if he could throw it and set something on fire with it, though he'd tried more than once when his cousins had teased him.

Trulliç concentrated on his palm, calling the fire within to the surface. To his surprise, the mage light sprang up immediately, much brighter than he'd ever managed before.

Huh. It must be because he was closer to his home here in the desert.

Feeling daring, Trulliç made the small light rise up, illuminating the interior of the rock cluster.

Just a couple of feet in front of him ran a small, clear stream. To his left, the water bubbled out of a collection of rocks, then disappeared again to the right.

Beyond the water lay long slabs of rocks, like rock stairs.

Would there be an altar at the top?

If there wasn't, Trulliç sure felt like making one.

He knelt gratefully at the edge of the tiny stream, then stuck his hand it. Lukewarm water caressed his skin. He cupped it with his palm and brought it to his nose. It smelled clean, not brackish. Plus, it appeared to be fresh running, not stagnant.

Hesitatingly, Trulliç brought the water to his lips.

The world exploded again.

———

Trulliç woke with cold stone under his back. Darkness filled the room. His muscles ached. His mouth felt as though he'd been swallowing sand. Without thinking about it, he set his mage light to glow beside him.

Then he remembered.

Trulliç sat up, his head still swimming. He'd been laying on the bottom most length of horizontal rock, just past the trickle of water. His pack sat neatly at his feet.

How had he gotten there? Had he climbed there himself?

The smell of water drove him to his feet. He staggered to the creek and knelt beside it again. Then he leaned to one side to look past the guard stone that partially covered the opening to the outcrop of rocks.

Trulliç shook his head. He must still be dreaming. Stars streamed through the air just past the rocks, like they were being blown by a strong wind. The desert itself reflected their light, sparkling like it was made of broken shards of glass, not sand. The night sky above was dark but not foreboding, more like a warm cover, finely woven. He thought he heard the cawing of a desert hawk, but they didn't fly at night. The smell of spices came to him as well, the pungent odors of mint and thyme.

That must mean he could take another drink, right? Since he was still dreaming and his body craved the water in front of him?

He found his right hand already sneaking into the water, his fingers wet.

With a grimace, Trulliç raised his hand to his face and licked off the water.

The world didn't explode again. But he found himself breathing heavily, as if he'd been covered in sand and just shaken it off. He could smell the age of the rocks, how they'd kept this sanctuary for centuries, even before the old kings. The water spoke to him as well, telling him of jewel-encrusted caves just under the surface.

Others had known of this place, nomads and desert people, even the star sisters.

They knew of the jewels, too.

The water was more precious. Digging into the caves would offend the water and kill the trickle.

Better to leave it and be alive than to be rich and dead.

Trulliç tasted the water again, letting it fill all his senses. His mind cleared and he felt as though he could truly think and see for the first time since starting his journey. He felt as though he could taste the minerals in the water, traces of the long underground stones it brushed by.

The stream asked him for a favor.

He could think of no other way to express it. But the idea grew in his mind, stronger, until he felt he must comply.

He rose slowly and gathered up his three water skins. Then he walked to the far side of the stream, just before it went back underground, and rinsed out the three skins.

Curdled yellow fluid poured from them, like rotten milk.

Trulliç shook his head. They'd been filled by Atça from the sweet well he kept behind his house.

Once the water containers were clean, Trulliç filled them with dream water.

Hopefully that would carry him through the next day.

After drinking his fill, Trulliç sat beside the trickling creek, humming a song of gratitude. The water seemed to sing along, playfully reaching up and splashing him once.

When Trulliç finished, the water grew very still. The night took a deep breath and held it.

Someone stood outside the archway.

Trulliç's heart beat hard. The pounding echoed in his ears. Fear filled him.

However, custom dictated that he welcome this stranger. There were far too many tales about the consequences of being a poor host, of not properly taking care of sudden guests who appeared at the door in the night.

Trulliç swallowed, his mouth dry.

"Welcome!" he finally said, his voice cracking. "Please come and share this bounty."

He didn't have any food out—the water filled his stomach completely —but he would still share what he had if the stranger was hungry. Plus, the trickle was a blessing.

Trulliç stiffened when a dog entered.

He set the mage light floating above him to burn brighter.

A blood hound stared back at him from across the tiny creek.

"Where's your charge?" Trulliç asked the dog once he'd drunk his fill at the stream.

The hound looked at him with his head tilted to one side, as if he didn't understand.

Trulliç didn't understand, either. Blood hounds only appeared when there was a pregnant woman carrying a baby of power, either male or female. They had short, dark, brown-red fur, tall ears that rose up to sharp points, a disproportionately large black nose, and eyes a lighter brown-gold color. Their muzzles were long and pointed, like a desert dog's, instead of square and solid, like a northern hunter.

Myrizhah had once told him that the dog who'd followed her had sad eyes, as if he had seen too many babies die.

This dog's eyes were the same.

But where was the pregnant woman the blood hound should be shepherding?

Trulliç gasped. Unless he was pregnant? He couldn't normally be pregnant. Though this was still a dream, right? Maybe he could be pregnant in a dream.

He reached down and probed his belly. It didn't feel any different.

The dog shook his head. He stayed on the far side of the stream and didn't show any interest in the pieces of the travel roll that Trulliç had carefully put out.

Stars still streamed past the door. Beyond them, the desert glistened with its own light. The night sky spread over them, vast and dark and empty.

Trulliç couldn't help but yawn. It had been a long day, strange and tiring. Though if this was a dream, how could he be tired? Maybe he needed to sleep again in order to fully wake up.

In the morning, he'd have to get his bearings. Figure out which way lay the caravan trail. See if he could either find his home or his way back to Gaadiwala.

He could admit that Atça was probably right. Trulliç would need many more journeys across the desert to find his true home.

"Good night," Trulliç told the dog.

He nodded to Trulliç as if he understood.

And maybe he did. The blood hounds were magical. They'd been conjured by the great emperor. After a woman gave birth, the blood hound who'd been following her ate the afterbirth, then went to the emperor and vomited it back up. The emperor fashioned a piece of the afterbirth into a scale and sewed it to the great cloak he always wore.

When the magician had found his or her power, he or she could never attack the emperor. It was impossible for a magician to fight their own blood.

Maybe the blood hound was between charges. But wouldn't he just disappear, then? Go back to the magical ether?

This is just a dream, Trulliç assured himself. It didn't have to make sense.

Atça read dreams. He'd be able to riddle out the meanings for Trulliç when he got back to town.

Trulliç lay down on the stone slab he'd first woken up on.

The dog watched him with soulful eyes. Then he turned three times, like a normal dog would, before also laying down.

Trulliç dimmed the mage light overhead. He left a flicker still glowing. It wasn't that he didn't trust the blood hound, not exactly. Blood hounds would protect the pregnant women they followed, killing any who might harm them.

At least until the woman started giving birth.

Then the blood hound would defend the babe, killing the mother if the birth went wrong, just so the child could live.

Trulliç felt his own belly again. Nothing growing there, not that he could tell.

Had the water made him pregnant? He sure felt full. But it was the richness of the desert he felt, not the stirring of another being inside him.

If he was carrying another soul, it would be the desert. It had found its way under his skin, the sand surging through his blood, his bones like the tough rocks, his eyes as clear as the desert skies.

He had to return to Gaadiwala. His family lived there. Atça hadn't taught him everything he needed to know about magic.

But he would return to the desert. Often. And he would find his home. Would find that special part of the desert that he could claim as his own.

Trulliç drowsed, thinking about the desert, its shifting sands, its cool nights, its blistering days. A soft *plop* made him look over toward the stream, then beyond. There weren't fish in the stream, were there?

The hound rose from where he had been sleeping. He shook himself, like a dog would shake the dirt from his fur after rolling in it.

Trulliç smiled. The action seemed like such a normal dog-like thing. He half expected the blood hound to sit on his butt and scratch his nose with his hind paw when he finished shaking.

But the dog kept shaking himself, twisting faster and faster.

A whirling noise filled the small space. The smell of bitter coal wafted to Trulliç.

What was the dog doing? Trulliç could barely make out his shape anymore—just four legs supporting a gray cloud that grew more white with every passing moment.

The air erupted with a soft exploding noise.

Trulliç sat up, startled.

A black and white dog now stood in where the blood hound had once been. Black patches covered its ribs—too irregular to be called spots. Plain white fur covered its—no, still his—legs. He had short black ears that stood up straight from his head, and smaller black and white spots all along his pointed muzzle.

The dog turned to look at Trulliç.

His eyes were the same impossible blue as the desert sky. Trulliç had rarely seen eyes that color before. Only the traders who came from Lydae had blue eyes, and even then, not very often.

Riyune, the dog seemed to say.

That was his name.

Then he did sit on his butt and scratch at his ear, before turning three times and laying down to sleep.

Trulliç stayed sitting upright. He glanced beyond the guard stone. Stars still streamed across the sand. So this was still a dream, right?

Magicians sometimes had familiars. Atça had told Trulliç about them.

However, that had been more than an age ago. Before the great emperor and the death of the old kings. Before the constant wars with the barbarians to the east that the widows complained about bitterly.

Trulliç shook his head and laid back down on the stone slab. Atça would have to spend a lot of time consulting his books to figure out *this* dream.

In the morning, Trulliç would have to find his way back to Gaadiwala, though he didn't want to. He felt so far out of his element, though. He needed more training—much more training—before he could live out in the desert on his own.

And he hadn't found that part of the desert that would be his home.

———

In the morning, Trulliç came all the way to waking. Outside, the sun had already kissed the sands. It looked like a normal day.

The white and black dog, Riyune, still lay sleeping on the far side of the trickle of water.

CHAPTER TWO

NADEEM

NADEEM CAME TO HER POWER earlier than most.

She sat on the dirt floor of the teaching tent, listening to Aunt Haneet tell the story of the great sister Arzhem and how she'd left the corrupt city to walk the desert. All the tent contained was a rug at the front for the teacher. Though Nadeem had been taught how to read and write, most of her lessons involved the great epic poems and memorizing the long history of the star sisters and the Tanesh empire.

Two other girls sat with her in the stuffy teaching tent. Jamak was only a year older. However, at age eight, Jamak thought *she* was going to be a big hero when she grew up. Nadeem would have to call them both "Aunt" after they had their coming of age ceremony, because they were older. Jamak wanted Nadeem to start calling her *Aunt Jamak* now. The other girl, Mojin, was ten, but at least she was nice and wanted Nadeem to use the term "sister," which Nadeem should use for all women her age or younger.

Nadeem hated lessons with Aunt Haneet. Yes, she was only seven, but she already knew most of the words to Arzhem's tale. She much preferred when Aunt Parayat taught them tales. She expected the girls to repeat every stanza exactly as she'd spoken it. It kept Nadeem on her toes, having to listen hard and pay attention, because Aunt Parayat sometimes mixed up the lines on purpose.

Aunt Haneet thought that having an illusion of Arzhem, tall and dark, showing her great tragedy and triumph, would be interesting and keep the attention of the girls. But Arzhem moved so stiffly, and Nadeem could see through the illusion to the wall of the tent beyond. Sometimes she could see Aunt Haneet through Arzhem, which was kind of funny. But Aunt Haneet didn't like it when Nadeem and the other girls giggled.

If only Aunt Haneet would finish! Aunt Parayat had promised to show Nadeem her latest blanket. She'd used a new technique for dying the wool threads, and Nadeem wanted to learn how to make that rich blue, the color favored by the goddess Barzhat.

Nadeem couldn't contain her sigh when yet someone else came to the door of the tent and called to Aunt Haneet. They were never going to get out of here! Aunt Parayat would be taking her afternoon nap by the time lessons were finished. Most of the older women napped in the afternoon, complaining of the midday heat.

Nadeem didn't really understand why. It was hot all the time. The *kabil* of star sisters lived in a desert oasis, all the women together, close to seven thousand souls with no men.

Aunt Haneet stood at the doorway to the tent arguing with someone in whispers. Just past the row of teaching tents stood an open area filled with benches and long tables. While some of the older aunts would eat in their tents, most ate at one of the three dining shifts. The aunts made a point of switching tables and eating with different girls, getting to know all of them.

A large flat area opened up to the east of the dining pavilion, where all important ceremonies would be held, like the coming-of-age ceremony for girls, the celebration of the goddess Barzhat's birthday, or the candle festival that happened midwinter.

North and south of the eating pavilion stretched rows of individual tents, as well as collective tents where the younger girls lived. The kitchen was at the center of the camp.

Though the *kabil* hadn't moved for as long as Nadeem could remember, the star sisters never built permanent structures. They stayed in tents so they could migrate whenever they needed to. Nadeem had already memorized some of the great epics that told of the time of persecution, when the star sisters always had to hide their camps carefully.

Aunt Haneet still talked with someone at the door of the learning tent. Nadeem couldn't hear what they were saying. Maybe they were arguing about the amount of salt used in the goat and cracked wheat stew they would have for lunch that day. Aunt Haneet did love her food. Her round belly and big hips showed that.

Nadeem snickered quietly to herself, but then sat up straight and tried to look innocent when Aunt Haneet scowled over her shoulder at them.

Aunt Haneet wore the same clothing that all the star sisters did: a long skirt made of a light cotton that hadn't been dyed that went to just above her fat ankles; a wide brown-leather belt that held mysterious pouches and the traditional three knives; a dark brown blouse that covered her from shoulders to wrists, though the neck wasn't as high as Nadeem's, and instead showed off Aunt Haneet's big breasts; and a low-cut tunic over it that even Nadeem had to admit was finely made, with thin black stripes between panels of pale red and gold.

Who was bothering Aunt Haneet during lesson time? Nadeem couldn't see who it was. She wanted to ask the other girls, but they were whispering to each other, and Jamak had purposefully turned her back on Nadeem so she couldn't join in.

Nadeem sighed and looked around. The illusionary figure of Arzhem that Aunt Haneet had created for their lessons stood as tall as a woman, fully grown, and as still as a statue without Aunt Haneet's attention on her. What would happen if she turned around and went back into the city that still appeared as a shadowy silhouette at the back of the tent, instead of walking to the desert?

Arzhem stirred, moving her head slowly, looking back the way she'd come.

The two girls beside Nadeem gasped, but quietly enough that Aunt Haneet didn't scowl at them again.

Go back Nadeem ordered the figure.

She sluggishly lifted one foot, then the next, turning around.

Too slow! Nadeem wanted the illusionary figure to walk all the way back to the city and maybe disappear there before Aunt Haneet noticed.

What was making the illusion move so slowly? Nadeem stared hard at the figure. She grew more transparent when Nadeem did so. She could now see everything through Arzhem, including the wall of the tent and even the ropes that held it down.

Ropes. Yes. That was what was making Arzhem move so slowly. There appeared to be ropes tied to her wrists and ankles, and two more tied up to the *chafiyek* she wore on his head, six total.

Six was a special number. All of the star sisters, once they came of age, had a six-sided star made up of two intertwined triangles carved into their left cheek. Each line had its own meaning, which Nadeem had learned so long ago she felt as though she'd always known about them.

Nadeem tugged at the ropes holding Arzhem, but they were too hard to break, like the leather straps that held on her own sandals.

Could she untie them?

Nadeem found the loop in the knots and quickly undid the binding on Arzhem's limbs. She swung her arms wide and moved her feet as if she was taking great strides.

The other girls giggled.

However, the figure of Arzhem still stood in one place. How could Nadeem undo the bindings of Arzhem's scarf? It was like the ropes were tied to her long hair underneath as well. There wasn't a simple, single knot for her to attack.

Nadeem frowned as she concentrated. It was tricky, like picking curved thorns out of wool without breaking the long strands.

The tent disappeared as Nadeem focused on the problem. It wasn't just that there were so many tiny threads. The problem was that they kept retying themselves. How could she undo those knots? She didn't want to shave Arzhem's head. Her hair was too pretty. But that might be the only way she could fully take control of the figure.

"Nadeem?" came a quiet voice.

Nadeem started, coming back to herself.

Shoot. Aunt Haneet stood right there, looking down on her.

"Could you let go of Arzhem please?" Aunt Haneet asked quietly.

Huh. Nadeem had never heard Aunt Haneet speak like that before, like she was talking to a wild hawk, trying to calm it and break it to the fist.

"Sure," Nadeem said, though she wasn't sure exactly what Aunt Haneet had asked. She'd just loosened the ties of Arzhem. She hadn't tied any of her own, had she?

Maybe she had, though. There still appeared to be twisting ties wrapped around the figure's wrists and ankles.

Shrugging, Nadeem willed the ties away.

"Thank you," Aunt Haneet said. "Now, where were we?" She made Arzhem turn, and turn again, and turn again, as if she was lost and didn't know which direction to go either.

"Ah, that way's the desert!" Arzhem proclaimed gleefully, pointing off to the distance.

Nadeem giggled with the other girls. She'd never seen Aunt Haneet be playful before.

Still, all through the rest of the lesson, Nadeem felt as though Aunt Haneet watched her, like a mouse keeping an eye on a poisonous snake.

Two days later, when Nadeem went to the lesson tent, Aunt Parayat sat waiting for her.

"Come in," Aunt Parayat said, gesturing for Nadeem to enter.

Nadeem gladly went and sat in front of Aunt Parayat. Her aunt sat on a teacher's rug—a small, square, braided rug made out of old scraps of cloth instead of the dirt ground.

Good. That meant Aunt Parayat would be leading the lessons that day.

Nadeem didn't know what had happened to Aunt Haneet. There hadn't been any lessons the day before. Had she gotten sick? Or was she still arguing with the stranger who had come to the lesson tent when she'd gotten so distracted?

Aunt Parayat sat straight and tall. Nadeem didn't know if she'd ever grow as tall as Aunt Parayat, but she hoped so. Her aunt wore a smart, sleeveless tunic dyed a pretty shade of blue over a clean white blouse and a brown skirt. Her hazel eyes stared at Nadeem, making her sit up even straighter. Aunt Parayat's nose was long and hooked at the end, like a desert hawk's. The dark skin of her face held many laugh wrinkles, and even now, when she wasn't smiling, showed wrinkles around her mouth and across her forehead. Her headscarf was woven out of blue, black, and white threads, the colors of the goddesses Berzhat and Serrit.

With a wave of her hand, Aunt Parayat closed the door to the tent. "It will just be us today," she said.

Nadeem didn't know if she should be happy or annoyed: Happy that she got to spend more time with Aunt Parayat, who always had the most interesting lessons, or annoyed at how hot the tent would get with the door flap closed.

Then she looked over her shoulder at the tent flap.

Wait.

How had her aunt done that?

The magic of the star sisters was illusionary. They couldn't affect the real world, not like male magicians. Men were trapped in a single place of power, while the sisters could travel to every land, equally comfortable roaming the desert or sailing the oceans.

Had the tent flap really closed? Or was it an illusion?

Nadeem stared, but couldn't tell.

She returned her attention to her favorite aunt. Though all the star sisters were supposed to love and honor each other equally, Nadeem still had favorites.

"Can you tell if the flap is open or shut?" Aunt Parayat asked.

Nadeem shook her head. Though stupid Jamak teased Nadeem when she didn't know something, Aunt Parayat had always said that admitting ignorance took more courage than faking knowledge.

And Nadeem always tried to be brave.

"How about now?" Aunt Parayat asked as she stared over Nadeem's shoulder at the tent flap.

Nadeem looked over her shoulder. She couldn't help her gasp. The tent flap *was* still open! She could see the illusion now, see how the flap looked both open and closed at the same time.

How did her aunt do that? Nadeem really wanted to learn.

"It's open," Nadeem told her teacher proudly. This was going to be so wonderful! Obviously, Aunt Parayat's lesson today was going to be all about illusions.

Aunt Parayat nodded slowly. "While it's not unheard of a girl coming into her power as young as you, it is unusual," she said.

Nadeem tried to keep the smug smile off her face. Given the way her aunt raised a single, beautifully arched eyebrow at her, she knew she'd failed.

"That just means you're going to have to work extra hard to make us all proud," Aunt Parayat continued.

Nadeem didn't like the sound of that. "What do you mean, extra hard?" she asked warily.

"More lessons. Oh, don't look so stricken! They'll mostly be with me and with the other aunts who are also strong illusionists," Aunt Parayat said. "In addition to learning all the stories of our people, the poems of the great heroes and heroines, the feast days and celebrations of the gods and goddesses, and the special arcane knowledge of the star sisters."

Nadeem nodded seriously. It sounded like a *lot* of lessons.

"The other girls will be jealous, you know," Aunt Parayat said in a conspiratorial voice. "Because you'll be learning magic years before they will."

Nadeem sat up straighter and tried to be proud. It would be fun to learn all about magic. To cast illusions. Not that she would try to trick the other girls.

Or at least, not too often.

Yet… "Will I still get to learn about weaving? And dying wool?" She really liked that. She enjoyed the way fibers slipped through her fingers as she spun them into thread on her drop spindle. She also loved learning the different combinations of ingredients that made up various colored dyes, as well as how to set them in the cloth so they'd be permanent.

Aunt Parayat laughed, sounding as young as Nadeem herself. "Of course!" she said, smiling. "I'm glad you want to. After doing magic, dying cloth is my favorite thing to do."

"I will learn all that you will teach me," Nadeem said, finding the ritual words the star sisters gave at the start of a new lesson series, how many of the call and response stories went as well.

"And I am glad to teach you," Aunt Parayat said. "To help you reach your full potential."

Nadeem liked the sound of that.

So maybe *she* could become a great hero, and not Jamak.

Aunt Parayat handed Nadeem a long wooden tray filled with three dozen *aǧrikat* shells. "You are now thirteen years old. You have started your menstruation. It is time for you to choose six shells for your coming-of-age ceremony," Aunt Parayat said. "Choose carefully, considering all I have taught you."

Though Jamak and Mojin were older than Nadeem, as Nadeem had the strongest magic, it fell to her to choose the shells for her ceremony first.

Nadeem and Aunt Parayat sat in the familiar teaching tent, just the pair of them, as usual. The black hand-held slates used for learning letters and numbers sat to one side, the precious chalk sticks carefully wrapped in waterproofed leather. Aunt Parayat sat on the teacher's mat, while Nadeem sat on the dirt floor. She kept her back hunched slightly so her head was lower than her teacher's, out of respect. It was easier to do with Aunt Parayat than with some of the other, shorter aunts.

The *aǧrikat* shells were oblong shaped. Each would fill her entire palm. A white, luminous substance covered the inside. The outside of the shell was a mottled gray and felt rough. It appeared to be made out of many layers, with the innermost layer breaking through the outer layers in places. The shells smelled of fresh raw fish.

Nadeem solemnly studied the shells in the tray that she held. The *ağrikat* mussel came from the Barzhat Sea, where the goddess Barzhat lived. They were extremely rare and hard to come by. They grew along deep shelves in the southeast corner of the sea. Divers couldn't get at them—the only time they were found was after a storm, blown up along the coast.

The goddess suffered men only to sail along the coastlines of the great inland sea, and only when she was in a good mood, her waters clear and blue.

When her mood turned foul, the waters of the sea blackened and all boats ran to the shore.

The goddess drowned anyone who tried to sail directly across the sea, killing them and dragging their souls into her golden court.

Once there, the stories told, all the bad deeds a person had done during the course of their life would manifest as teardrop shaped weights sewn into a vest, weighing the person down. A person had to dance for the goddess and keep dancing until all their weights fell off. Only then would the goddess would give them the true kiss of death and the person would be reborn without sin, their soul clean and light.

When properly prepared, the *ağrikat* mussel caused vivid, wild visions. When not fixed the right way, they were deadly.

If the correct amount of the crushed shell was applied during a star sister's coming-of-age ceremony, it made the magic of a star sister more powerful.

Nadeem examined the shells on the tray. Which ones were the strongest? Which ones weaker? And what did Nadeem want? She knew she didn't have just herself to consider, but the others sharing her coming-of-age ceremony as well.

"May I touch them?" Nadeem asked.

"You may," Aunt Parayat said. She held herself aloof and stern.

Nadeem knew that it wasn't because her aunt was angry with her—in fact, her aunt was very pleased with Nadeem and her progress. But she couldn't influence Nadeem's decision of which shells to choose and could only advise her about the properties of the shells.

Aunt Parayat had been strict about that during all of Nadeem's training, insisting that Nadeem think for herself, come up with her own solution, always questioning what she'd been told, finding new answers to old problems.

So now, it was up to Nadeem to choose the right shells. Though Aunt Parayat had never said so, Nadeem was aware that this was one of the most important decisions of her life. Did she pick the strongest of the shells, which might enable her to cast stronger illusions? The downside was that the shells could cause her to have permanent visions and make it difficult for her to distinguish between reality and her dreams.

If Nadeem picked the weakest of the shells, she might not reach her full potential. While she was only thirteen, she was already a stronger magician than all but a handful of the aunts in the *kabil*. Aunt Parayat was stronger than all of them, as far as Nadeem could tell.

Outside the tent, the *kabil* of star sisters stirred. The cooks started preparing the evening meal, which wouldn't be eaten until after the sun had firmly set and the temperatures had started to drop. A group of younger girls carefully prepared the ceremonial space to the east of the eating pavilion, sweeping the ground and placing sweet incense in the braziers around the edges of the space, preparing it for Nadeem's coming-of-age ceremony that she would share with Jamak and Mojin.

The other two would choose their shells after Nadeem had chosen hers. So she also had to consider their powers as well, how strong they might become. She shouldn't greedily take all the strongest shells for herself. The tribe must work together if they were to survive. No matter how powerful of an illusionist Nadeem might become, she was nothing by herself. It was only with her sisters and aunts that she was strong.

Or at least that was what Aunt Parayat had tried to beat into Nadeem's skull when she got too proud, or fought too hard to win one of the combats the girls regularly fought with illusionary beings.

Nadeem carefully set the tray on the ground in front of her and picked up one of the three dozen shells. It was slightly smaller, barely covering her palm. The back of the shell felt rough and cool, while the faintly luminous interior felt smooth against her fingertips. The faint smell of fish made her hungry.

Feeling daring, Nadeem lifted the shell to her ear. Could she hear the goddess Berzhat's sad, lonely sighs, as Manisat had?

Nadeem caught her breath when she heard a faint *whooshing* sound. But that was all she heard. It almost sounded like a sigh, but not quite, more like the echo of a long forgotten sigh. Disappointed, she brought the shell down.

When she looked up, Aunt Parayat smiled at her. "I did the same at your age," she confessed, "when the *ağrikat* were presented to me."

That made Nadeem feel better.

The great heroine Manisat had led a huge *kabil* of star sisters in ancient times. At that time, the star sisters were faithful and honored the goddess Serrat, the mother of them all. However, Serrat wasn't well loved. It was difficult to love such a trickster, especially when the star sisters prided themselves on keeping their word and their blood oaths.

Manisat had heard the sad sighs of the goddess Berzhat when she'd picked up an *ağrikat* shell. She'd made her way to the goddess' golden court while she'd still been alive and had promised the goddess that the star sisters wouldn't merely venerate her, but love her. They would welcome her at all their feasts, big and small. A bowl was always left empty at every meal, a welcome place for the goddess.

And sometimes the goddess came, bringing capricious death with her. The star sisters persisted though, in loving the goddess. They'd given their word, and continued to do so at every coming-of-age ceremony, taking a blood oath, binding the star sisters and the goddess of death together.

In return, the goddess promised Marisat and the rest of the star sisters a boon, once in their lifetime, when a woman asked in her truest hour of need.

Nadeem put the shell she'd been holding back on the tray and focused her attention on them again. Which were the strongest shells?

She couldn't tell. Normally, Nadeem saw magic well. Then again, she was used to seeing through illusions, not physical magic.

Were the shells magical, though? Or did they hold some other property? The bark of the *meslit* thorn tree looked brownish red. It could be boiled down and reduced to a sweet syrup. It could also be used to dye wool. However, the wool didn't turn out a dark color but a very pale brown, almost golden colored.

The *meslit* thorn tree didn't have any magic. The golden color it gave to thread was just a quality of the bark.

Nadeem paused, reconsidered, then reposed her question.

Which of the shells held the least amount of the luminous inner substance?

That was much easier to figure out. She would bet that they were the thinnest shells, the ones where the white inner surface didn't rise to the lip of the shell, sometimes the dark grey backs poking through the white.

Nadeem picked out the half-dozen weaker shells and put those to one side.

Then she graded the rest, from what she assumed to be the weakest to the strongest, those that appeared to have the least of the inner white shell to those with most.

She ended up with four piles, with a few in between.

Then she sighed.

Now, she had to choose six.

What would be the best combination? What would help her win? Though this wasn't a contest or battle, she generally thought in those terms.

She chose what she hoped were the three strongest shells—those with the most luminous material—and she put those to one side.

Did she balance those out with the three weakest?

But that would make her merely average, a difficult numerical concept, but she'd finally figured it out after many examples had been given to her by her aunts.

Nadeem wasn't about to be average. She had to be better than average. That was the only way to win.

Instead, she chose one shell from each of the remaining three piles, weakest, next strongest, and next.

This left strong shells for the other girls so they had options as well.

She assumed Jamak would choose the strongest shells, if she could figure out which they were, merely because she always wanted to be the best at everything.

Nadeem tried not to take pleasure when she won at their battles, but she couldn't help it. Jamak had always assumed that she would be the most important star sister and bitterly complained when Nadeem proved that she wasn't.

While Mojin…Mojin would be balanced. She would choose shells from each of the piles. She was smart enough to figure out the difference, of that, Nadeem felt confident.

Satisfied, Nadeem put the rest of the shells back flat on the tray, leaving them roughly grouped in her categories. Then she looked up.

Aunt Parayat didn't smile at her or show any outward signs of what she felt. "You have chosen well, my sister," she said.

Nadeem heard the pride in her teacher's voice. She had done the right thing. She was certain.

Nadeem swayed with the beat of the booming drums, the wild wailing of the flutes. Most of the *kabil* still danced on the ceremonial sands behind her, their undulating calls ringing through the desert night.

Sweat covered Nadeem from her scarfless head to her naked torso, down to her bare feet, showing that she was purified and ready.

A huge bonfire burned in front of her, out under the stars. Aunt Parayat stood beside it, along with the other elder aunts. They were naked to the waist, with blue and white stripes in protective patterns drawn across their skin. They wore long skirts with thick leather aprons tied over them and sturdy sandals.

The heat from the fire blasted Nadeem's front, causing more sweat to trickle down between her small breasts, while the coolness of the night tickled her back and raised chicken flesh across her shoulders.

Jamak and Molin stood behind her. The three of them would be scarred together, the shape of a six-sided star carved into their left cheeks as part of their coming-of-age ceremony.

This part of the ceremony wasn't private, but it wasn't done in front of the entire *kabil* either. A girl had to be allowed her tears before she returned to show her new form for everyone to see.

All of the star sisters wore this mark. The goddess Serrat who had born them had such a mark. Plus, the emperor required it. There were only a couple of stories from ancient times, before the times of persecution when the old kings ruled, when the star sisters could choose whether to bear the mark or not. But those stories were told in whispers, passed from older sisters to the younger ones, not in the learning tents taught by the aunts.

Once marked, a star sister could never hide her origin. Few could change their appearance enough to disguise themselves. None could hide the mark after it was set.

Nadeem would never hide the fact that she was a star sister! She couldn't imagine why anyone would. She was proud of being a star sister, a powerful illusionist and mighty fighter.

Aunt Parayat's dark eyes stared at Nadeem from across the flames. She held a large knife, its edge sharper than a desert gale. Rare cherry wood made up the handle: Like most of the desert *kabil*, Nadeem had never even seen a cherry.

But the red wood made it appropriate for the ceremony.

Nadeem stepped forward, past the fire, facing Aunt Parayat. The blue and white stripes across Aunt Parayat's chest and down her arms were done in groups of three, vertical lines to represent Enkat, the goddess of rain, as well as horizontal lines that represented her husband, Xannil, the god of the sun. The single line around Aunt Parayat's torso, at the bottom of her ribs, was for the goddess Barzhat. Aunt Parayat's small breasts were still firm, and Nadeem admired her aunt's wiry muscles. Even though Aunt Parayat was older than most—in her sixties, or so it was rumored—she still was a force to contend with in the physical arena, like wrestling matches.

Nadeem hoped to be that strong and solid when she reached that impossible age.

Aunt Parayat held up the knife, tip pointing toward the stars, then she kissed the hilt. "Do you swear to uphold the honor of the star sisters? To stay true to your promises and your blood oaths? To fulfill the oaths of your sisters and your aunts if they cannot?"

"I do," Nadeem said solemnly. She'd already sworn such oaths in front of the *kabil*.

"Do you swear to love the goddess Berzhat, always welcoming the easy death she brings, not just for others but for yourself as well?" Aunt Parayat continued.

"I swear," Nadeem replied. She'd kissed the statue of the goddess that afternoon in front of the *kabil*, promising not to merely venerate the goddess but to love her unreservedly, as one might love a sister or even a son.

Aunt Parayat stared at Nadeem, judging her, weighing the truth in Nadeem's vows.

Nadeem stayed standing straight and unflinching. This was the most important time of all, in the entire ceremony.

If Aunt Parayat didn't consider Nadeem worthy, she would be in her right to kill Nadeem at this moment. There were many stories of girls who didn't apply themselves, who were judged too lazy to be allowed to live.

Or too powerful and uncontrolled, like the mighty Sahrilla who had too much male in her and could call the desert winds, her magic not just illusionary but real as well.

"I welcome you to the challenge," Aunt Parayat said after a dramatic pause, "the challenge of being a full member of the *kabil* of star sisters."

"Thank you," Nadeem said humbly. "It is my honor." She felt the weight of her choices resting on her shoulders as she stepped forward and kissed the knife held before her.

Two of the aunts suddenly grabbed Nadeem's arms, holding her still and ready to support her.

The first cut of the knife, across the bottom of her left cheek lengthwise, took Nadeem's breath away.

Earth.

That was the base of all life, the basest element of all.

Nadeem breathed through the pain. She'd experienced this much pain before when wrestling with her sisters, learning how to grapple and fight.

The next cut was another long, lengthwise cut, a parallel line at the top of her cheek.

Sky.

The stars above them, where the home of the goddesses and the gods lay.

Nadeem took another deep breath, sweat pouring down her back. She would handle the pain. She would not cry out. She would make her sisters and aunts proud.

Now another cut, going from the base of earth up past the line for the sky.

Water.

Without water, there was no life. It was as essential as earth.

Nadeem swayed when the night breeze touched her ravaged skin. The pain beat like the pulse of the drums in her head.

But Aunt Parayat wasn't finished. She had three more lines to cut.

Nadeem tried to brace herself for the next cut of the knife, trying to recall the songs about the blade's sweet kiss.

All she felt was fire, her blood burning with pain.

The next cut came, from the other side of the earth line up to join the water line, the last cut of the base triangle.

Sand. It wasn't essential. But it was a central element of their lives. Nadeem's *kabil* lived in the desert.

Other star sisters who lived in places other than the desert, used a different line, whether that be mountain, ocean, or even forest.

Wherever the *kabil* of star sisters lived shaped every aspect of their lives. So it had to be included.

Courage. The fifth cut. Coming down from the sky and bisecting the earth line.

Courage in all things, in the face of desert gales or even the fierce joy of the star sisters.

Nadeem took a deep breath, swallowing against her dry throat. Only one more cut remained.

Dream.

She'd asked Aunt Parayat why that was the last cut. Was it because it was the most important? Or the least? It completed the triangles, the ritual cutting.

The star sisters were master illusionists. Could they only create illusions of what they could dream?

Nadeem created the most beautiful, fanciful landscapes.

She still had difficulty mastering the most simple of illusions, a tent flap appearing shut.

Aunt Parayat had merely told her to meditate on it. And Nadeem had, but she'd never been able to figure it out.

Aunt Parayat wiped the blade clean of Nadeem's blood, using a clean, white cloth. The other two would also have their blood on the one cloth, their blood mingling together literally as well as figuratively, before the cloth would be burned in the bonfire at the end of the scarring ceremony.

Then Aunt Parayat nodded at the two aunts holding Nadeem. Their grips on her shoulders and arms tightened.

Nadeem blinked, the pain making her hazy. Wasn't the ceremony over? Except, no. She still had to be given the *ağrikat* mussel shells. She knew they'd been ground into a fine paste after she'd chosen her six.

She'd also assumed that she'd be eating them, next.

Aunt Parayat brought out an oversized *ağrikat* shell. It easily filled both her hands, cupped like a large bowl. Inside glittered a thick, whitish paste.

Nadeem assumed the paste had been made from the *ağrikat* shells she'd chosen.

Aunt Parayat scooped out a small bit of the shell paste.

Instead of asking Nadeem to open her mouth, she reached out and gently applied the paste to the bloody wounds on Nadeem's cheek.

The pain tripled, as if a flaming sword ripped into her skin. Nadeem barely choked back her scream. She didn't mean to flinch and try to pull away from the aunts holding her. She couldn't help herself. It was an animal instinct, to get away from such pain.

She wasn't about to fail at this ceremony, however. She tried to make herself stand still and proud.

Aunt Parayat's firm fingers held Nadeem's chin still while she applied more of the shell paste. The abrasive shells cut open Nadeem's wounds further, slipping into the bloody mess.

Nadeem shuddered, the pain eating at her soul. Tears streamed from her eyes, the saltwater stinging the cuts.

Finally, Aunt Parayat stepped back, satisfied.

"Let your power be full," she said stiffly.

The aunts holding up Nadeem let go of her shoulders. She sank to her knees, shaking.

Then the world exploded and the visions began.

CHAPTER THREE

TRULLIÇ

TRULLIÇ WAITED UNTIL THE SUN had kissed the western horizon before he left the outcrop of rocks.

He'd spent the day inside the rocky outcropping with Riyune. Trulliç had napped when he could, knowing that he'd be traveling at night, trusting that he could follow the stars like the goat herders had taught him. Though he nibbled at the sweet travel roll that his mother had baked him, he found he wasn't very hungry. The water from the stream continued to satisfy both his thirst and his hunger.

Riyune stayed on his side of the little trickle of water. He sniffed at the pieces of the travel roll that Trulliç offered him but didn't gobble them down like a normal dog would have. Riyune seemed quite content to sit and wait out the heat of the day as well.

Had he really first come into the little space as a blood hound? Or had Trulliç just dreamed it? Riyune looked like a regular dog, maybe a little smaller than the ones the herders used, coming up roughly to Trulliç's knee, with a broad head and pronounced eyebrows. Riyune's jaw looked strong, though he had the pointed snout of a desert dog.

However, Riyune's white and black coloring was odd. Most of the dogs Trulliç knew were some shade of mud brown or black.

Plus, those eyes. That searing blue. They appeared as soulful as his mother's when she looked out across the yard, up toward the mountains and the desert beyond.

And yet…Riyune lolled to one side of his butt while he scratched at his neck with his hind legs, like a normal dog. He also grumbled in his sleep, his legs twitching. Beyond telling Trulliç his name, Riyune hadn't spoken or given Trulliç any messages.

Trulliç would have thought that a familiar would communicate more.

Then again, Atça had more than once accused Trulliç of being too fanciful. Atça denied that Trulliç could see magic or someone's power.

Trulliç stubbornly kept trying, however. He doubted himself mightily, but the ability came naturally to him.

Throughout the day, every time Trulliç slept, he dreamed of the desert. Endless sands stretched before him. He tasted the sweetness of cool mists that came at night during the rainy season. He smelled the fear of the tiny mouse hiding while a desert hawk flew overhead. He felt the age of the dunes, constantly shifting in the wind but still solid at their core.

To the east he felt a nearby oasis, a stream that had crested the sands for a patch, feeding the palms and other hidden desert life. It felt different than the place where he rested—more open, easier to find. The outcrop of rock where he currently rested was more aware, as well as more shadowy, and would only show itself to travelers in dire need.

Atça hadn't wanted Trulliç to spend too long in the desert the first time if he didn't find his home right away. The desert was dangerous. No one traveled alone in the desert. It was a sure way for a traveler to find the goddess Barzhat's court, dancing for true death.

That much Trulliç believed, particularly since he'd gotten so sick the day before.

He *knew* better than to try to cross the desert sands in midday, even if it was just after the rainy season and cooler than usual. Why had he gone out in the heat like that the day before? What had made him so impatient? At least his skin stopped feeling as if he had ants crawling all over it.

Had that been part of the dream? Some trick of the god Serril? Trulliç would have to be sure to ask Atça about it.

Still, Trulliç wanted to visit at least one oasis before he traveled back to Gaadiwala. He didn't think the one just to the east was his home. He didn't feel drawn to it, just as he didn't feel as though one particular corner of the desert called to him either.

This time, Trulliç waited until he sensed a change in the air, the desert cooling around him as the sun continued to set. Only then did he tie his sleeping roll to the bottom of his pack, look around to make sure that he hadn't forgotten anything, and take one last, long drink from the water in the creek.

"Ready?" Trulliç asked Riyune.

The dog just looked at him expectantly, as if he had been ready to go all along.

How much did Riyune understand? Trulliç felt uncomfortable talking to the dog like he was a person. How had Riyune found the rocks? Had he really been a blood hound? Trulliç had never heard any stories about blood hounds transforming into real dogs.

However, Riyune had told Trulliç his name. That much Trulliç believed.

Squinting, Trulliç stepped from the small outcrop of rock back onto the desert sands.

A sense of longing filled him. His feet wanted to wander. Why did he want to travel so? It didn't make sense to him. He should be heading toward his home, or town, or something. Not just aimlessly walk over dunes of sand.

Riyune sat next to him, looking up at him.

Obviously, the dog thought they needed to travel together. Or something. Probably looking for easier food.

Trulliç set off to the east, to where he'd dreamed had been an oasis. It seemed easier at night to keep his focus, to make his feet travel in the path he'd set, rather than wandering, though he still felt the tug of the sands.

Riyune walked beside him. However, he frequently looked up at Trulliç, as if waiting for instructions.

Finally, Trulliç told Riyune, "We're going to the oasis to the east."

The dog nodded as if he understood, then walked ahead of Trulliç, aiming a bit more south than Trulliç's original course.

Trulliç stopped and closed his eyes.

Riyune was right. If Trulliç's senses could be believed, the oasis actually lay in that direction.

Trulliç would have corrected his course in a while. Probably.

Disappointment stabbed Trulliç's heart as he trudged along.

Stupid dog knew more about the desert than Trulliç did.

Still, Trulliç couldn't stay disappointed for long. Heat rose from where the sun had beaten down on the sand all day long. Though there weren't any bushes or shrubs for Trulliç to run into, he still paid attention to the shadows, making sure he didn't twist an ankle or something.

The sky turned to a deep purple, the royal cloak of night. Trulliç understood the poetic image better out here in the desert. A few stars winked at him from the east. He could already make out the one the goat herders called the "shepherd's light"—it shone constantly from the east, the brightest star on the horizon. It was just past the rainy season, and the star would stay closer to the horizon for another month or so.

Hawks flew high in the sky, twilight hunters, seeking small game hidden ahead.

When Trulliç looked behind him, he wasn't surprised that the outcrop of rocks where he'd spent the last day had disappeared.

He had a feeling that if he was ever in desperate need again, it would show up wherever he was.

Maybe he was making things up, dreaming too much, as Atça had accused him more than once.

He decided right then that he wouldn't tell Atça about the outcrop disappearing.

Sweet winds blew from the east, carrying the scent of water. Riyune still walked just a few feet ahead, his nose and ears forward, his short, pointed tail wagging slightly as he strode along. His white fur made him seem like a small cloud drifting across the sand.

Or a ghost.

Maybe that was what Riyune was. A ghost dog. Maybe only Trulliç would be able to see him. Maybe he wasn't a familiar at all.

Trulliç looked down at his own dark skin. Was he already dead? Had he turned into a ghost as well? A ghost dog with a ghost boy, forever trapped in the desert?

He pinched himself. *Ow.* No, he appeared to be real. And Riyune left footprints in the sand.

Whether people other than Trulliç would be able to see the dog was a question that would just have to wait until they returned to Gaadiwala.

Even in the dimness of the night, the oasis stood apart. Tall palm trees guarded the banks of the tiny stream. Reeds crowded the water, sucking up the moisture with all their might. Not as many *meslit* and other thorns grew here. The air smelled sweet, and the dampness soothed Trulliç's dry throat.

Riyune walked directly to the stream. He stood for a moment at the edge of it, staring into the water. Trulliç realized the dog was sniffing mightily.

Could Riyune tell if the water was bad just by smelling it?

After another moment, Riyune lowered his head and took great gulping laps of water.

Trulliç knelt down beside him, cupped his hands in the lukewarm water and drank as well. Then he sat back on his heels and looked around.

The oasis wasn't large. He could stride across the tiny spot of greenery in a dozen steps. All the life crowded around the water.

After drinking his fill, Riyune lifted his head and sniffed the air.

"Anything interesting?" Trulliç asked after a moment.

Riyune glanced sideways at him, then trotted deeper into the scattered palms.

Trulliç followed, curious.

He smelled the ash before he saw the circle where other travelers had had a fire. It made him smile and draw a breath of relief.

This *was* a real place. Other people had been there. It might even be located on a map somewhere, though Atça didn't believe in maps, claiming that the land changed too often for any of them to be true.

Trulliç had to agree. For all its permanent sand, the desert felt as though it was in flux, as changeable as the seasons and the night sky. Different from day to day, though with deep patterns that Trulliç felt he could tease out, given a lifetime or two.

Trulliç called up his mage light easily again, setting the golden light burning above his head. Though the oasis was tiny, he still felt a touch of regret that this wasn't his true home. He looked around eagerly, but there really wasn't much to see: a few trees, the stream, some bushes. If he listened, he could hear mice scurrying close to the water, and a cloud of gnats, buzzing.

That was it. Just him, alone, in the oasis.

As if reading his thoughts, Riyune came and sat next to him.

All right. Fine. Just Trulliç and this strange dog.

Was that what it meant to be a magician? To always be alone? Was that why Atça had welcomed Trulliç and the other boys that he taught into his home?

At least Atça's true home was a town. He'd always be surrounded by people. Particularly if he did right by them.

Atça only took his fair share of what the town produced, sending the rest on to the emperor. He kept order in the town, and held court once or twice a week, listening to everyone's complaints and meting out justice.

Trulliç's life wouldn't be like that. He'd be alone in the desert, living in his little oasis.

His heart ached with the thought of it.

Sure, travelers would come by now and again. And maybe, once he'd found his true home, he could entice a woman to marry him and come and live with him there, despite it being in the middle of the desert and just the pair of them.

In the meanwhile, he was all alone. Already homesick and tired of adventures.

Riyune whined, as if he, too, felt Trulliç' anguish.

Trulliç just shook his head and sat up straighter.

This was his manhood journey.

He would face his future tall and proud, like a man.

Even if it made him want to weep like a little boy.

Trulliç left the oasis early in the afternoon the next day. The heat of the sun had passed, and Trulliç was determined to make it back to at least the foothills of the Kinarak mountains by the end of the night.

He'd eaten a bit more of his travel roll, though Riyune had turned his nose up at it still. Instead, he'd gone hunting mice, making a nice meal for himself.

So the dog did eat. Trulliç had woken up with Riyune curled up at his side, sharing heat during the cold of the night. He smelled like a dog, that earthy scent that came from always laying in the dirt. He breathed normally as well, and Trulliç was glad for the warmth.

Still, he wasn't sure if he could trust Riyune or not. His appearance had been too strange, even if he did mostly act like a regular dog.

Trudging across the sand was easier the next morning. Trulliç felt he was finally getting the hang of how to cross the sand. He wasn't walking on his toes, not exactly. He did consciously try to keep his feet lighter, so he didn't sink as much. That seemed to be working, as long as he kept part of his attention on it.

The rest of his mind wondered about the desert, where his true home lay, what type of magic he could really do. Atça had insisted that most magic needed to be taught—a real magician performed magic not just in his true land but elsewhere.

It wasn't that Atça hadn't done his best to try to teach Trulliç spells. It was just that Trulliç wasn't a very good magician.

Yet, Trulliç felt stronger here in the desert. His mage light was certainly a lot more powerful. He didn't want to experiment, however. Atça had told him too many stories about mages who had ended up blowing themselves up.

Trulliç still tried a few things. Atça would never know. Like calling up a soft wind that kept Trulliç cooler, even with the sun beating down on the oasis. As well as stretching his senses, seeing how deep the water lay under his feet, if any was there at all.

The winds carried scents Trulliç couldn't identify. Something spicy, not mint, but close. Did Riyune name the scents the wind brought to him? Trulliç couldn't tell. However, Riyune seemed content walking beside Trulliç, while every now and again wandering off to chase some other scent.

The hills rose on the horizon sooner than Trulliç had expected. Had he really only gone such a short ways into the desert itself?

Next time, he would be better prepared. Maybe hire a guide or something.

Though where would he get the money? It wasn't as if he had any skills he could barter. Not like Atça, who read dreams and always told the farmers when the rainy season would start, as well as how long it would be, predicting it down to the day, so the farmers and the rest of the town were always prepared.

Trulliç was just going to have to find his own place in the world.

Someday.

The harsh line demarcating the true desert from the foothills of the Kinarak mountains shown as clearly in the night as it had in the early morning sunlight.

Trulliç hesitated. He didn't want to go back to Gaadiwala. He didn't want to have to tell his mentor what a failure his manhood journey had been. He didn't want to see the look of disappointment on his mother's face when he arrived home so soon. He really didn't want to face his cousins, or their teasing.

But he couldn't stay out in the desert. He hadn't found his true home. Though he felt certain he would always be able to find water, if his senses were to be believed.

Food was another matter. He didn't want to subsist on mice and small prey, not like Riyune seemed to do. Though he'd thought about setting up a cricket trap at one point. If he could find a large enough oasis that supported big enough insects.

Trulliç looked over his shoulder. Riyune had sat down a few feet behind him, butt on the sand, front paws too, head raised high. He had a stubborn look to his eyes, the way he held his jaw.

It was obvious Riyune didn't want to leave the desert either.

"You don't have to go with me," Trulliç said softly. It wasn't as if he owned the dog or anything. Riyune wasn't some kind of purebred that the emperor's court in Atayurtkah kept. He was a desert dog, despite his large snout and unusual coloring.

Riyune didn't reply, of course. Just sat there like a statue made of white stone.

"It was nice to meet you," Trulliç told him.

Maybe the next time Trulliç came to the desert, Riyune would find him again.

Taking a deep breath, Trulliç took the final step over the border, returning to the foothills.

It felt as though blankets had suddenly been put over all Trulliç's senses. He couldn't see as well or as far. His nose only told him about the nearby bushes, not the smells that came on the winds from miles away. His skin ached and his bones felt chilled, as if the desert night had abruptly grown much colder.

Trulliç stopped for a moment. Longing for the desert filled him. He knew if he didn't pay attention his feet would turn him around, march him right out back over the sands.

He belonged in the desert. That much he knew. His mother had been right about that. He was a desert magician.

He had to learn more first, though. About being a magician. About how to survive out on the sands.

About being a man.

Trulliç swallowed against the lump in his throat. He felt worse than when he'd been alone in the tiny oasis, more homesick.

He shook his head and gave a tiny, cawing laugh.

How could he be homesick for a place that he'd never dreamed about before, that he'd only spent two nights in?

It didn't matter. He needed to go home.

Or at least back to Gaadiwala.

Determined, Trulliç strode forward, not even glancing back once, his anger boiling over.

He couldn't live there, in the desert. He couldn't live in the foothills either. He needed to get to the Ladikah pass, where he'd spend the rest of the night, then travel into the town in the morning.

A white wind rushed past, at knee level.

Riyune had decided to join him.

"I'm glad you're coming along," Trulliç whispered. At least for now. Riyune may or may not be a familiar. What he represented to Trulliç was a permanent reminder of the desert and what it had felt like.

Riyune glanced over his shoulder at Trulliç as if to say, *Of course. Idiot.*

Then the dog trotted forward, automatically heading for the trail that led to the pass.

Trulliç didn't feel like a hero on his return journey. He didn't feel like he should break into song.

He still hummed a tiny prayer to Serril, thanking him for his life and his new companion.

Atça seemed surprised when he opened his door and found Trulliç standing there.

"My dear boy!" he exclaimed. "Welcome home!"

Atça still wore his lounging robe made from a pale green silk. No one else that Trulliç knew had any silk, let alone a piece of clothing just for breaking your fast and drinking tea in the morning.

As always, Atça stood tall and proud. White hair fringed his long skull, making his broad forehead seem even bigger. His dark eyes had faded with age to a pale brown that looked golden in the right light, making him seem more magical. He had a large, bulbous nose and fat lips. Because he spent as little time as possible outside, he had the lightest skin of anyone Trulliç knew: Not white like the travelers from Lydae who stayed at the tavern sometimes, but several shades lighter than anyone else. It made Trulliç sometimes want to hide his rough hands and dark skin.

"Thank you," Trulliç said. "May I come in?" Atça liked it when Trulliç used the formal forms.

"Eh? Yes, yes," Atça said. He seemed distracted, staring at Riyune who stood beside Trulliç.

Atça backed out of the doorway. Before Trulliç could take a step forward, Atça added, "Not the dog."

Trulliç blinked, surprised. Then disappointment struck. If Atça didn't want Riyune to accompany Trulliç, it meant that Riyune was just an ordinary dog.

"I won't have that mangy mutt bringing fleas and who knows what else into my home," Atça said harshly.

Trulliç stood still, stunned. Riyune was the cleanest dog Trulliç had ever known. He didn't have fleas, even if he did scratch himself sometimes. And he wasn't a mangy mutt. Trulliç had to chase away ownerless dogs from the back of the tavern sometimes.

Still, Atça was his mentor. With a sigh, Trulliç looked down at Riyune, waiting until the dog turned his face up, those impossibly blue eyes staring into his. "I'm sorry—"

No.

The word came through loud and clear.

Trulliç blinked in surprise. It was only the second time he'd heard Riyune speak, the first being when the dog had told Trulliç his name. Both times, Trulliç couldn't mistake the words for anything else.

Trulliç looked up at Atça. "Did you hear that?" he asked eagerly.

"Hear what?" Atça asked sourly. "Come. Either come in or stay out. Stop letting flies into my house."

Trulliç looked again at Riyune. The pale blue eyes that looked into his didn't say anything else. However, Trulliç knew he shouldn't leave Riyune behind. He felt it as deeply as the sand that sifted through his blood, the memories of the desert heat that still warmed his soul.

"Riyune is my familiar," Trulliç said, willing the words to be true, though he knew they weren't. "He goes where I go. If he isn't welcome, then I'm not coming in."

Fear made the core of Trulliç tremble, but he wouldn't back down. Riyune was too important.

"Familiar? Bah," Atça said. "You've always been too fanciful." He looked critically at Riyune. "There's nothing magical about that dog," he declared loudly.

Trulliç reached down and touched his fingertips to Riyune's warm head. It was the first time he'd voluntarily touched the dog, permitted bare contact between Trulliç's skin and Riyune's fur. Riyune had come and found him at night, both when they'd been traveling as well as in the small shack Trulliç shared with his mother. They'd shared heat in the cold of the night, through blankets, Riyune getting up as soon as Trulliç stirred.

The world didn't suddenly change when Trulliç touched Riyune, as it had when Trulliç had first stepped onto the desert sands.

Still, Trulliç felt the blankets that covered his senses lifting slightly, as if a strong desert wind had blown away the first layer of fog.

Was Atça scared of Riyune? The way he held his mouth, how his eyes narrowed, spoke of fear.

Trulliç shrugged, withdrawing his fingers but still feeling the warmth they'd brought. "Maybe he has magic. Maybe not. He still belongs with me."

Atça pressed his lips together and glared at Trulliç.

That was a look Trulliç was familiar with: That glare which spoke of how stupid Atça thought Trulliç was being.

"Fine," Atça said after another moment. "He can come in. But if he ever messes my rugs, I'll skin him alive."

The thrill of having won an argument with his mentor startled Trulliç. They weren't competing, were they? He'd fought with Atça a few times in the past, with Trulliç always backing down. This was Atça's territory, his true home, not Trulliç's. Besides, Atça was older and wiser, and Trulliç had been taught to respect his elders.

Trulliç stood on the threshold and waited until Riyune looked up at him. "You heard him," Trulliç warned.

Riyune didn't nod or in any way acknowledge what Trulliç had just said.

"I need to be able to trust you," Trulliç added. He knew that Riyune understood. He also suspected that Riyune was the type of dog who knew better than to soil the inside of someone's house, but who might do so anyway out of spite.

Finally, Riyune did the dog equivalent of rolling his eyes as he turned his head to the side.

"Thank you," Trulliç said.

Again, nothing from Riyune. Though if Trulliç were feeling as fanciful as Atça always claimed, he would have said that Riyune did give off a strong sense of smug satisfaction.

Here we go. Trulliç didn't like feeling as though stepping into his mentor's house was more fraught with danger than stepping onto the desert sands.

He still braced himself as he stepped across the threshold.

Nothing happened.

Trulliç looked around the entrance hall of Atça's house, expecting to feel different.

He was in another magician's true home. Shouldn't he feel more magical himself? Or perhaps less magical?

What was wrong with him? Was he really such a poor magician? Why didn't this house ever strike him as magical, though he knew it was?

Dark wood paneling covered the walls in the front hall. Wood that could be used for planks didn't grow in or near Gaadiwala: It all had to be imported. So much wood in a simple room was a sign of extreme wealth.

Two scrolls hung from the walls. The one directly in front of Trulliç held a welcome poem written in the Lydean tongue. The one on his left held warnings and an incantation in Tadnesh against demons.

Riyune trotted over to the scroll to the left and gazed up at it, unfazed.

So maybe Riyune wasn't a demon, something that Trulliç hadn't even considered. Then again, all the demons who both Atça and Trulliç knew about were just from old stories, when mighty foes battled even mightier heroes.

A plain, dark-blue rug made of braided cloth covered the floor in the entrance hall. To the right side stood a cleverly made wooden structure. It was only as high as Trulliç's knees, but it took up half the wall and held many cubbyholes. Trulliç leaned over and untied his sandals, then put them into their usual spot, close to the floor, on the right side.

Atça thoughtfully provided his guests with house slippers made of black felt. They lay jumbled together in a basket woven together out of reeds with a geometric diamond pattern on its side. Trulliç grabbed a pair, wiped the soles of his feet with his hand to make sure they were (mostly) free of dirt, then slid the slippers on.

Atça had already left through the doorway at the back of the front room. Trulliç walked down the hallway next. Atça never bothered to light this hall. It always felt closed in to Trulliç. Sometimes, he would swear the hall grew longer as he went down it. He walked quickly through it. Riyune's claws clicked as he walked behind Trulliç, giving him comfort.

Trulliç knew his mentor's habits and went past the teaching rooms on the right and left of the hallway, and instead walked to the room just past the staircase leading to the upper levels.

The room wasn't much bigger than the front room. However, light poured in from the windows that filled the wall on the left. This morning, Atça had them thrown wide open. The window had two parts: A solid cover that Atça used at night and during the rainy season, as well as a second covering that was made of panes covered in a translucent paper. Trulliç always wondered if the diffuse light that came through the panes was similar to what light coming through tree leaves might look like.

Against the right wall, Atça had many pillows and a comfortable rug for his guests to sit on. Atça himself had settled back in, leaning against the wall and nibbling on a piece of cheese. A brass tray sat on the ground next to him, carrying the remains of his breakfast: A cup that held milky trails of yogurt, a couple of tops from dried figs, a half-eaten piece of flat bread, and the rind of the cheese.

"May I offer you tea?" Atça asked as Trulliç settled himself down, leaning against the wall himself, a comfortable pillow supporting his back.

"Thank you," Trulliç replied.

Riyune stayed close to the door, laying down just inside it, close to Trulliç but out of the way.

Atça poured a small cup of the herbal tea that he drank every morning for Trulliç. It smelled spicy, of cloves and dried *golangie* berries.

Riyune lifted his head and sniffed the air when Trulliç accepted the cup, then lay his head back down again.

Trulliç took a sip, the warm tea clearing his throat.

"Tell me of your great journeys, so that I may learn," Atça said, using the ritual formula that a storyteller sometimes used to gather a greater crowd.

Except that no storyteller Trulliç had ever heard sounded so sarcastic.

He ignored the sting, though. That was just Atça being Atça. He couldn't be genuinely excited about anything.

So Trulliç told him all about his journey, including how Riyune had first appeared as a blood hound. He admitted his weaknesses, such as not waiting until the heat of the day had passed before traveling out on the sands that first morning, of feeling so lonely the second day at the tiny oasis.

Atça merely listened, refilling their cups when needed.

"You have had a great dream," Atça proclaimed when Trulliç finished. "I will have to meditate long and hard to wriggle the meaning out of it."

Trulliç breathed a sigh of relief. His mentor agreed! He *had* had a great dream.

Atça stared at Riyune, considering him carefully, before he shook his head. "Still can't see anything magical about that dog," he said, sounding exasperated. "Just an odd colored dog with strange eyes."

Riyune didn't bother to stir or even to look at them, staying as still as a statue of a dog.

"Maybe that's how familiars work," Trulliç said. He'd been giving this some thought as well, since Riyune hadn't appeared magical at all to him, either. "If a familiar looks magical, then other will know it instantly. They could exploit the familiar. Maybe it would be a weakness in the magician. If the familiar just looks like a normal animal, that protects the magician."

"Perhaps," Atça admitted, though he didn't look pleased. "It is unnerving, though, how still that animal sits."

Trulliç looked over his shoulder at Riyune. The dog lay completely motionless. Trulliç hadn't seen him do that before, but he didn't think it meant anything.

"You have given me much to think about," Atça added, sitting up. "I will spend the day meditating on the symbols from your dream."

Trulliç swallowed down his disappointment. Atça didn't want him to spend the day, learning.

"Thank you for listening to me," Trulliç said, sitting up straighter, then bowing his head.

"Come back tomorrow, no, the day after tomorrow, to hear what I have discovered," Atça said firmly.

"I will," Trulliç said. He didn't add anything like *I will count the hours.* That sounded way too mushy, even in his own head.

Trulliç rose and bowed to his mentor one last time before he left. Riyune followed right behind him on his heels.

What did Atça really think about Trulliç's journey? About Riyune?

It would be at least two days before Trulliç found out. If then. Atça was a master of not answering questions he didn't want to.

Trulliç walked down the dark hallway in his mentor's house, back toward the front hall. Atça would see him in a couple days, tell him what he'd teased apart from Trulliç's journey of the desert.

The hallway grew, as Trulliç suspected it might. If he was being fanciful, as Atça accused him of being, he'd say the hallway didn't like Trulliç, didn't want to allow another magician through.

The light at the end of the hallway winked out. Trulliç stopped, panicked, and looked behind him.

No light there either.

Total darkness.

Trulliç called up his mage light.

It was like trying to do magic through a blanket. Trulliç struggled to bring more magic to his hand, to cut through the darkness with his light.

Riyune's claws clicked in the darkness. Trulliç felt a warm pressure against his calf, where Riyune leaned against him.

The mage light flared suddenly, as bright as it had been in the desert.

Trulliç felt as though he was channeling the energy from somewhere else, not just drawing it from himself. Was it coming from Riyune? Or from some deeper well, further away?

The end of the hallway appeared again, just a few steps away.

Trulliç scurried to the front room, extinguishing his light as soon as he crossed the threshold and stepped out of the hallway. He slipped off the house slippers and grabbed his sandals, tying them quickly.

Riyune waited patiently beside the door.

"Thank you," Trulliç said as he opened the door for the pair of them.

Riyune didn't say, *See? I told you so.*

But Trulliç knew the dog could have said those things, as well as much more. Such as how important it was for Riyune to accompany Trulliç everywhere he went. How Riyune could help Trulliç with his magic.

How Atça, or at least his house, didn't like Trulliç.

Atça had been Trulliç's mentor all his life, had shown him the wonders of magic, taught him what it could be like to be a town magician.

But Trulliç wondered as he left Atça's grand house, what things his mentor had never taught him, had never planned on teaching him.

What things Trulliç now needed to learn on his own.

CHAPTER FOUR

NADEEM

SWEAT POURED DOWN NADEEM'S BACK, though she sat as still as the carved rocks west of the oasis.

Izmet, the star sister Nadeem battled, sat the prescribed three feet in front of her. The pair of them were naked in the center of the ceremonial circle. A small pavilion protected them from the sun overhead. Aunt Parayat and Aunt Karalit watched critically from the sidelines. No one else was allowed to stand close to watch this battle, though several sisters from other *kabils* waited outside, curious.

It was the *panayirat,* the annual celebration and meeting of the seven star-sister tribes. Everyone spent months preparing for the games: contests to determine the strongest illusionists, the cleverest storytellers, the most inspirational dancers, the finest cooks.

Any girl who had just passed her womanhood training and had been marked could go. Often, mentors brought their most talented protégées to compete in private games.

Like Aunt Parayat and Aunt Karalit.

Both Nadeem and Izmet neared the end of their training. They were both sixteen, the strongest at their age of their individual *kabils*. Izmet was the most powerful girl Nadeem had ever met. She had a deep well of magic that Nadeem found difficult to match.

Above the seated girls two illusionary figures wrestled one another.

Nadeem had chosen her favorite figure—a tall blue-skinned girl with a human body and the head of a desert hawk. Brown and white speckled feathers covered the sleek head and faded out across her shoulders. She also had large golden eyes and a bone-white hooked beak.

Izmet battled using a dog-headed boy with a pointed black snout, soft looking ears that rose up just a little from the top of his head, and pale brown eyes. He had a longer reach than Nadeem's hawk girl and a terribly strong bite. However, Nadeem's hawk girl moved faster, sliding out of any hold the dog-boy put her into.

Both figures bled freely when struck, the drops falling out of the air and disappearing before they touched the ground. Then the wounds healed, the imaginary creatures whole again.

And while Izmet's dog-boy couldn't wrestle Nadeem's hawk-girl to the ground for the count of three, neither could Nadeem get the upper hand. They were too well matched. The battle continued.

When Nadeem had a spare moment to think, her figure circling Izmet's, she wondered if they'd fight for the rest of the day and into the night, only giving up when they'd reached complete exhaustion.

No.

Nadeem had to win.

She always had to win.

Nadeem felt herself grinding her teeth in frustration as the dog-boy slipped away again, out of her hawk-girl's grip. There had to be a way to stake him down!

She knew that she could win if she cheated. She'd have to cause permanent damage, however. Or come close to it. Impale the dog-boy on her hawk-girl's beak. Bleed the illusionary figure dry.

That was against the rules. Just as a star sister couldn't kill another when they wrestled, imaginary foes couldn't permanently damage each other either.

Izmet had considered it once, Nadeem could tell. Had thought about tearing out the neck of her hawk girl, but had pulled back at the last minute.

Was this fight worth breaking the rules? Nadeem would win the battle. Izmet would have the moral victory. Would it count? Did it matter?

Nadeem found her body swaying. She didn't want to cheat. But they'd been fighting since the first light of morning. She just wanted this to be over. Her focus wavered for a moment.

The dog-boy flipped her hawk-girl onto her back. Nadeem felt the hit as if it had been physical, the breath forced from her body by the impact.

With a twist and a flip, Nadeem's hawk girl found her feet again, then stood there, swaying, instead of attacking immediately.

Nadeem was going to lose if she didn't do something quickly.

Lightning fast, Nadeem's hawk girl leaped forward. She feinted with her right hand, as if going to grab the dog boy's upper arm.

When he rolled his shoulder back, out of the way, Nadeem's hawk girl struck with her beak, sinking the hooked end deeply into the soft skin, where neck met shoulder, that spot that a lover might touch, causing chicken flesh to raise across her bare skin.

The hawk girl dropped to her knees, forcing the dog boy down as well. He flailed at her, punches that Nadeem felt but ignored.

He had to go down. Now.

Nadeem flipped them, throwing the boy onto his back, withdrawing the beak and grabbing his wrists.

One. Two. Three.

Done.

Nadeem's hawk girl regained her feet. The cry of victory she gave sounded feeble and hollow to Nadeem's ears, as if the figure was really as insubstantial as she appeared.

Then the battling figures disappeared.

"You cheated!" Izmet loudly proclaimed.

Nadeem took a deep breath and merely stared at the other girl. *So?* "Non-lethal force," Nadeem said slowly. "I didn't tear his head off. I didn't even nick the jugular. He could have lived through that wound."

Izmet glared at her, then turned to appeal to the aunts standing beside them. "She cheated," she said again.

Nadeem sat still and breathed, grateful that the battle was over. She felt dizzy with relief. She looked around, then blinked.

Why was it so dim? Then she realized that she'd been so focused on the battle she hadn't noticed the light changing. She looked out of the pavilion, toward the west. What was the sun doing way down there? Had they really fought all through the day and into the evening?

When Nadeem looked back, she saw Aunt Parayat and Aunt Karalit glaring at each other, as if they'd been the ones battling, not Nadeem and Izmet.

Then again, since they were the mentors for the girls, they had been, in some ways.

"He could have recovered," Aunt Parayat said slowly.

Aunt Karalit nodded, resigned. "Only if he had immediate help," she added.

Aunt Parayat shrugged. "They did battle longer than expected. By attacking as she did, Nadeem saved their physical selves."

"True," Aunt Karalit replied sourly. "We could call it a draw."

"But she cheated!" Izmet complained.

"Yes, and all will know it," Aunt Parayat said, her eyes drilling into Nadeem's.

Nadeem stared back defiantly. She'd won. That was all that mattered.

"I declared Nadeem the winner," Aunt Parayat said slowly.

"I agree," Aunt Karalit said.

"Cheater," Izmet said without a sound.

Nadeem shrugged. She'd won. That was what was most important.

And she was willing to accept the consequences.

<hr>

Nadeem tried to rest in hers and Aunt Parayat's tent. She'd depleted most of her body fluids during the fight—always a danger when battling using illusionary figures—and still felt light headed, despite the salty tea she'd drunk.

However, she couldn't rest. She paced the dirt floor between their two sets of blankets. Three steps, turn, three more steps, turn. She tried to sit, to rest, but found herself jumping to her feet again and again. Oil lamps made out of baked clay hung in the corners of the tent, casting as much shadow as light.

She wore a sleeveless tunic that fell to her knees, unbelted so the front slid open as she walked, letting the cooler air touch her heated skin. Nadeem had dyed the linen herself, using the bark of the *meslit* thorn bush. The thread had turned the palest gold, and Nadeem thought it looked good against her dark skin. She wore her hair shorter than most, well above her neck and ears. Generally, only married women let their hair grow long.

The door to the tent stood wide open, allowing in what few breezes the desert night brought. No one would look in, though: Nadeem had finally mastered the simplest yet hardest of illusions—making the tent flap still appear closed. She kept track of that illusion with a thread tucked away at the back of her mind, so she could focus on other things.

Where was Aunt Parayat? Who was she meeting with? Nadeem knew she'd won her battle by a mere technicality. What were the consequences?

She wouldn't be banished, that much she knew. She would have had to commit a much more egregious act for that, like murder. Would they be asked to leave the *panayirat* gathering? When Nadeem had been fighting, she'd been willing to accept the consequences. She'd been too tired to think beyond ending the battle.

Now, with fluids in her and time to think, she worried.

She kept trying to tell herself that it didn't matter. She couldn't survive in the desert on her own forever. But if she needed to do a purification ritual, go into the sands for a week, she could do that.

Finally, Nadeem felt the thread of illusion for the tent flap be cut.

Aunt Parayat entered.

Though Nadeem knew her aunt was only in her sixties, she looked as ancient as the old crone in the Tale of Marisat—the one who'd been dancing forever in Goddess Berzhat's golden court.

Nadeem stopped pacing and crossed her arms over her chest. She stood in the middle of the tent, her legs spread and her weight equally balanced over her feet so she could either take a blow or pivot away.

"Sit," Aunt Parayat directed.

Nadeem stayed standing.

Aunt Parayat merely shrugged. "Or don't." She collapsed on her blankets then rolled her shoulders stiffly.

Nadeem bit her lips together. Obviously, her aunt had been arguing with the others for a while, her whole posture still tense.

But Nadeem knew that Aunt Parayat wouldn't take it easy on her. She saw no reason to be easy or gentle in return.

"You deliberately injured another player," Aunt Parayat said slowly as she flexed her back. She still had wiry muscles through her arms. But she was no longer as flexible as the young girls when they first came in for training, and she wasn't as strong.

She also took longer naps in the afternoon.

If Nadeem had one fear, it was going to wake up her aunt, only to find her gone and already dancing in the goddess' golden court.

"I need to understand why," Aunt Parayat said as she finished working her shoulders and ribs.

Nadeem had so many answers prepared. She knew that would be the first question her aunt would ask.

"I don't know what to tell you," Nadeem said honestly. The

restlessness that had driven her to move all evening left, as abruptly as an illusion, the strings cut.

Nadeem collapsed on her own blankets, sitting across from her aunt. She didn't bother with trying to lower her head beneath her teacher's out of respect. This was more important.

"I was hot. Tired. I had to win. I couldn't let the battle go on," Nadeem said all in a rush.

Aunt Parayat nodded slowly. "But you chose this. You weren't delusional, or having visions."

Nadeem shuddered. "No," she said firmly. "I chose the final action, to bleed my opponent dry rather than continue the fight."

"Are you certain?" Aunt Parayat said. "Sometimes your visions—"

"I'm sure," Nadeem said firmly.

Yes, since her womanhood ceremony she'd had visions, more than most.

Violent, dark visions, with her footsteps turning to ashes as she walked across the sand.

However, she'd learned to never drink more than a mouthful of the palm wine served at ceremonies, and to never touch the *igrat* that some of the older aunts drank, claiming it helped ease their aches and pains when in fact, it generally made them gibber and snooze.

Aunt Parayat looked at her closely, then nodded. "That's what I told the others. That you'd made a choice." She paused, then added, "But why?"

"Why did I choose to end the battle? Beyond being tired, being out of patience? Why?" Nadeem asked, her voice raising.

Aunt Parayat nodded. "Yes. Why. Tell me the true reason for the darkness around your heart."

Nadeem sat up taller, her back stiffening. What did Aunt Parayat know? What had she heard?

Nadeem started to shake her head. No, she wouldn't tell her aunt.

But she was already in so much trouble. The sand was already piled up over her head. What harm could another cupful be?

"Why do we battle each other?" Nadeem asked. Instead of shouting the words with the force she felt behind them, she found her voice lowering to a whisper. "What's the point? We battle and prove our worth, but for what? So we can be the best among equals? There has to be a reason. Something else. Something *more*."

All the nervous energy flowed out of Nadeem. There. She'd said it.

Those words she'd only whispered to herself on a still night, when no wind could carry them away.

It didn't make sense to her why she had to work and improve and try so hard. It would be years before she was an old, respected aunt. Sure, she could work hard all her life, be a respected part of her *kabil*, but there had to be more. More to struggle for, more reward.

Aunt Parayat had always taught her to question.

She'd never found an answer to this, though.

Aunt Parayat looked at her sadly. "That's what I thought," she said softly, her tone almost matching Nadeem's. "You're restless, more than most. Striving. Questioning." She gave a bitter laugh. "More my daughter than any other."

Nadeem blinked, tears welling up. Aunt Parayat had *never* called her "daughter." Not once. Aunt Parayat was Nadeem's mentor, her teacher, her aunt. Not a friend, a confidant, a mother.

Aunt Parayat nodded, as if Nadeem had just answered a question. "Come!" she called.

Nadeem wondered at the power behind her aunt's tone. If she didn't know better, she would have said that there was something magical about it.

But the star sisters could only do illusions. They couldn't use real magic.

Could they?

A few moments later, the tent flap flipped back and Izmet entered.

Nadeem gasped. What was she doing here?

Out of habit, Nadeem rose to her feet to welcome a stranger to her tent. "Please join us," she said formally. There was no seat of honor, no separate setting.

But strangers *must* be welcomed. Always.

It had been many years since Goddess Berzhat had taken human form and walked among them. But she could return at any time.

Better to always welcome the stranger.

"Thank you," Izmet said.

Izmet and Aunt Parayat exchanged a look that Nadeem couldn't interpret. Why did Izmet seem smugly satisfied? And Aunt Parayat so sad?

Nadeem stood, shocked, when Izmet sat beside Aunt Parayat. She shouldn't do that. Izmet wasn't any older than Nadeem. Surely she knew better? She should sit across from all the aunts, her head lowered in respect. She should never presume to be as important and sit *beside* an aunt. Particularly not one as revered as Aunt Parayat.

"Please, sit," Izmet said, as if this were *her* tent.

Nadeem sat carefully, cautiously. She wished she had belted her tunic, that she had a knife at hand, that she wore strips of leather tied to her feet so could run easily if necessary.

Then she stared defiantly at Izmet. She'd beaten the other girl at the battle that afternoon. Sure, it had been more of a technical win than anything else.

Nadeem could do it again, either physically or with illusions, if the other girl challenged her.

"Oh, go on," Aunt Parayat told Izmet when the girl looked at her again. "I swear she loves the drama of this as much as you do, Nadeem," Aunt Parayat added crossly.

Nadeem sat, waiting. What drama? What was going on?

Wait. What was happening?

Izmet's face began to change.

Nadeem watched, fascinated. Of course, she'd tried to change her own appearance, secretly, away from her aunts and everyone else. She'd figured out how to make the skin of her arms and hands appear lighter, and even how to make her hands appear larger, stretching out her fingers until they were thin and delicate.

There weren't any mirrors in the oasis where Nadeem had grown up. She'd been told she was beautiful by the two lovers she'd had, both other sisters in the *kabil*. She knew she had a small nose, thin lips, and a wide smile. Her eyes were dark brown. The cuts on her left cheek formed delicate scars, darker than the rest of her skin.

She'd never been able to see, though, if she could change her face and disguise her appearance. Most star sisters couldn't.

None of the star sisters had the ability to hide their scar. Though Nadeem couldn't imagine why a star sister would want to hide her mark, that didn't mean she wasn't interested in seeing if she could. It was strictly against the law, though. The emperor decreed that any star sister who hid her mark was to be executed immediately. The rest of the sisters would enforce that rule strictly, stating that they never wanted to return to the times of persecution.

Izmet's skin kept its dark color. Her eyebrows stayed like two wings, thick and solid, over her eyes.

But the color of her eyes changed, from a dark brown to a more faded color, similar to Aunt Parayat's.

Wrinkles sprang up around Izmet's eyes, growing deeper, then spreading like water around the edges of her cheeks and around the corners of her mouth. Darker spots spread across her skin—age spots. Streaks of white sprouted in her dark hair, and her hair suddenly spilled down, caught up in a braid that fell to her waist.

Nadeem couldn't contain her gasp when Izmet's change was complete. "You're not a girl," Nadeem accused her. "You're an aunt!" She looked between Aunt Parayat and Aunt Izmet. "You're the same age," she guessed.

Izmet gave her a sharp smile. "Very good," she said. "Parayat told me you were smart."

The compliment didn't make Nadeem feel any better. "Why the disguise?" she asked. Could any of the other aunts see Izmet's true face?

Aunt Izmet said, "We needed to test you. To see if you had the right instincts."

"I couldn't have won the battle, could I?" Nadeem asked bitterly. "Not without doing what I did."

She wouldn't admit that she'd cheated. Just that she'd been driven to an extreme.

Aunt Izmet's laugh rang through the tent. "She is just like you, isn't she?" she asked, nudging Aunt Parayat.

"Including questioning why the games, why the battles, why isn't there something more?" Aunt Parayat replied.

Nadeem blinked, surprised. Others had these same thoughts and questions? She'd assumed she'd been the only one.

"Have you ever heard of the stars of the emperor?" Aunt Izmet asked.

Nadeem shook her head no. She knew the names of many of the stars in the sky, their history, how the great heroes still watched them from above.

"There are a very select few star sisters who receive special training and work just for the emperor," Aunt Izmet said proudly.

"The *Padisha-i-Ghazi*, the great emperor, himself?" Nadeem asked, shocked.

She'd never even heard rumors of such a group!

"Yes, him," Aunt Izmet added dryly. "The emperor himself."

Nadeem sat back, stunned.

The star sisters worked with the emperor? For the emperor? The stars of the emperor? She remembered the change of prayers during the great feasts, only two years before, where they now had to thank the emperor at every meal. And at least once she'd heard an aunt grumble about the amount of tribute that the star sisters had to pay the emperor, that it had increased every year.

Nadeem didn't say anything, however. She bit her lips together so she wouldn't ask more. They would have to tell her everything.

Aunt Izmet let the silence between them gather weight.

"You passed the first test," Aunt Izmet finally replied. "Would you like to continue? I can't guarantee that you'll become one of the few," she warned, then paused, "though your aunt here thinks you'll be one of the best."

"You were one of the emperor's stars," Nadeem said, turning to her old mentor.

"I was," Aunt Parayat said gravely. "It was an honor."

Nadeem wasn't sure what her aunt meant by that. Her voice held no emotion, as though she was discussing the weather.

Nadeem turned back to Aunt Izmet. "It would be my honor to continue," she said, making sure that she sounded as awestruck as she felt.

Aunt Izmet gave her that sharp smile again. "I'll make sure it is," she purred. "Come. We need to celebrate."

A bag suddenly appeared beside Aunt Izmet. Had it been there all along, just hidden with illusion?

Nadeem shook her head. She wasn't as strong as Aunt Parayat, though she knew that in time, she would be.

Would she ever be as strong as Aunt Izmet? She didn't know. It would be good to test herself, though, and push.

Maybe there was a reason behind all the tests, the struggles.

From her bag, Aunt Izmet pulled out a leather flagon of *igrat*. Nadeem smelled the sour alcohol from where she sat.

"I don't drink—" Nadeem started.

"I know. Parayat's told me," Aunt Izmet said. "If I'm taking you on as an apprentice, this is the next step. To walk you through your visions, see the worst they can become."

Nadeem shivered as if a cold wind suddenly blew through the tent. She'd never purposefully gone hunting her visions, had always felt ashamed anytime she'd had one.

Given her day and how little food she had in her stomach, she suspected any vision brought about by the *igrat* would be overwhelming.

However, Nadeem didn't fear getting lost in her vision world. Particularly not now, when she had so much to look forward to: a new mentor, new training, the possibility of working for the emperor himself.

"Let us walk, then," Nadeem said, sitting up straighter. It was the call of a storyteller to an audience, to get them to travel along the tale's trails with her.

"Let us walk," Aunt Izmet said, raising the flagon and taking the first sip before passing it to Aunt Parayat.

"May you gain wisdom on your journey," Aunt Parayat replied, also taking a drink then handing the flagon to Nadeem.

Nadeem weighed the leather container in her hands. "Let me be your guide," she said as she raised the sour drink to her lips.

Fire water poured down her throat. It burned all the way to her stomach. Nadeem lowered the flagon and coughed, her eyes watering.

Determined, she took another swallow.

Willed the vision to begin.

The sky changed from the soft blanket of night to the purple of an old bruise. Nadeem walked on blackened sand. It crunched under her sandals as though she was breaking tiny bird bones with every step. When she turned back to look, her footprints appeared as white as ash. The air smelled of rotten eggs.

Clouds boiled on every horizon, angry and threatening. The rain they carried would wash the land clean, but the desert wouldn't allow the storm across its border. Every once in a while Nadeem caught a whiff of sweet rain, but she knew she'd never see it.

So it was the desert vision today. Nadeem had visions of other locations as well—a place where water as far as the eye could see came crashing into the shore, chasing her away from the buried chest she needed to rescue. The water itself was composed of tiny, stinging darts that shredded her skin if she let it touch her. Or the forest one, when she raced beneath trees taller than any she'd ever seen, something awful pursuing her. She almost always took a wrong turn and ended up being cornered, the only way to escape to tumble down the mountain-side herself.

In the desert, to her right, ran a long wooden barrier. It had rotted in places, the wood falling to dust. In others, it stood taller than her head by several yards. She walked beside it. In the areas where it was still whole, she could tell that it had at one point been round, like the shaft of a great spear.

Once, when she'd reached the end of it, she'd found a huge piece of metal, as big as the entire oasis where she'd grown up.

It sloped on either side, triangular in shape.

Like a spear head.

Beyond what Nadeem called the Spear Mountain lay the heart of this vision place, the desert. A tiny outcrop of rock that sprang up out of nowhere. The rocks looked haphazardly piled, one on top of the other, though they were a single piece. It was smaller than the teaching tent, and only had the single opening.

Gibbering black shapes lived inside the prison created by the rocks, teeming masses of shadows that threatened to tear the world apart. They howled when Nadeem approached. If she wasn't careful, she'd find herself tearing at her own clothes, marking her own skin, their hatred of all living things overwhelming her.

A flimsy red rope was strung across that opening, holding all the creatures in.

In Nadeem's worst visions, she was the one who cut the rope or untied it, unleashing madness on the world.

The creatures would always destroy her first, showing her the ugliness inside her own soul so she would take her own life. Or they'd tear her to pieces when Nadeem refused to believe their illusions.

This vision was more awful than those, however.

As Nadeem neared the end of the Spear Mountains, the darkness came rushing at her.

Someone else was there. He'd already released the black hordes.

Stupid boy. He was obviously a magician trying to rein in the darkness, but his mage light wasn't strong enough to contain the creatures. The shadows cringed, yes, but they didn't stop. Instead, they poured out of the rocks, destroying the boy before he could blast them.

So Nadeem fought them instead. An endless stream of opponents. She was already tired, the day's events blurring into her dream: Her hawk-girl battled beside her, along with the dog-boy, but they were still restricted and couldn't do fatal damage.

Nadeem, however, could kill. She used her knife like it was an extension of her hand and sliced apart the shadows she fought, or cut their throats, or when her knife shattered, broke limbs and clawed out eyes.

It was a battle worthy of songs or poems, but Nadeem lost in the end as she always did, falling under the onslaught of so many creatures.

With a cry, Nadeem woke, finding both Aunt Parayat and Aunt Izmet looking down at her. Worry lined their faces.

"What?" Nadeem asked as she looked from one to the other. She blinked, her eyes gritty with sand. She took a deep breath, smelling her own sour sweat. When she tried to push herself up, she found her head even more dizzy than after the long battle that afternoon.

Aunt Parayat helped Nadeem to sit up, then Aunt Izmet held the water jug while Nadeem took great gulps.

"You went far, my sister," Aunt Parayat said softly when Nadeem finally was able to push the jug away, her thirst sated for the moment.

Nadeem shrugged. She always did.

Wait. Did Aunt Parayat just call her sister?

Before Nadeem could ask about that, Aunt Izmet added, "You walked the dreamlands for more than a day. Went places I couldn't follow." She sounded put out by that.

That was interesting. Could other aunts follow Nadeem's visions? Dream beside her? Was that what the dream readers did? That was a skill she wanted to learn.

"It was a long time for a vision," Aunt Parayat said. It sounded as though she was scolding Nadeem. "Too long."

Nadeem nodded. She was aware that her visions had not only grown more violent, but stronger as well.

Aunt Izmet sat on the ground beside Nadeem, looking at her sourly.

Was Nadeem not worthy of becoming one of the emperor's stars? Because of her visions? Had she chosen the wrong shells for her coming of age ritual? If only she'd taken the weakest!

But Aunt Parayat had pointed out to her that weaker shells might not have prevented her from having visions—it might have only prevented her from being able to return from the dreamlands.

Aunt Izmet appeared to be reconsidering her offer.

Nadeem held her breath. She wasn't sure what she'd do if Aunt Izmet refused to keep training her. She wouldn't walk the desert looking for the goddess, though she knew other girls who would. There was honor staying at the *kabil* as well.

"It's a good thing you're going to continue your training with me," Aunt Izmet finally said. "One of the first things you're going to learn is how to pretend to drink, and get drunk, while not taking a sip of alcohol."

Nadeem sighed, relieved. That actually sounded like a very useful skill for her to learn.

She couldn't wait to get started.

CHAPTER FIVE

TRULLIÇ

TRULLIÇ WOKE WITH A START. He'd been dreaming of the desert, as he had almost every night since he'd returned from his first manhood journey four years before.

Of course, he never dreamed of his true home. He despaired of ever finding it. His dreams were full of oases, hidden streams, caves that held ancient secrets, foothills that towered over the sands, the cry of the desert hawk filling his ears and sweet dates tickling his tongue.

He'd never determined how he was supposed to live on the sands, either. His dreams didn't show him secret fields of wheat or trees full of fruit and nuts. He couldn't choke down the small rodents that Riyune found so effortlessly, either. If he found a desert hawk chick and raised her by hand her entire life, maybe she could have gone hunting for him, but how could he afford to feed her while she was young? He didn't have the time or the money for such an expensive pet.

Trulliç pushed aside his blankets, sat up and stretched, his shoulders popping. He stood over six feet tall now, taller than most of his cousins. He kind of hoped his latest growth spurt had been his last—it was such a pain being so hungry all the time!

Riyune looked up from where he'd been sleeping, curled up beside Trulliç, his back warming Trulliç's left thigh.

"Yeah, yeah, I'm getting up," Trulliç said. Gaadiwala wasn't big or rich enough to have proper temples with bells to mark all the hours of the gods. They still had the morning bells—bell, really—that had just started to ring.

That was another change since Trulliç had been younger—the bell that marked the morning was no longer rung just for Xannil, the sun god, but also in honor of the emperor.

In a week's time, Trulliç would take another journey through the desert. He didn't know how he felt about that. Or rather, he had too many feelings and couldn't sort them out.

Trulliç stood and threw the blankets back on his sleeping pallet—just a collection of soft sheepskins with the wool still attached that he needed to air out again. He'd worn his plain brown shirt and short pants to bed so he'd stay warm through the cool desert night. Now he threw his workman's tunic over them, its soft gray cotton still clean from the last time his mother had washed it, belting it with the broad leather belt that Atça had given him at the end of the previous year.

After slipping on his sandals, Trulliç picked up two of the four clay water jugs that rested beside the door. His first chore every morning was to walk up the street to the neighborhood well and get water for the day.

His mother still slept in her blankets in the alcove that held her sleeping pallet in their one-room hut, farthest away from the door and closer to the hearth that was never enough on cold winter nights. Their few goods, scattered along the base of the wall. They couldn't afford cupboards or even fine pillows to lean against. They mostly sat on the dirt.

Myrizhah worked until after dark most nights at the family tavern. She wouldn't get up until after he'd gotten the water. Then she would clean herself and go into the tavern and work, baking the flat bread that the customers would eat for that day. It kept her near the fires, where it was warmest. She brought home the leftovers, or the burned pieces if there were no leftovers, for her and Trulliç to have with their supper.

Trulliç hung the two pots over a yoke and trudged down the hill to the well.

Two people stood in line already, with a third drawing her water: Widow Jarkat, who'd lost not one but two husbands to the wars, and so constantly wore the blue-and-black striped scarf of mourning around her neck; Old man Somlekçi, who'd once been Gaadiwala's main potter but whose hands were now too twisted with arthritis to throw pots anymore; and young Erzalat who hauled water out of the well.

Erzalat was a few years older than Trulliç and lived with her parents up in the foothills where they tended a huge flock of sheep. She kept her head covered with a soft gray *chafiyek* to keep the sun and wind out of her face and the sand out of her short, dark hair. Under her light blouse, her biceps bulged as she pulled a full bucket up out of the well. Her mouth was set in a grim line, her jaw hard and square.

Trulliç always assumed that Erzalat could beat him at any wrestling match, and his cousins to boot.

"There's water," Erzalat told the others as she lifted the bucket and poured it into her waiting water jug. "But it's low. And slow in coming."

Fear shot through Trulliç.

Gaadiwala couldn't live without water. The punishment for stealing or blocking another man's stream was death. Atça took all accusations of water theft very seriously. Though he hated leaving town and grumbled the entire way, he'd make the trip out to a farmer's residence to verify claims of water stealing.

Though Gaadiwala wasn't *his* home, not like it was Atça's, Trulliç still had tried to find the water under the town once, like he had in the desert.

It had been *much* harder to find. And then Atça had yelled at Trulliç for wasting his time—until Trulliç found his true home, he could never trust his senses or his magical ability.

Still, Trulliç worried about the lack of water at the neighborhood well. They'd just passed through the rainy season and there had been plenty of rain. The well should be full.

"Can't you do anything?" Widow Jarakat asked, turning to Trulliç.

"Me?" Trulliç asked, surprised.

"You are a magician, after all," old man Somlekçi added.

"But I'm not Atça, the town's magician," Trulliç told them.

Erzalat snorted. "Exactly," she said. She shot a hard glare at Trulliç as she dropped the bucket back into the well. "You're likely to actually help."

Trulliç opened his mouth to defend his mentor, then closed it again. Atça had explained more than once that the town owed him their tithe, that they were unaware of all that he did for them, how he protected them. The tithe had been growing though, both the emperor's portion as well as Atça's.

"Fine," Trulliç said. It would be awhile before he could draw his own water. What could it hurt? He wouldn't be wasting his time, since he had to wait anyway.

Trulliç took a deep breath, closed his eyes, and pushed his awareness under the hard-packed earth.

The smell of rich, wet loam filled his senses as he pushed down. There *was* water below them.

He tracked the cold shaft of the well down into the reservoir below.

Water trickled through the stones into the northern end of the reservoir. Though Atça had told Trulliç more than once that he couldn't believe his senses, it still felt to him as though the water meant for this place had been diverted.

But where was the start of the underground creek? Where had it been blocked off?

Trulliç tried backtracking past the stones, up the small trail of water.

Instantly, he got lost.

Instead of following the main spear of water, he found himself tricked again and again, following the little fingers of water that divided off of the primary stream. He couldn't tell which direction was up, or down, or east, or west. He bumped into the hard rock when he tried to leave the water trail, unable to push through it and rise to the surface.

Trulliç lost all awareness of his body above him. It grew into a faint memory. He'd had fingers once, and toes, but they were long gone. The ground breathed air into him, kept his hungering belly full, drew his attention along, instead of allowing him to float back up, above the ground.

Was this how the hero Arzhem felt when she first left the corrupt city and wandered lost in the desert? Trulliç's feet had meandered every time his sandals had touched the sands, but it had never been as bad as this.

Something hard pinched his cheek. The pain drew his face, his attention, away from the underground water trails and back—ah, there! Back toward the surface.

When Trulliç opened his eyes, his mother stood in front of him. He blinked, surprised.

He was taller than her. When had that happened?

"Are you all right?" Mother asked. Her dark features were pinched with worry.

"Yes," Trulliç said, nodding. *Ow.* Had she slapped him? He put his hand up to his cheek. "What happened?" he asked.

"You got lost in your head," Mother said simply.

Trulliç nodded. It hadn't happened to him for a while, but it had happened before. He looked at Riyune who sat beside his mother.

"Couldn't Riyune help?" he asked. Before, the dog had licked his fingers or something to bring him back.

Mother shook her head. "He came to get me."

"Oh," Trulliç said. Mother and Riyune avoided each other. They both pretended the other didn't exist most of the time.

That Riyune voluntarily went to go get Mother meant that Trulliç had been truly lost.

"Let's get some water," Mother suggested. "Then you need to get to Atça's and tell him what happened."

Trulliç nodded, though he didn't agree.

He didn't want to tell his mentor about how he'd gotten lost in his head again while he'd been looking for water sources, something Atça would chide him for.

All Atça needed to hear about was the lack of water at the well outside of town, so he would hopefully do something about it. And not demand more tribute in payment from the poor neighborhood.

"Have you come with a great vision this morning?" Atça asked Trulliç as he walked into the learning room, Riyune at his heels. "Some new grand prophecy to entertain us with?"

"No, master, I have not," Trulliç replied. He tried not to sulk. Atça was just being Atça, as usual, though it stung every time Atça asked such questions in front of Ordu and Çirmal, the two paying students.

With a sigh, Trulliç lowered himself to the floor beside the others. He sat on bare wood while the other two boys had their own rugs, provided by their families. Riyune lay down just inside the room, next to the door, as if guarding the occupants from any who might enter.

Trulliç had made the mistake once of asking Atça if maybe, since he never dreamed of a single place in the desert, if perhaps the *entire* desert was his home.

Atça had not only laughed himself silly, he'd told the other students about it. They teased Trulliç mercilessly about it, calling him King of the Sands and other titles.

"Since you've decided to join us, even with your lack of stories to entertain us, perhaps you could recite the lines assigned for this morning?" Atça continued.

Trulliç wasn't a paying student. Atça took Trulliç on only because of his magical abilities, no matter how feeble they'd turned out to be.

Fortunately, Trulliç liked the poem they'd been assigned. It told of the hero Lyons, who stole an egg from a stone eagle, then hatched the great rock himself by roasting it in the fires of a mountain of flame—a volcano, or so Atça had explained. Lyons and his eagle then flew to the courts of the gods, where he became their messenger.

Trulliç pushed himself back up to his feet. Atça insisted that they do all their recitations standing. Even if that meant going from seated to standing and back again all day long.

After taking a deep breath, Trulliç recited the next stanza of the poem. He was just getting into the interesting part, where Lyons turned the egg in the coals by using a lever, when he noticed Ordu and Çirmal working hard to keep straight faces, trying not to giggle.

Trulliç found his words tumbling off.

"That's very good," Atça said sourly. "But that's also not where we were in the poem."

Trulliç thought back. Where had they left off?

"Ordu, if you can?" Atça said, sounding bored.

Trulliç sighed and sat back down.

Ordu stood. He gave Trulliç a smug smile, his fat face beaming with satisfaction. Then he started reciting, just two stanzas after where Trulliç had started.

Trulliç recognized his mistake instantly. He'd been thinking about the poem while he'd been walking to Atça's, wondering about the amount of force needed to turn such a heavy object. Since discovering the blocked off trail of water below the well that morning, he'd been wondering what it would take to open up that flow again.

Of course, Atça would deny that the poems he taught had any application to *work*. The poems and songs they learned were to stir the soul, not to teach people how to build or to live more productive lives.

Trulliç kept his back straight and his face neutral as he made himself listen to Ordu, who spoke with a nasal, flat tone. He never added any of the passion that Trulliç felt needed to be in the tale. Ordu would never give Blind Giresul, the market storyteller, a run for his money.

But Ordu was accurate and didn't miss a single, droned out word.

After Ordu finished three stanzas, Atça indicated that he should sit down. "Çirmal? If you could continue to catch Trulliç up?"

Trulliç bit his lips together and didn't say anything. It was just Atça being Atça. Trulliç knew where they were in the poem—he already had the entire thing memorized! He was also aware, though, that he was in trouble for the entire day. Atça would assume that Trulliç hadn't done any of the lessons. Despite the fact that Trulliç *always* did his lessons and never missed any assignments, even when that huge caravan had come into Gaadiwala and he'd spent most of the night working in the tavern with his mother and cousins.

Çirmal stood and continued from where Ordu had left off. Atça had to prompt him a few times when he stumbled over words and phrases, but Atça still heaped praise on Çirmal when he finished.

"For next week, start with the birth of the stone eagle," Atça told the students. "If you think you could remember that, this time?" he directed at Trulliç.

"I will," Trulliç said. "I promise." He really liked that part of the poem as well.

Atça merely raised one eyebrow at him but didn't comment.

Trulliç kept his sigh to himself. He did everything he could to make his mentor proud of him. It never seemed to be enough, though.

He would just have to try harder to please his mentor and his mother, and not be such a disappointment to everyone.

"So why was the King of the Desert late this morning?" Ordu asked as he came out into Atça's back garden. The late afternoon sun still hung on the horizon, but the day had grown cool already. Since the rainy season had just ended, all the flowers along the edges of the garden bloomed. Bees and other insects buzzed, trying to finish their gathering before the hot weather returned. Palms shaded the center of the garden, and the light breezes made it close to perfect.

Trulliç sighed. If only he didn't have to deal with the others! He also wished the paying students wouldn't call him that. But he didn't have any way to make them stop, no leverage. "I had chores," he replied truthfully.

He checked over his shoulder. Riyune lay on the dirt at the edge of the shade, watching everything as always. The dog raised an eyebrow at Trulliç, as if to say it was his call what he wanted to do, to stay and deal with the other students, or to just get up and leave.

"Chores?" Çirmal chimed in, coming to sit on the other side of Trulliç. "Surely you have servants for those kinds of things."

Trulliç shook his head but didn't reply. The paying students *did* have servants, and lived richer lives than anyone else Trulliç knew.

Besides Atça, of course.

"What kind of things did you have to do?" Ordu asked. He sat on the other side of Trulliç.

Trulliç recognized a trap. They didn't actually care about him or anything in his life. They were just looking for another opportunity to make fun of him, something else they could tease him about.

He had to answer them, however. Despite Trulliç's slight abilities at magic, as paying students they held higher rank than he did. On judging days, Atça paid careful attention to rank when he listened to the complaints of the people of Gaadiwala.

Towns that didn't have a local magician had a magistrate appointed by the emperor who did the same thing, listened and held judgment, declaring fines as necessary.

Atça also counted all the baskets of flour, flagons of sweet *meslit*, clay tiles and jugs, pelts of sheep's wool, and everything else the town produced for the emperor, making sure that all the produce was accounted for and the town properly tithed.

Trulliç accompanied Atça one afternoon a week, carrying the books where he kept track of everyone's input. Trulliç didn't like keeping the count, though he could read and write his numbers and letters well enough. There had been too many farmers that winter who were short, who'd offered just about anything not to go into debt.

Atça had been firm, but he'd also tried to be fair, counting extra barrels of palm wine against the family's total, though those didn't make their way to the emperor but to Atça's cellar instead.

The farmers didn't complain to Atça's face about the amount that the tithe had increased every year, but Trulliç still heard their grumbling, particularly when they came into the tavern and had had too much to drink.

"I had to wait beside the well for water this morning," Trulliç told the boys. He wasn't about to tell them about trying to trace the water trails, then getting lost underground. They'd just tease him more, maybe call him the king of the caves or something.

Atça would address the problem. He was good at raising water. He could direct people to the exact location where they should dig their wells.

Gaadiwala was Atça's town, where the magician drew his power from.

However, if Trulliç allowed himself to be fanciful, Atça's powers actually diminished the moment he stepped across the threshold of his house, growing weaker and weaker as he got further from his home.

Trulliç didn't remember how he'd cried and screamed as a young boy when they'd first come to live at the tavern with the rest of his mother's family. However, she'd told the story—often—about how he spent days and nights screaming. Even the horseshoe over the doorway of the tavern didn't calm him, though he supposedly spent a lot of time staring at it as a child.

It hadn't been until Atça had come into the tavern that she'd realized the pair of them couldn't live in the town, that they had to go find a shack out on the outskirts so that Trulliç would have some peace.

Trulliç did remember how he felt like he couldn't breathe. Even now, the tavern still felt all closed in, like there was no air in the smoky main room.

When Atça had taken Trulliç from his mother, he'd calmed down immediately. Then, Atça had taken the boy outside.

As soon as Trulliç could see the stars again, he'd started breathing fully.

That was when Trulliç and his mother had moved to the very edge of Gaadiwala, so Trulliç could see the stars more easily at night. They lived in a mere shack instead of the much nicer rooms at the inn.

Trulliç knew that his mother was just waiting for him to find his true home so she could move back into the tavern.

But Trulliç had disappointed her in that as well.

"Can't you just call water to the surface? Enough to fill your jugs?" Ordu asked reasonably.

Trulliç nodded and lied to the boys. "Of course I can. But who wants a well in the middle of the street?"

Wells needed to be in their proper place. Atça had declared that place to be where the neighborhood well currently existed.

It wasn't Atça's fault that the reservoir under the well was no longer filling properly.

Could Trulliç create a well in his own backyard? Possibly he could call the water to the surface—he'd certainly been able to track it well enough when he'd been out in the desert. That wasn't the same as laying down all the rocks that needed to be placed to create a proper well.

Plus, as his adventures had shown him that morning, if he directed water to his own backyard, he was directing it *from* somewhere else. He'd be the one responsible for the neighborhood well not filling properly.

Erzalat had seemed to accuse Atça of not doing anything, that he wouldn't do anything to take care of their well.

Trulliç had failed when he'd tried, getting so lost.

But maybe if he wasn't right above the water trails, maybe he could stay grounded…

"I don't believe you," Çirmal said dismissively. "If you could call a well, why wouldn't you?"

Trulliç shook his head. Being a magician wasn't all about power, though he doubted the other two boys would understand that. Being a magician was about proper application of power, or so Atça had drilled into Trulliç's head day in and out. It was like the hero Lyons, how he'd applied leverage to turn the stone egg. Just turning the egg over in the wrong direction would have sent it careening down the mountain's edge.

"That's the real reason you were late, isn't it?" Ordu said. "Because your magic failed. As usual."

Trulliç flushed but didn't try to deny it.

"It's okay," Çirmal said, trying to be reassuring. "We know that Atça has just taken you on as a charity case."

Trulliç bit his lips together. He *wasn't* a charity case. Though he could well imagine Atça telling the other boys that.

"Tell you what," Ordu said. "You call up some water, right here, right now, and we'll leave you alone for the next month."

"Week," Çirmal said.

"Month," Trulliç said immediately.

"Deal," Ordu said.

Trulliç knew the boy wasn't telling the truth. He could see it in the way Ordu's skin turned slightly red around his jaw, in the way his aura flared.

Trulliç had tried to describe his ability to Atça, but his mentor had just dismissed Trulliç as being too fanciful, as usual. Atça maintained that Trulliç couldn't trust his vision, all those signals that his magical ability gave him, just as he could only sometimes rely on his senses. Until Trulliç found his true home, he wouldn't be able to calibrate anything he felt or saw, wouldn't know what was real or true.

Trulliç kept his judgments to himself and tried to pay attention to his mentor, but he knew that in this instant, Ordu was lying.

Despite that, Trulliç still agreed to Ordu's challenge. He needed to prove to himself that he wouldn't get lost this time. Particularly since he was just about to go back out to the desert.

If he got lost there, he'd never find his way back home.

"Deal," Trulliç said. He looked over his shoulder, then beckoned for Riyune to come closer.

Riyune didn't quite roll his eyes, but he did stand slowly, stretching his back by placing his front paws on the ground and raising his butt in the air, then shaking himself before he walked over to where Trulliç sat and lay down next to him, the dog's side lightly touching Trulliç's knee.

Trulliç had found that if he started a journey touching Riyune, he tended not to get lost. Or at least as lost.

Then Trulliç reached for his cup of water and poured it over the thirsty ground.

"That's cheating!" Çirmal exclaimed.

"No, it's not," Trulliç said firmly. "It's just always easier to call like to like." One of the reasons why he'd been able to find the reservoir under the ground so easily was because he'd traveled down the rock path of the well. He hadn't just stood in the middle of the village square and tried to direct his senses down under the earth with nothing to guide him.

Water lay in a large reservoir just under the ground in Atça's back garden. Trulliç had found it before. He'd never tried to do anything with it, however.

Before Trulliç sent all his attention underground, he looked at the other students.

Ordu always had a golden aura around his hair, as if he'd come from a bath in the sun. Trulliç didn't know what that foretold, if it meant the son of the richest man in town was destined for riches, or if he would have to find his way in the desert.

Çirmal was the exact opposite, as usual, like he carried his own gray cloud with him. Was he destined for the sea? To live in the rain? Or was it something completely else?

Atça had told Trulliç he couldn't believe what he saw, that it wasn't real.

But Trulliç saw it every time he looked. It *had* to mean something. But what?

Trulliç also saw that it didn't matter to Ordu or Çirmal if he succeeded or not. The boys would claim that Trulliç failed, even if he brought a huge geyser blasting out of the ground.

They didn't realize that this test wasn't about them, but a test for Trulliç against himself.

Could he trace the water without getting lost this time?

Riyune was a solid weight against Trulliç's thigh, warm and comforting. The dog never looked like anything other than a dog. He never had an aura, no matter how often Trulliç checked. The dog wasn't a familiar, though Trulliç still claimed he was sometimes.

Mostly Riyune was just like any other dog. Except he never barked. Never showed his teeth. Always managed to avoid Trulliç's cousins when they would try to kick the dog or if they threw something at him.

Trusting that Riyune would keep him grounded, Trulliç sent his senses down into the cool earth.

Again, he found that layer of clay that lay just under the dirt. He felt it was why the garden grew so well—the water gathered near the roots of the plants instead of sinking further into the thirsty ground.

Further down, Trulliç followed the water to Atça's well. It fed off the main water pool that Trulliç felt spread out under most of Gaadiwala.

He headed north, following the main pool, trying not to get tangled in all the smaller streams that fed the main reservoir. Could he find the offshoot that led to his neighborhood well?

Was that it? It felt familiar, that closed off bladder. Rocks had tumbled into the stream that fed the smaller reservoir, blocking off the flow.

Trulliç backed up along the main stream. When he felt his attention drawn by one of the smaller streams, the steady warmth of Riyune against his thigh brought him back.

Why was it all so distracting? Trulliç wished he could ask Atça about it, but he knew that Atça would tell Trulliç that he couldn't trust his senses, so why was he bothering with this?

Finally, Trulliç found where the main stream of water had been blocked. Another underground chamber had been opened up. It felt new to Trulliç, and it had a regular shape, not the long, skinny, natural shapes of the existing water reservoirs.

Why was the water for his neighborhood well being siphoned into there? No wonder the water at the well had been so low!

He didn't like this new place. The water belonged to his neighborhood well, not to this greedy opening.

Riyune nudged Trulliç's thigh. He caught a sense of urgency from the dog. He didn't have a lot of time.

He still didn't have a lever to nudge the rocks aside. Did he have to be gentle, though?

Trulliç pushed himself into the ground, imaging that he had roots growing out of the bottom of his spine, then with all his force, he focused his will on the rocks blocking the flow of water and *pushed*.

The rocks dissipated into the earth, leaving a large space behind them.

But Trulliç wasn't finished. He traced the main trail of water back to *his* well, shoving rocks out of the way so the water had a clear path.

When Trulliç came back to the afternoon in Atça's garden, he found the other two boys had left. Which was good, because Trulliç hadn't actually raised any water up, like he'd boasted he would.

Atça stood over him, his face as thunderous as the first rain of spring.

"How dare you change the water flow?" Atça yelled at Trulliç.

"Everyone needs water," Trulliç said stubbornly. Water rights were important. They caused blood feuds.

But it meant that Atça knew about how low the water level had grown in Trulliç's neighborhood well. *He* had probably been the one who had directed the water elsewhere.

"Are you the town magician for Gaadiwala?" Atça asked angrily.

"No, sir," Trulliç said, shaking his head.

"Did it not occur to you that I might have had a plan for the extra water? That it might have been put to better use in the new area?" Atça said.

"No, sir," Trulliç said. "But—"

"Yes, I know, you've started seeing less water out in your slum," Atça said. "I would have taken care of you as well."

"Really?" Trulliç asked sarcastically, then instantly regretted it.

Atça raised his hand but didn't strike Trulliç like he normally did.

"Go. Now. And do not return until after you get back from the desert," Atça said sternly. "If you come back."

"What do you mean?" Trulliç asked, alarmed.

"You get lost in your head too often," Atça said. "Trusting your *magical* senses instead of paying attention to what's right in front of your nose. I predict the desert will take you before you figure out how to live there."

Trulliç nodded but didn't say anything. He had hoped his mentor would give him more instruction for his time in the desert.

It scared him, though, for Atça to voice Trulliç's deepest fear. He trudged away from Atça's house, his heart heavy.

The desert was his home. But he couldn't live there. Couldn't live in town, either. This hadn't been the first time that Trulliç's magic had interfered with Atça's. And Atça was the town magician. Trulliç had no standing in Gaadiwala. The emperor and everyone would always side with Atça, no matter what Etzalat and the others might think.

What was he going to do?

CHAPTER SIX

A HAND ACROSS NADEEM'S MOUTH brought her instantly out of her deep sleep.

She didn't start, however, or struggle. Her training took over instead —the three long years she'd spent working hard to become one of the emperor's stars. She wouldn't be *the* youngest at nineteen, but she would be one of the younger sisters.

Before Nadeem opened her eyes, she took a deep breath and tried to assess the situation. The hand across her mouth felt small and solid. Strong enough to choke her if that had been her assailant's intent. It smelled of dirt. Blood. And familiar sweat, too.

Çara. The youngest of Nadeem's team of six. The newest member assigned to them by the aunts, still wet behind the ears and unsure of herself, her place.

Nadeem opened her eyes but didn't struggle to get away.

Çara looked scared. The whites of her eyes shone, reflecting the single torch that burned just beyond her. Her mouth looked bruised, and dirt lay in streaks across her forehead, as if she'd brushed away sweat with earth-covered fingers. The left shoulder of her unbleached, plain chemise had torn and flopped down, exposing her breast. Wild curls, tangled with twigs, circled her head.

The cave roof above Nadeem looked the same—full of harsh rocks and beaded stalactites that she always feared would break off and kill her some night. This meant she was still in her own quarters out in the training zone, on the eastern coast of the Tanesh Empire, just east of the Qaenev desert.

Other than Çara's harsh breathing, Nadeem couldn't hear anything. Not the faint breath of wind that generally blew up coast, across the fertile Nusaybil valley and up into the foothills, nor the occasional drip of water caused by the condensation of moisture from sweaty bodies and humid breath, not even the murmuring or gentle snores of her team who lived in the cavern beside hers.

Nothing.

"They're gone," Çara whispered. "Taken."

Nadeem nodded sharply, showing that she was awake and understood. The drugs the aunts had given her earlier that night to help her sharpen her vision hadn't really worn off, but Nadeem wouldn't let that stop her. She aggressively pushed back against the fuzzy feeling inside her head, forcing saliva into her mouth and swallowing past the dryness there.

"When?" Nadeem asked as she sat up. Every muscle protested as if she'd been running and climbing for the last few hours instead of passed out, dreaming.

"Just after you left with the aunts," Çara replied. "Two, maybe three hours ago." Çara shuddered. "Slavers."

Nadeem's breath caught. How had they gotten so far inside the defenses? Who had they bribed? How many of her sisters had been killed?

"I got away. You must go rescue the others," Çara said fiercely. Her eyes held a wide-eyed stare, as if the horror of what she'd seen still lived with her.

"You must go," Çara repeated.

Nadeem looked at the girl closely. Had she been drugged? She didn't appear to be fully herself. Nadeem leaned closer to her for a moment, disguising the movement as a stretch. She didn't smell anything sweet or acidic in Çara's breath.

Then Çara tapped her right knee with her middle finger three times.

It was a signal that Nadeem and her team had come up with, part of their private language so that they could communicate among themselves and not even the aunts would know.

Test.

"I will rescue them," Nadeem said clearly.

She and her team knew that the final test was coming. They were near the end of their training.

Nadeem had assumed that the test would involve all of them from the start. She should have known better and run more individual drills.

But the aunts wouldn't kill the rest of Nadeem's team if she failed. Or actually sell them to the slavers who trolled the coast, looking for innocent girls to cart off to the decadent courts of the east or service the barbarian hoards.

Probably.

"You stay here," Nadeem told Çara as she got off her sleeping platform, stretching as she stood.

What had the aunts given Nadeem to make her so sluggish? This had to be part of the test, to see how Nadeem functioned when she wasn't at her peak.

They'd be surprised at how fast she'd recover. Since assembling her team, Nadeem had taken to building tolerances to most of the soporifics that the star sisters commonly used.

"Tell the aunts what happened if I'm not back by dawn," Nadeem said. That gave her at least three hours to track down the slavers and rescue the remaining four members of her team.

Nadeem quickly dressed in black pants that clung to her legs, giving her more movement, as well as a plain black blouse. She tied a black scarf around her head, low on her forehead to keep the sweat out of her eyes. She chose to tie plain leather strips to the soles of her feet—she might need to climb up or down rocks, so the strips would be better than sandals. Last, but not least, she packed up her knives and blowgun.

None of what she had on was proper or what women generally wore.

However, it was what a star sister wore when she was training or on a mission. Nadeem could always disguise her outfit using her magic if she needed to, to make it appear that she wore something more suited for traditional women.

Çara had already laid down on Nadeem's bed, her eyes closed, her breath regular and deep.

The aunts had probably given her something so Nadeem wouldn't be tempted to ask for Çara's help.

It didn't matter. Nadeem would rescue her team. Bring all four of the others back safe and alive. Even if this was just a test.

However, tests given by the aunts often had a bite. Nadeem was prepared to be bitten as well.

Nadeem tasted the night as she stood in the shadows at the entrance of the cave her team used for shelter.

Even this far inland, the air carried more moisture than Nadeem was used to. It felt soft against her cheeks. The aunts didn't set watch fires at night. Though they could have hidden the light easily enough, it was better to train the girls to work in darkness.

Still, Nadeem smelled something burning. She took another moment to glance up, placing the Shepherd's Light—one of the stars that stayed in the east and was generally visible. The moon had already set, but the stars abounded, giving her enough light to see.

Nadeem slipped from the entrance of the cave, heading for the shadows of the grove of *meslit* trees that grew to her left, along the ridge. In the desert, *meslit* didn't grow much past knee height. Here, where there was more moisture, they grew far above Nadeem's head. The thorns increased in size as well—instead of being spindly and not much longer than a thumbnail, they were as thick as a stake and easily the length of Nadeem's palm.

Though Nadeem had her customary three knives, plus a few others, she still plucked two thorns and stuck them at the back of her head scarf. They'd break easily if she tried to use them like a dagger, and their sharp sides made them difficult to hold onto without cutting her hands to shreds. However, the thorns had just enough weight to be used as throwing knives, and accurately too, if one had enough practice.

Nadeem made sure that all of her team practiced.

Just beyond the trees, Nadeem took the path down, toward the valley. A few feet to her left lay the abrupt edge of the cliff. Off that was a short way down to a sure death. To her right, the path stayed open for a bit, then, as it descended, cliff walls rose above her.

Slavers traditionally sailed up the east coast of the Tanesh empire, occasionally storming undefended towns. Mostly they kept their larger ships out in the Uluborlu sea and sailed smaller boats closer to shore, slipping up channels and attacking farms and communities.

The star sisters' training camp stood close to the top of Knife Ridge; a small mountain range that ran between the coast to the east and the Qaenev desert to the west. The slavers wouldn't take the captives west toward the desert. No, they'd go back to the coast.

Nadeem skimmed along the beaten dirt path, glad for her foot coverings. They wouldn't last more than a couple hours before they'd be torn to shreds once she started going across the rocks. Knife Ridge grew along a sharp line. Its stones were black, sharp, and brittle. Many looked like cloth that had been attacked by moths, full of holes.

In a pinch, the sharp rocks could also be used as weapons, but Nadeem hoped it wouldn't come to that.

Far below Nadeem, where the path switched back, she saw a fire burning.

Stupid of the slavers to light such a bright beacon.

A dark shape lay across the path.

Nadeem had no place to hide, so she went for the element of surprise and took off, running as quickly as she could toward the shape.

The shape resolved itself into a prone body. Nadeem recognized the clothes first—a plain tunic, shirt and long full pants—a star sister.

Nadeem's pulse suddenly sounded loud in her ears. Was this one of her team?

She stopped and squatted down next to the body. The girl lay on her side. Nadeem tugged her onto her back while reaching for the pulse at her neck.

Zarahat.

Nadeem took a deep breath of relief.

She was one of the younger girls, not one of Nadeem's team members. She'd probably been guarding the path and had been surprised by the slavers coming up it. Blood covered the right side of her face. No pulse.

May your dance before the goddess be short, Nadeem mouthed silently as she closed Zarahat's one open eye. It was the most common of all blessings. The aunts could have a full service for the girl later, when Nadeem would pay her proper respects.

In the meanwhile, she had to make sure her team didn't end up in the same condition.

Nadeem took off again, skimming lightly along the path, keeping to her toes. She knew she could run like this for half a day, maybe longer if the terrain was mostly flat. She watched the ground carefully. It wouldn't do for her to trip or break an ankle because of some errant rock.

Just around the next bend, Nadeem slowed. There was only a single path up the hills. It zigged and zagged, narrow and steep, with parts where the cliff fell away on one side, while rising steeply on the other.

The star sisters always had it guarded, generally with more than one guard.

If the slavers were smart, they'd hide a guard just past the next bend, someone equipped to make noise to warn the raiders of anyone approaching.

Nadeem stopped briefly, examining the few feet of open space to her left.

One of the things Nadeem had excelled at since coming to the training camp was climbing. She had a great sense of balance and could always find finger and toeholds in the rock. Wrestling continued to be her worst sport: though Nadeem had a long reach with her six-foot height, she didn't have the weight of the other girls. Nor did she generally exercise the patience to wear down an opponent.

If this was a test—the final test—then the aunts would expect her to use all her skills, both those she was good at as well as all the others she'd trained in.

Without looking back, Nadeem walked to the edge of the cliff. She'd never tried this climb, at least not at this point—she had climbed the face of this rock before, but further up, closer to the camp, and in full daylight.

If she fell—no one would rescue her.

Nadeem took a deep breath and swung herself over the edge. She couldn't see anything, the night and the rock were too dark.

She just had to trust her instincts.

Just as her team trusted her to get them out of this.

Her feet scrambled, seeking out the first toehold with her left foot.

Found it.

Then she lowered herself, finding the next toehold, her fingers digging into the rock.

She trembled, her muscles already exhausted.

Nadeem pushed herself, taking another deep breath to calm her fear, focusing on the task at hand.

She could defeat this rock. Rescue her team. Finish this test triumphant.

Become one of the emperor's stars.

<hr>

Nadeem looked over her shoulder again. It was so hard to judge just how far above the path she was! She cursed the aunts again.

But she couldn't find any more toeholds in the rock. The cliff face had been sheared off, like a fine sheep's coat. Nadeem knew if she landed on something or didn't have solid footing, she'd tumble down the rocks and land broken at the bottom. If she pushed out too far, she wouldn't land on the narrow path below her, and would instead tumble off and keep falling.

She opened her jaw, making sure she wasn't clenching it. She needed to be loose for this. With one last large exhale, she pushed off, dropping down.

The fall went on for much longer than Nadeem expected.

Or maybe she just so scared that time seemed to stretch and expand.

Impact.

Nadeem's ankles twinged. She rolled, absorbing the shock. Forced herself to a stop.

The path was very narrow here. The cliff's edge going down lay inches away.

Nadeem took a deep breath. Stood.

Her ankles still hurt, but she hadn't broken or sprained them either.

Stop shaking, she ordered herself.

Her knees felt weak and her head swam.

At least two toenails had broken off in her climb, and a fingernail had split. The skin on the tips of her fingers had been sliced open by the sharp rocks. Nadeem had stopped more than once to suck the blood away, shaking her hand to dry it quickly.

She couldn't afford to lose her grip.

Focus.

Where was the slaver's fire?

Nadeem couldn't see it from her vantage point. She still smelled it, off to her right.

She checked her knives, her blowgun, the thorns still stuck into her scarf. Then she took off along the path again. The night felt more quiet to her, the light of the stars dimmed. How much time did she have before dawn? The climb had taken her longer than she'd expected.

Fortunately, after a short while, Nadeem passed above the raiders. She dropped to the dirt, then crawled to the edge of the cliff to look down.

The raiders had camped at a broad spot. The path ran straight along the climbing rock face, but there were several feet between it and the edge of the cliff going down. The place they'd chosen would be easy to defend, both from above and below the path.

They'd banked their fire, but Nadeem could still see the embers, still smell the smoke.

Where was her team being held? Nadeem couldn't see enough of the camp to determine how many raiders waited for her. Half a dozen? Maybe more?

She decided the slavers would place her team as close to the edge of the cliff as possible. That way, there would be one less direction for them to escape, unless they decided to throw themselves off and kill themselves.

It also meant the raiders could easily intimidate their hostages by threatening them with the cliffs below.

Could Nadeem get past the raiders, then climb up the cliff to rescue her sisters? Not before dawn. She could climb down the bit of rock just below her, so she could avoid the guards on the path at the next bend. But then she'd have to climb up another cliff face, and if she remembered correctly, it was more sheer than the one she'd just negotiated.

Nadeem made herself wait and watch for another hundred heartbeats. No one stirred at the camp. The guards must be the only ones awake, and they were on the path, above and below the camp. No one stood guard in the actual camp itself.

That would make it easier.

Nadeem didn't care what happened once she'd freed her team. They could fight their way out. They'd trained well and hard and were good enough to defeat two dozen untrained men, even if they carried swords and whips.

After another hundred heartbeats, Nadeem slipped over the next cliff edge. If this was the final test, the aunts were certainly putting her through her paces.

Nadeem's muscles trembled as she found the first toeholds. She couldn't see. She was going to fall. Going to fail.

No.

Nadeem found the next finger-hold. She balanced on her left foot and swung her right across the rock, banging her knee.

But she found a tiny ledge, a place where she could stand and breathe for a moment.

Then she forced herself to continue, her heart pounding hard in her ears.

She felt like saying a blessing every time she found the next toehold, every inch she traveled closer to the ground.

This time, there were holds all the way down the rock.

The smell of feces rose as Nadeem got closer to the path. Ugh. She tried to move to the side, and barely managed to avoid stepping in a huge pile of shit.

The slavers had been using the wall for doing their business. Were these men barbarians? Why didn't they dig a proper latrine? Or were they just too lazy to do so much work for a single night?

Nadeem stayed crouched down next to the wall, forcing herself to adjust to the stench. She didn't cover herself in their filth, though she considered it for a moment. Then she realized they wouldn't be smelling anything over their own filth, so it really wasn't necessary.

No star sister had enough talent to make themselves invisible. Nadeem was as good as most, though, when it came to being unnoticed.

The guards standing at the top and bottom of the path would be watching the dark carefully, so she wouldn't be able to slip by them.

Hopefully, though, she could get up close enough to rescue her team without being seen.

Nadeem put her hands wide in front of her, willing the flesh to *blur*. The edges along her spread fingers grew less distinct. Anyone trying to spot her would have more difficulty figuring out exactly where she started and where the night ended. Then she scurried across the path, heading directly for their fire.

Three mounds circled the banked embers: one pack and two bodies.

A mule brayed into the quiet night. Nadeem crouched down and froze.

No wonder they'd been so bold, climbing up Knife Ridge. Pack animals would make it much easier to cart away unwilling victims.

Nadeem would still bet that they'd been paid—and paid well—by the aunts to enact this test. And Çara had known it was a test. She'd probably gotten away before the slavers had made it too far down the path, before they'd camped for the night. Slipped away before anyone had realized she was gone.

The slavers didn't realize the death that awaited them. Even if Nadeem failed, the aunts would still never let them leave the ridge alive.

It must have been some bribe to have gotten them there…

Focus. Nadeem had to get to her team and get them out of there first. Then she could worry about how the aunts had arranged all this. It seemed awfully elaborate for a final test.

Nadeem stayed crouching and waddled across the open space, moving slowly but steadily. The snores (as well as the stench!) of the slavers rolled over her, but she willed it not to stay with her.

Pay attention to the night. The soft sighs. The smell of the fire.

The smell of her team.

There. To the right.

Nadeem had guessed correctly—the other four members of her team had been placed close to the edge of the cliff. Bound tightly with thick ropes. Gagged. Unconscious. Bruised and beaten.

Galbril. Duzhen. Yalovreen. Nikzhar.

Nadeem went first to Galbril. She was the wrestler of the team, big boned and strong as a mule. Stubborn as one, too. She'd been the first one that Nadeem had been paired with by the aunts, the first of their team.

Nadeem woke her like she'd been woken, a hand over Galbril's mouth, though she also pinched the other woman's nose.

The eyes that opened looked startled and crazed, moving from side to side rapidly, trying to take everything in at once.

When Galbril's eyes finally slowed, staring straight at Nadeem with sanity again, Nadeem lifted her hand off. She untied the gag and used her first knife to saw through Gabril's bindings around her wrists.

When Galbril had rubbed circulation back into her hands, Nadeem handed her a second knife so she could free Duzhen. Another wrestler, though not as big as Galbril. She had the best sight and often scouted for the team, seeing traps and illusions that the other missed. Gabril had asked for Duzhen to be partnered with them, and after watching her win more than one sprinting contest, Nadeem had agreed.

Duzhen woke more quietly, her eyes immediately focused on Nadeem and burning with anger.

Despite the seriousness of the situation, Nadeem felt a smile cross her lips for the first time that night. The only thing that kept Duzhen from spouting obscenities and cursing all the gods was her gag.

Nadeem waited another moment, getting an eye roll from Duzhen before she undid the gag. Duzhen would either wait and start her cursing later, or she'd begin right away, but silently.

Gabril went to work freeing Duzhen's hands while Nadeem woke the others.

Guards, Nadeem signaled them once they'd were ready. She pointed up and down the path.

Gabril nodded. *Ten more*, she signaled.

Nadeem nodded. A dozen men in all, then, at least. She pointed to Nikzhar, then indicated their strongest illusionist should take out the guard going up the hill.

Nikzhar nodded, then grimaced and shook her head. She motioned for Nadeem to come closer.

"My leg is broken," she whispered against Nadeem's ear.

Nadeem looked down, alarmed.

Wait.

Nikzhar's legs looked fine. They weren't covered in bruises or swollen.

Nadeem reached out and pushed against Nikzhar's left thigh.

The girl didn't cry out, but she did gasp. Her eyes welled with tears. "I'm sorry," she whispered. "Just leave me behind."

"But your leg isn't broken," Nadeem whispered back.

"Yes, it is," Gabril said.

Nadeem looked at the wrestler, then looked back at Nikzhar.

Her leg now bore massive bruises and had swollen to twice the size it should have been.

Nadeem cursed silently.

How much of this test was actually real? How much of it was merely an illusion, cast by a group of aunts working in concert?

How much could Nadeem ignore? How much did she have to play by their rules?

The roaring of a barbarian slaver from behind her answered her questions. At least for now, all she could do was fight.

<hr>

Nadeem dodged the blow of the ugly, hairy slaver in front of her, then used her momentum, turning, to lay a solid blow across his ribs.

But the stupid barbarian didn't go down.

Nadeem had the reach on him. She could dodge most of his blows. But he was frighteningly strong.

Her team wasn't doing much better. They all fought to the best of their abilities, Nikzhar using a stolen bow to keep at least some of the barbarian hoard at bay.

But more slavers kept coming. Nadeem knew it wasn't right. There weren't that many men to start with. The others just appeared, though.

The aunts had to be behind this. It was an unwinnable battle. Just like the first one that Aunt Izmet had designed to test Nadeem, to see if she was willing to go beyond the rules and join the emperor's stars.

A desert hawk cried out above Nadeem's head, distracting her.

Thunk. The barbarian landed a solid blow against Nadeem's ribs.

They didn't crack. But she knew she couldn't take much more. She'd started weak, and the fighting had only weakened her further.

The hawk, though. It was her personal totem. The symbol of her team. Her favorite illusionary fighter.

If this battle wasn't real (despite how her ribs hurt, her legs trembled, her ragged fingertips bled) then Nadeem should be able to call up her hawk-girl.

"Cover me!" she shouted to Gabril as she took two steps back, withdrawing from the melee.

She could do this. She could find the thread. Pull them out of this illusion. Before they all suffered permanent damage or died.

Nadeem focused back on Nikzhar's leg. It looked broken, swollen, and bruised. Nikzhar's face was pale, sweat running freely from her forehead and down her back. She watched the battle with ultimate concentration, before she hefted another knife into the fray.

It didn't matter if she took out her mark or not. Another barbarian would just step up.

Nadeem turned away from Nikzhar. She couldn't let herself get distracted by guessing if the girl's leg was actually broken or not.

Instead, Nadeem raised her head and her arms toward the sky. "Hawk sister!" she cried. "I call to you. Come join our battle. Fight with us toward glorious victory!"

A desert hawk's warning cry echoed across the sky.

She would not come closer. This wasn't her fight.

Desperate, Nadeem changed her call. "Transform me! Give me your golden eyes! Your bone-breaking beak! The feathers that protect and defend you!"

A stillness passed through the air above Nadeem, like an impossible cloud crossing the eye of the sun in the middle of the desert.

Nadeem started to change. Her bones grew lighter as she expanded. Blue skin traveled from her outstretched fingertips and up her arms. The world grew sharper and the day grew brighter.

Instead of giving words of thanks, Nadeem issued a great, loud *CAW!*

When Nadeem turned back to the battle, she realized she towered over the others. With graceful movements, she reached out and one by one touched the heads of her team.

Gabril turned into the mule fighter she resembled, her braying laugh echoing out over the valley as she landed a solid kick on the barbarian in front of her.

Duzhen took on the features of a mountain cat, spitting and hissing at her opponent, still cursing in her own way.

Yalovreen surprised Nadeem. Instead of becoming more like the lizard creature she generally fought illusionary battles with, she grew a great set of butterfly wings, colored every shade of blue, from the palest white-blue to the darkest blue-black.

Spiked wings that could slice an opponent in two.

Even Nikzhar changed, her leg mending itself as she rose up, her skin growing woody and covered in thorns—a walking *meslit* tree, set to do as much damage as she could.

The barbarians gasped, as if they shared a single breath.

Then they surged forward, ten, twenty, thirty or more.

Nadeem gave her cawing battle cry again.

It didn't matter how many opponents they faced.

Now, they could win.

"No one has ever figured out the final test was an illusion so quickly," Aunt Izmet said proudly, squeezing Nadeem's hand. "In fact, most of the teams have to be tested more than once before they pass. How did you do it?"

Nadeem stirred sluggishly, searching for the words. Every muscle hurt. Her fingertips actually had been torn to shreds by her great climb. That part of the test had been real. She would have died if she'd made a single misstep.

The aunts had expected her to fight her way through the guards to her team. Not to avoid them and go around.

Nadeem lay in Aunt Izmet's tent on a well-cushioned pallet stuffed with feathers, with soft furs propped up behind her to help her sit. Diffuse sunlight lit the brown cloth, making the tent seem more open and airy. Not only did the tent flap stand propped open, Aunt Izmet's tent had window openings as well, letting the cool afternoon breezes in.

"Nikzhar's leg wasn't broken," Nadeem finally said. She slowly reached for the tea beside her, taking a deep sip. Her lips had split open, and all the exposed skin on her face and neck had blistered and burned—she and her team had evidentially fought the aunt's illusions in the bright sunlight for far too long.

"Interesting," Aunt Izmet said. "I'll have a talk with the council later to see what happened."

Nadeem shrugged. It would never occur to Aunt Izmet that the problem had been that the aunts had underestimated Nadeem and her team.

Aunt Izmet believed too much in her own power and the power of the emperor. She didn't question things like Aunt Parayat had taught Nadeem.

It made Nadeem uncomfortable sometimes, the unquestioning loyalty that Aunt Izmet demanded, that Nadeem tried to give.

The battle had been glorious, and one that poems should be written about.

But no one could hear the details of it. It was part of her secret training.

A question nagged at Nadeem's fuzzy brain. She had to take two more sips of the sweet and salty tea before she found the words. "Did I pass?"

Aunt Izmet's grin answered her. "I already have your first assignment. From the emperor himself."

Aunt Izmet's voice took on a fanatical fervor that it often did when she talked of the emperor.

Nadeem had learned to parrot the tone back, but Aunt Parayat's voice, questioning everything, still sounded at the back of her mind.

For now, though, Nadeem didn't have to question. She'd passed. It was enough.

"Good," Nadeem said, as she lay back down.

She'd finally made it. She was one of the emperor's stars.

There was that voice again. Aunt Parayat. Warning Nadeem about being careful what she wished for.

Today, Nadeem decided she couldn't be happier that one of her wishes had finally come true.

CHAPTER SEVEN

TRULLIÇ

TRULLIÇ SAT ABOVE THE DESERT. Riyune sat beside him. Trulliç had brought sticks and a heavy piece of brown tent cloth in his pack, then built an impromptu lean-to, so he sat in the shade on the final Kinarak foothill, before scrub and dirt transformed into sand.

The desert called to Trulliç. It promised soft paths for his feet, sweet dates and cinnamon bark, an endless blue sky to bring joy to his heart.

The desert lied.

Trulliç knew as soon as he stepped one foot onto the sands, he'd be lost. He'd wander, drawn on by the promise of shelter or water, only to have the desert laugh cruelly at him.

Maybe not this trip, but perhaps the next, or the one after that, the desert would take all of Trulliç, strip his skin from his bones, greedily drink his blood, absorb all of him into itself and then go looking for its next victim.

The desert didn't give life. It only took.

Trulliç now understood the bards in the marketplace who sang of a cruel mistress, who stole their hearts and then didn't return their love.

Trulliç couldn't look away from the desert. Even when he closed his eyes he still saw its golden sands spread out before him. If he wasn't careful, he'd wander from his camp straight down the hill.

But why should he go into the desert this time? It was his fourth trip since his initial manhood journey. He was sixteen. He wouldn't find his true home. Despite all his dreams of the desert, it never showed him the same place twice.

Maybe it was finally time to put aside boyhood dreams and fancies and grow up, like Atça always told him. Stop daydreaming about the desert, face the reality that he would never become a powerful magician. His glass horseshoe was just another trick, an illusion cast by the blood hound. Trulliç needed to accept that he would only ever do small magics on the fringes of another magician's territory.

Trulliç angrily pressed his palms against his eyes, pushing out the tears welling up. He wouldn't cry, not for the desert. It was his true home, he couldn't deny that.

He'd never be able to live there, though.

He gave himself the rest of the day to watch the sands, to dream of tiny lizards who scuttled from one rock to the next, to listen to the desert hawks and their lonely cries, to taste the sweet water from hidden rivers, to feel the scorching winds and the abrasive sand they carried.

When the sun was on the far horizon, Trulliç finally stood. He rolled up the cloth and sticks, carefully tying them to his bag. After one long last look, his eyes sweeping all the way across the sands, he firmly turned his back on the desert and started back up the hill.

An eerie, high-pitched noise came from behind him.

Was that the desert calling to him? Was she finally ready to show him all her secrets, give him the ability to live on her sands?

But no. It was merely Riyune, whining.

Trulliç had never heard Riyune make a sound. The dog never barked or growled.

"I'm not going," Trulliç told Riyune. He kept his attention focused firmly on the dog, not even sneaking a peek at the golden sands that still beckoned at the foot of the hill. "I can't."

Trulliç sniffed but didn't let any more tears come. He was done with his mourning for his true home.

Time to move on.

Riyune whined again, looking from Trulliç to the desert and back again.

"You can go if you need to," Trulliç said softly. He'd miss Riyune terribly, he knew. The dog strengthened his magic and was always there when Trulliç felt alone.

Riyune had come from the desert. He belonged there, more than Trulliç.

Trulliç had never believed that Riyune was his familiar. In the ancient stories, the familiars interacted more with their magicians, talked plainly, and cast their own magic.

Riyune had never done any of those things.

Plus, Trulliç believed that he'd feel some sort of bond with Riyune if the dog was truly his familiar. He'd never be able to suggest that the dog just go.

Riyune sat stubbornly in the path, growing perfectly still, as if he'd turned into a statue. Trulliç had seen him do that more than once.

Would the dog stay frozen this time? Or just disappear, like a ghost?

"I can't," Trulliç said again. He figured Riyune would know what he meant.

Though it broke his heart, Trulliç turned away from the desert and started walking up the hill.

Riyune didn't whine again.

After twenty steps, the dog also hadn't joined Trulliç.

A second ache settled in on top of the first wrapped around Trulliç's heart.

He was on his own, now.

He didn't drag his feet, or start walking more slowly.

He'd made his decision like a man. He would have to face the consequences on his own as well.

When Trulliç reached the top of the foothill, he was tempted to turn and look back. But he knew he wouldn't see the desert from there—the path wound back and forth up the steep hill to the pass. He did pause and breathe for a moment. His mage light shone above his head, giving him enough light to continue walking

Just ahead he knew there was a small shelter where he could spend the night before he walked back down the other side to Gaadiwala.

Suddenly, Trulliç's mage light flared.

He looked up, startled.

A white streak flew past his legs.

His heart beating hard, Trulliç looked down.

Riyune sat in front of him, looking as though he'd been waiting there all along. He nodded once to Trulliç, as if to say, *Come on, then*. Then he turned and trotted down the path, toward the shelter.

For the first time in a few days, Trulliç felt his heart grow lighter.

It would be hard, he knew, turning his back on the desert as he had.

Perhaps, though, his journey forward would be a bit easier with a friend by his side.

———

Atça looked like the cat who'd just gotten into the cream when he opened the door and saw Trulliç standing there. He wore his green silk morning robes. "Didn't even step on the sands, did you?" he asked.

Trulliç shook his head, ashamed. "I would have gotten lost," he said. Atça had even said that was what would happen to him. "I decided not to get lost," Trulliç added, looking up. Instead of stopping at home, he still had his pack on his back, coming straight from walking down the pass.

"So you're leaving the desert for good?" Atça purred.

"For now," Trulliç told him firmly. He didn't think he could ever leave the desert for good. She was in his heart, her sand in his blood, her rocks adhering to his bones.

Atça gave him a sour look at that. He cross his arms over his chest and stared at Trulliç for a few moments.

Would his mentor reject him? Because he wouldn't completely refuse the desert?

"I see you still have that mangy mutt with you," Atça added.

Trulliç nodded. He wasn't going to tell Atça of how Riyune had almost left him.

Riyune would leave him, someday. That much he knew.

At least it wasn't now.

"I may, just may, have an assignment for you," Atça told Trulliç after another long moment. "Come back at dusk."

Trulliç nodded, then backed away when Atça firmly shut the door in his face.

An assignment? So maybe Atça had forgiven Trulliç for messing with the water flows under Gaadiwala?

Trulliç took a deep breath, relief trickling over him.

He knew he was still on Atça's "troublemaker" list.

But maybe if he did well with this assignment, he could get back into the good graces of his mentor.

———

Trulliç dreamed he was walking over a sand dune when the ground started shaking and the sand started skittering away.

It took him a moment to realize he'd been asleep and his mother was shaking him awake. He brushed the sleep from his eyes and swallowed against a dry throat.

"What happened?" Mother asked, pushing aside his blankets and looking at his body and legs. "Are you hurt?"

"No," Trulliç said, pushing himself up to sitting. "I…I couldn't stay. In the desert."

Mother went from frantic worry to icy stillness. "I see." She sat back, pushing herself away from Trulliç. She still wore her *chafiyek* scarf covering her gray-streaked hair, the blue and gold one that she'd received from her husband so many years before. Her gray tunic bore smudges of soot from the ovens she worked behind the tavern, and the sleeves of her plain muslin blouse were tied up and out of the way.

"What are you doing home?" Trulliç asked. The light through the door was still bright, still daylight. Normally, Mother didn't get home from the tavern until it was dark, and frequently after it was night.

"Someone saw you in town," Mother said. "Asked me how your journey had gone."

"Oh," Trulliç said. He felt like squirming, but Mother didn't like it when he did that. "I did go talk with Atça already. He may have an assignment for me."

"An assignment?" Mother asked. She pursed her lips together in disapproval. "A *job*?"

"Yes?" Trulliç said, unsure of what Mother was unhappy about now.

"So instead of going into the desert to become a real magician, you've decided you're content with being another magician's lackey?" Mother asked angrily.

"That's not fair," Trulliç said hotly. "I can't live in the desert. Can't find my home. I need to do *something*."

"Did you even try?" Mother asked.

Trulliç sighed. She wouldn't understand. He would have gotten lost if he'd set foot on the sands. Never found his way back. The desert would have absorbed him, eaten him alive.

"I had such great hopes for you," Mother said quietly, turning away. "All those miles I walked with you strapped to my back. Telling myself that it would all be all right if I could just get home."

Trulliç nodded. She'd told him her heartache more than once. It wasn't his fault that he wasn't a better magician, more powerful.

Mother shook her head. "'Children will lead their own lives'," she said. "My mother told me that before I went north with Alpheais, your father." She pushed herself up, brushing off her long skirt. "I thought I knew what she meant. I didn't realize it might mean that they would choose *not* to live."

With that, Mother swept out of the door.

Trulliç stayed where he was, trying to breathe. It wasn't that Mother had taken all the air out of the tiny shack with her, but it suddenly felt closed in and confining.

Mother had talked more than once about how Trulliç had howled when they'd first reached Gaadiwala, how he couldn't stand to be indoors. It was why they lived outside of town.

Trulliç threw back his blankets and strode out of the shack, standing in the yard, the chickens scattering in front of him, then settling down again quickly to their quiet clucking and scratching.

Riyune appeared beside Trulliç, as if summoned. He stood with his head cocked to one side. What was he asking?

"I can't," Trulliç whispered. He realized he was standing with his back directly to the desert, that it stretched out behind him, calling to him, even over the foothills and through the pass.

Trulliç reached down for the glass horseshoe that he always carried, that emblem of his birthright.

Was it, too, a lie?

The smooth glass brought him no comfort, as well as no hint of his destiny. He clenched it tightly in his fist. Raised his hand. Shook with anger, disappointment bitter on his tongue.

Then he made himself lower his hand.

He would not throw the glass horseshoe across the yard, send it skittering through the chicken poop and dirt.

Instead, he secured it away again. Best to keep it out of sight.

There was nothing magical about the talisman. Atça said it was plain glass. Trulliç believed him.

Trulliç still held onto it. Maybe as a promise that one day there would be more for him. That the desert would welcome him, tell him her secrets, not just consume him and keep him all for herself.

That there was hope, as fragile as the glass might be.

Evening stole gently across the sky, darkening the clear blue to a softer color, then turning slowly to black. Trulliç felt odd, walking through the town as the lights went on in people's houses. He heard children crying for their dinner, old men saying evening prayers as they knelt before altars, young women chasing the chickens back into the yard.

He knew that the town would soon sleep. Not much happened in these neighborhoods after the sun fully set. The tavern would keep going for a while, full of the first travelers of the spring and good ale.

Atça opened the door before Trulliç knocked, issuing him into the house. Trulliç paused momentarily to change out of his sandals into house slippers before following his mentor.

They didn't turn into the learning room, or the front sitting room. Instead, Atça led Trulliç to the meeting room, where he sometimes held private court with rich merchants and farmers who could pay his fees.

Trulliç hadn't been in this room often. It smelled of sweet frankincense burning on the altar to Serril in the corner. Wood covered the walls, of course. Shelves, also made out of wood, held Atça's many folded books, as well as scrolls and maps. A rich red-and-gold rug covered the floor. In the center lay many pillows and backrests, so guests could lounge comfortably.

Maybe Mother would be less disappointed with Trulliç's choice when he told her about this meeting. Then again, she'd probably just make a snide remark about bribes and cheap whores. She'd already made her displeasure known about Trulliç doing an assignment for Atça.

Atça already had his tea set ready. The pungent odor of mint, cardamom, and fine black tea wafted toward Trulliç as he sat. Riyune stayed near the door, as was his habit. But instead of laying down and sleeping, he took on his statue pose, legs in front of him as if ready to accept offerings.

Atça looked at Riyune, then back at Trulliç. "I swear he does that just to disturb me," the old magician muttered.

Trulliç bit his lips together to hide his smile. Riyune had never hidden from Trulliç just how much he didn't care for Atça. He'd never made a mess on Atça's fine carpets or chewed any of the pillows. But he'd make sure he lay just exactly where Atça would trip on him. As well as turning completely motionless when it was just Atça and Trulliç.

Riyune was wrong to not like Atça. Atça had been Trulliç's mentor and teacher for a long time. Without him, Trulliç would have been lost the first time he'd stepped on the sands. He owed his teacher a lot.

"How may I serve you?" Trulliç asked after Atça had served the tea. The bitter taste washed through his mouth, leaving his senses clear.

Atça looked at Trulliç seriously. He wore his judging robes, fine black and blue silks, the color of the goddess of death, Berzhat. A golden girdle around his waist held the ceremonial dagger of office, presented to Atça by the emperor himself. Pearls from the far away sea encrusted the dagger's sheath, and fine silver covered both ends.

"What I am about to tell you can never leave this room," Atça told Trulliç.

Trulliç stiffened, sitting up straighter. "I swear to never tell a soul," he promised.

Atça nodded after staring at Trulliç for another moment, giving his words weight. "I've discovered a conspiracy. Of magicians. Against the emperor."

Trulliç swallowed against his suddenly dry throat. Magicians? Fighting against the emperor? They couldn't win. The emperor protected himself against all magicians by using the blood hounds to collect the afterbirth of every magician, then made himself a great cloak of scales from them.

No magician could fight against his own blood. In ancient times, the times of the old kings, weaker magicians were required to give the stronger magicians who lived nearby a vial of their blood.

Atça had never asked Trulliç for one. He'd assumed it was because he was such a weak magician Atça didn't need the extra protection.

"How may I help?" Trulliç asked. He would fight this beside Atça. Maybe this was his destiny!

He shook himself. No. He didn't have a grand destiny. He was a failed magician. He could only do his tiny part.

Hopefully it would be enough.

"I want you to travel to Çandekili and meet with Yerkoyliç, the town's magician." Atça leaned closer and whispered, "It's rumored that he's one of the ringleaders."

Trulliç blinked, confused. Why would Atça be sending him into this snake pit?

Atça leaned back and took another sip of his tea. "I want you to see how true this Yerkoyliç is. How loyal."

Trulliç nodded. He could probably do that, though he wasn't sure.

"And to deal with the matter, once you make your judgment."

The room suddenly grew very hot, as if the summer sun had just crept back over the horizon.

Atça wasn't looking at Trulliç anymore, but at Riyune.

The dog continued to do his impression of a statue.

Except—was that a glow coming from him?

No. Trulliç had to have just imagined that. Let his overly fanciful nature take over.

Then Atça turned his attention back to Trulliç. "So how is your dear mother?"

Trulliç knew that Atça wouldn't say another word about the matter. He wouldn't be so direct as to say how he intended Trulliç to deal with the matter.

But Trulliç knew.

If Yerkoyliç was not faithful, it would be up to Trulliç to kill him.

"You're going where?" Bekbel, Trulliç's oldest cousin, asked as he carefully tipped one of the dozen barrels of beer that crowded the cellar over onto its side. It came up to his mid-chest, made out of precious wood, reinforced with metal bands. A huge cork about the size of Bekbel's hand stayed connected solidly to one end.

Bekbel's muscles strained through his thin work shirt as he struggled with the barrel. The shirt was made of gray muslin and came down to mid-thigh. He wore loose brown pants and plain straw sandals. He had the same nose as Trulliç, small and sharp. His dark eyes didn't miss much, and his tongue was always biting.

"Çandekili," Trulliç bragged. He shivered despite himself. The rough rock walls kept the cellar cool even on the hottest days. It smelled musty, not like clean dirt, stale even though rinds of cheese were aging on racks along one side and the barrels of beer lined the other. "Atça wants me to meet with the town magician." He wasn't about to tell anyone that he was supposed to kill this other person.

Bekbel gave a low whistle. "Some secret magician's meeting, hmmm?" he asked.

"No, nothing like that," Trulliç assured him, lying through his teeth.

Bekbel nodded. "Right," he said, obviously not believing a word Trulliç had just said. "Little light here?"

Trulliç raised his mage light higher, sending the golden ball to float above Bekbel's head. Trulliç noticed with surprise that he was almost as tall as his oldest cousin. Bekbel was five years older, the oldest son of his mother's sister, and had always been one of the tallest cousins.

When had Trulliç gained that much height?

And what was he going to do about Yerkoyliç? What if he turned out to be in a plot to harm the emperor? Trulliç had never really considered killing someone. How was he going to do this? How could he make Atça proud of him?

"Sorry?" Trulliç said when he realized that Bekbel had asked a question.

"I said, is that why your mother's so angry? Because you're going to Çandekili?" Bekbel asked as he tipped over another barrel onto its side.

"She's just…disappointed in me. That I'm not living up to my destiny or something." Trulliç couldn't disguise the bitterness of his tone.

Bekbel nodded. "I remember one night last year, when your mom and mine got really, really drunk."

"Wait, you're talking about my mother? Myrizhah?" Trulliç asked, clarifying.

"Yup. They didn't know I was there. They were both bragging about their sons, trying to outdo each other." Bekbel paused, considering. "Of course, my mother had more to brag about than yours."

Trulliç snorted. "Of course." He'd never been good enough for his mother, for Atça, for anyone.

"It was before your third trip to the desert," Bekbel said. "And your mom was sure that that time, you'd find your home. And that she'd be able to escape Gaadiwala and the tavern and everyone and go live with you in the desert."

"Really?" Trulliç said, surprised. His mom had never even hinted that she wanted to live somewhere else.

"My mom teased her about shaving her head and becoming a nun or something," Bekbel said. "But your mom—she's always had dreams. Bigger than yours. Why else would she go off with some stranger she'd just met and get married?"

That made sense, actually. That his mother would want more than Trulliç, more than anyone else. "Well, I'm afraid I'm just going to disappoint her," he said, trying to swallow down his bitterness.

Bekbel shrugged. "Maybe. Maybe not," he said. "She might just go off and live in the desert without you. Or at least that's what she's threatened Grandma with."

Myrizhah had never gotten along that well with her mother. Then again, Trulliç hadn't known his mother to get along with anyone. She was too quick to speak her mind, too fast to storm out in anger, too slow to forgive. Atça had warned him that Trulliç would have to be careful around her, and would have to leave her behind someday.

Trulliç knew Myrizhah hadn't merely threatened to go live in the desert. If she'd mentioned it, that meant she already had a plan in place and was just waiting until she could put it into effect.

He swallowed around his pain.

Mother would abandon him. Particularly since he wasn't off doing his own magic, but doing the bidding of another magician.

"Hey, it's all right," Bekbel said. He was suddenly standing beside Trulliç.

"I'm fine," Trulliç said bravely. He noticed his mage light had dimmed considerably. "Let's get these barrels upstairs," he added.

"All right," Bekbel said slowly. "But you know, you have family, here in town. If you ever need anything."

"Like I would need help herding goats or something," Trulliç said.

"Might find an attractive one," Bekbel teased.

Trulliç helped Bekbel roll the first barrel to the foot of the ramp leading up, out of the cellar. While Trulliç helped physically push the barrel, he also applied his magic, making the barrel lighter so it rolled up the ramp with ease.

After they'd gotten the second one up the ramp and into the courtyard, Trulliç left his cousin and walked over to the ovens back there, to see what other work his mother might have for him since he was leaving the next day.

All the while, a single question rolled around and around in his head.

Would you help me go kill a stranger?

Trulliç couldn't ask his cousin that. Couldn't ask any of his family.

Could only hope they wouldn't hate him if he failed.

Or worse, if he succeeded.

Trulliç noticed the weather ridge right away. In a very short distance the scrub changed from scraggly and wide spaced to taller and fuller. The leaves grew from finger thin to palm sized. The green of the leaves didn't change, and continued more gray than green. But grasses sprang up beside the bushes, as bright as the one season when Gaadiwala had had so much rain everything bloomed at the same time.

Then flowers started showing, hooded with bright yellow and white petals, followed with open-faced pink and gold flowers, then tiny pink and red clusters, and others, more flowers than Trulliç had ever seen. And not growing in gardens! But covering the ground. He couldn't name half of them.

Bees buzzed beside the road, along with flies and crickets. As Trulliç walked, he even passed a hidden pond that held belching frogs.

The closer Trulliç got to Çandekili, the more crowded the trade road grew. He passed at least three caravans with a dozen or more camels slowly ambling along. Other merchants ambled along with large packs on their backs.

When the trade road crested a slight rise, Trulliç got his first real look at Çandekili. He'd thought that it wasn't that much larger than Gaadiwala —he was wrong. It stood, walled and proud, in a green valley. He could barely see from the front gates to the back. How long would it take to walk from one end to the other? Half a day? Maybe more?

Stone houses cropped up like weeds, though the ones at the center appeared to be on some sort of a grid. The roofs slanted either one direction or another, making the placement of the houses seem even more random. Dark brown and reddish rock made up most of the houses, though there were a few yellowish ones as well, and closer to the center of the town, some of the rock had been whitewashed.

The grand house in the very center of the town shone in the morning light, reflecting it as if it were coated in gold. Was that Yerkoyliç's house? Probably. Other large buildings stood beside it, though it was at least a story taller than them.

To the right, just inside the gate, stood an open square. Trulliç assumed that would be the marketplace. But what was that other open area, just inside the gates?

Suddenly, Trulliç was even less sure about his mission. Obviously Yerkoyliç was a powerful, important magician.

How could Trulliç even think about questioning his loyalty?

Or possibly kill him?

Trulliç stepped inside the gate of Çandekili with trepidation. He knew what Atça's magic felt like. He'd grown up with it. He didn't remember a time when his own magic wasn't influenced by it.

Yerkoyliç's magic had a sweeter flavor than Atça's. It felt lighter, too. Trulliç couldn't tell if it was stronger or weaker. Those didn't seem to be the right terms, either. Instead, Atça's magic felt dry, like the packed dirt that made up the streets of Gaadiwala, and it was as solid as the rocks of the foothills. Not laced with *meslit* syrup, but the fires that refined it, more smoky than sweet.

While Yerkyolic's magic felt like a garden, full of jasmine, gardenias, and other fragrant flowers. Instead of hard rock, there were soft breezes and fertile earth. It felt busy, too, like all the bees and ants and other insects that worked constantly all through the spring.

Houses crowded close to the street, looming over Trulliç. He took deep breaths, though the smell of so many people crowded close, so many fires and different smells, made him want to gag.

He told himself that there was enough air. He just had to keep breathing, despite how closed in everything felt.

The people here were different, as well. They seemed better dressed than the people in Gaadiwala, though they had the same look to them: tall, thin, with dark hair and dark eyes, wearing tunics over long-sleeved shirts. Some of the women wore full pants, though many wore long skirts. More than a few had aprons on. Almost everyone wore headscarves, though most were of flimsy material, not heavy enough to protect them from the sun.

No one bumped into Trulliç, or each other. He still felt hemmed in by so many bodies. He could count over a dozen nearby, with a dozen more scattered in the street in front of him and behind him.

Trulliç looked away from the crowd and up at the houses. Banners hung from the walls of every third one or so. He recognized the sandal maker, the lamp maker, as well as the oil merchant. He nearly stopped at the tinsmith's store, wanting to look at the horseshoes for babies.

A banner with a barrel painted on it adorned the next building, though the front windows and the door were closed. Was that a tavern? Why weren't they open yet?

Though Trulliç didn't see anyone looking at him—they must be used to strangers here—he still felt watched. Was it Yerkoyliç? Did he know that another magician had come to his town? Though Trulliç was only a minor magician, at best. He was probably too insignificant to be noticed.

He didn't know if that made him feel better or not.

Trulliç glanced down at Riyune. The dog clicked as he walked, his nails scraping the stones. Anyone else looking at Riyune would think he was a normal dog, walking along, just with unusual coloring and very strange eyes.

Trulliç knew better, however. Riyune was tense. Nervous. On guard, his head up, looking around, trying to keep track of everything around them.

"It'll be all right," Trulliç said softly.

He didn't need to see Riyune to know how the dog rolled his eyes at him.

The magic Trulliç felt swimming around him suddenly surged. It was like walking along a path and happening across a large flowering bush. Everything seemed brighter suddenly, and the smell of flowers was briefly overwhelming.

Trulliç stopped to sneeze, once, twice, three times.

When he looked back up, a large man hurried down the street toward him. Trulliç hadn't seen many of the emperor's guard—they rarely made it to such a small village as Gaadiwala. They had come a few years back, though, to collect the town's tribute to the emperor.

This man had the same look to him, built broad like a building, head shaved, all muscles. He wore a red-and-black striped tunic, and now that Trulliç had thought about it, he'd seen others in that same tunic, those same colors.

That answered that question.

Yes, Yerkoyliç and his magic did sense Trulliç. And had sent someone to deal with him.

CHAPTER EIGHT

NADEEM

NADEEM KEPT THE LOOK OF disgust off her face with ease, pretending instead to listen with great care to Aunt Izmet and her instructions for Nadeem's first assignment as one of the emperor's stars. They sat in Aunt Izmet's tent in the training camp, sipping tea in the cool evening. Soft breezes came up from the coast. The smell of spices came with them. Occasionally the *thunk* of knives hitting a target from the range next door wafted in.

It had taken Nadeem most of a week to heal from her final test to the point that she felt as though walking from her cavern to the eating tent no longer made her want to take a nap. It took a second week before she had regained her strength and felt as though she could try running or climbing again.

Luckily, Aunt Izmet had taken pity on her and brought her a small drop spindle she could use while still seated. Nadeem had always liked the feel of the thread slipping through her fingers, growing long and smooth as she spun thread from coarse hunks of wool.

Nadeem took another sip of her tea despite the revulsion rolling through her stomach. Aunt Izmet had sweetened it with *meslit*, but it still had a bitter aftertaste on the back of Nadeem's tongue.

She'd expected her first assignment to be easy. Though Nadeem had trained hard for three years to win her spot among the emperor's stars, she was still new. She accepted that, took the ribbing the older aunts gave her about being wet behind the ears as good naturedly as she could.

But this? Killing an old man in his sleep, so his death looked natural? Where was the honor in that? She hadn't expected they'd be rescuing orphans or looking for lost sheep in the Kinarak foothills. She had expected to be sent into battle somewhere, maybe in the barbarian lands to the north or east.

The emperor still fought the northern barbarians. Surely there was something that Nadeem could do that would be more useful than this assassination.

Aunt Izmet frowned at Nadeem as if she could read her thoughts. "This is strictly a political move by the emperor," she said sternly. "It isn't personal."

Nadeem contained her snort at that. Everything was personal. She'd learned that as a young girl at Aunt Parayat's feet. Her aunt had always insisted that Nadeem look beyond the first layer, to the second, or third face that lay beyond.

They were supposed to be masters of disguise, after all. What good was her magic though, if she couldn't see through to the true heart of something?

Did this man, Malik, have friends who were too powerful? Had he refused to pay some tax of the emperor's? Was he too popular? Nadeem was going to have to learn all she could about her assignment. She was already justifying her research in her head, all in the name of doing a thorough job, in case one of the aunts asked.

Layers upon layers of illusion and lies.

Aunt Izmet added, "It is for the glory of the emperor that you should be chosen for this task."

"For the glory of the emperor," Nadeem repeated, perfectly mimicking Aunt Izmet's fevered tone.

Surely there would be some glory in it, right?

"You'll take Gabril and Duzhen with you," Aunt Izmet said.

"Have they already been told about the assignment?" Nadeem asked, curious.

"They have. In separate briefings," Aunt Izmet assured her.

Why wasn't her team being briefed together? Was it so that secret information could be given to Gabril and Duzhen? Things that they were being told that they'd never tell Nadeem? Additional assignments that they'd also be expected to fulfill while on the primary one?

Nadeem was certain it was another damned test.

She'd passed the big one. She could pass all these little ones as well.

"We'll leave in two mornings' time," Nadeem said as she put her tea to the side. "Thank you for trusting me in this matter. It will be done."

Aunt Izmet nodded. "You'll need to swear it."

Nadeem paused and blinked. Star sisters took their oaths seriously. If a sister took an oath, all the rest of them were bound to uphold it. "Really?" she asked, surprised. "Surely this is a private matter, and not for all the sisters?"

Aunt Izmet nodded. "There's a special oath, just for the emperor's stars."

That made sense. So if she failed, it wouldn't be all of the star sisters who would be held responsible for fulfilling her oath, but just the emperor's stars.

Nadeem wouldn't fail, however.

Aunt Izmet pulled out her ceremonial dagger. It had a red wooden handle with a black obsidian blade. Had it been made from the rock near here?

"I need your blood oath, that you will take care of this matter for the emperor," Aunt Izmet said, handing the knife to Nadeem, handle first.

Nadeem weighed the blade in her hand. It was well balanced. Sharp. The stone would be brittle, given how thin it was.

"I swear to you that I will kill this man, this Malik," Nadeem said. "Or die trying. I give my oath on that."

After kissing the tip of the blade, Nadeem turned it, then sliced a fine cut along her left palm that stung only a little. Beads of blood sprang up along the cut. Nadeem swiped her finger along the blood, held it out to Aunt Izmet.

Instead of daubing the blood onto a ceremonial cloth, or directing Nadeem to smear it back on herself, marking her forehead or cheeks, Aunt Izmet leaned forward and took the proffered digit in her mouth, sucking the blood off.

Nadeem held herself very still. No one had ever done this before. Her revulsion suddenly came back, her stomach rolling.

"I take the blood of your oath upon myself," Aunt Izmet said. "I, or one of my sisters, will succeed if you fail."

Though Aunt Izmet spoke in a neutral tone, Nadeem couldn't help but wonder if there was more to it, if there was an acknowledgement that Aunt Izmet was already convinced Nadeem would fail.

Nadeem met with Gabril and Duzhen out in the training tent after breakfast the next morning. She had no illusions that the aunts weren't somehow listening in.

Or that one of the other two wasn't going to report back on every word that was said.

She still didn't want Çara or the others listening in to the details of their first assignment. It would be up to them to face their own assignments in the future, and they were likely to be very different.

Plus, Nadeem wasn't sure how she felt about the assignment now that she'd had a night to sleep on it. She'd been disgusted at first, but she'd managed to come up with a few scenarios that explained away her hesitation. Perhaps he was a powerful man but corrupt, and so needed to be dealt with surreptitiously. Or perhaps he was a traitor to the great emperor, and by dying would kill an entire conspiracy.

That morning, under the long tarp, Nadeem had set up targets at the far end for knives. Though she didn't believe in throwing away her only weapon, throwing knives could be used as a good stealth defense. She was more accurate with a blowgun, so she wanted to practice with the throwing knives.

The day had dawned with summer heat, despite it still being spring. She wore a dull red and green striped tunic without a blouse underneath, along with a pair of very loose pants that gave her full movement. She didn't expect to have to wrestle with either Gabril or Durzhen, but she wanted an outfit that would let her flow and move and do whatever needed doing.

She felt as though she would need that ability a lot in the upcoming days, the ability to change and flow and move as necessary.

Malik lived in the town of Koruli, just north of Gaadiwala on the trade route coming out of the desert. The town was a little smaller than Gaadiwala, and though it had a better water source, it was less important because it had no magician.

Nadeem had readied three targets so all of them could practice at the same time, then take breaks and watch each other, critiquing movement and stance. "You've all been told about our first assignment by the aunts, correct?" she asked as she threw her first knife.

It made a nice *whump* as it hit the target. However, it landed in the fourth circle out. There were five rings around the center. Nadeem would have to do much better. She must still be tired. That must be why she hit so far out.

She took a drink of her tea, pausing while the others answered. She'd made it sweet that morning with a large dollop of *meslit* syrup, needing the extra energy.

Gabril replied. "I have," she said. She threw her first knife, which landed on her target in about the same location as Nadeem's. She wore a similar outfit to Nadeem's, just a tunic and pants, though she'd tied her hair back with a band instead of a standard *chafiyek*.

"Yeah," Durzhen said. "Completely stupid if you ask me." She threw her knife with precision and hit the exact center of the target. She wore all black that morning and moved like a shadow, her gray eyes cloudy.

Nadeem pressed her lips together so she didn't grin too hard. Of course, Durzhen would have spoken her mind not just to Nadeem, but probably to the aunts as well when they'd told her of the assignment.

"I can kill someone one from halfway across a goddamned town and make it look like an accident," Durzhen continued. "Where's the challenge in that?"

"It is to not be seen," Gabril said solemnly. "To come into town as ourselves and leave as ourselves, with no one suspecting our involvement."

Nadeem nodded. That was part of the challenge, particularly when dealing with a smaller town. Strangers would get remarked on. Remembered. Particularly a group of star sisters.

"We could stay a couple of days after the death and spread rumors of other deaths that happened in the night," Nadeem said.

"I agree," Gabril said. She threw another knife that landed in the second circle, much closer to the bullseye. "We need to make sure that no suspicion lands on us, or our other sisters."

Durzhen snorted and threw another perfect bullseye. "Townspeople are always going to suspect us. 'Where the sisters go, trouble follows'," she said, obviously quoting someone.

Nadeem wondered when Durzhen had heard such a thing. She believed it, however. The aunts always warned them about outsiders, and taught how little the star sisters were trusted, despite their blood oaths and kind deeds, the number of children they took in that the townspeople abandoned. She'd never met her own birthmother. She'd been raised in the *kabil* of star sisters.

This assignment would be the first time she'd experience such prejudice firsthand.

She took the time to throw her own knife, again landing in the fourth circle.

She really needed to practice more.

"There are soporifics," Nadeem said slowly, "that in large enough doses are lethal."

Gabril grimaced. "And anyone with a lick of knowledge would know those and be able to trace them back to us. No, we need something else."

Her next hit went way off the mark, barely nicking the target.

"All we have to do is smoother him," Durzhen said. "He's an old man. Old men die in their sleep all the time."

Nadeem's third knife landed on the outer ring of the target, exactly where she'd intended for it to go. She nodded. "True, old men do just die. But I don't think it will be that easy. Otherwise, why would the aunts send all three of us?"

Gabril grinned. "They're sending me so I can look after the two of you and make sure you don't get into too much trouble."

Nadeem believed that. Either the aunts had told Gabril that was her responsibility, or she'd just taken it on herself as one of her duties, as she generally did. She was

"Yeah, well, I'm supposed to keep y'all on the straight and narrow. Make sure you honor your oaths. As if," Durzhen said.

Nadeem didn't have to see Duzhen's expression to know just how hard she was rolling her eyes. She always pushed the limits set by the aunts. If she could figure out a clever way around a problem, she would go that way, even if it involved more work, rather than do what was expected of her.

"And you?" Gabril asked after throwing another knife that was very close to the bullseye. "What is your task?"

Nadeem blinked. Aunt Izmet hadn't given her a specific task in the group beyond killing the old man. "To keep an eye on you two, of course," she said.

"Of course," Gabril said, her eyes narrowed.

She obviously thought Nadeem had lied and had some other task that she'd been given, like the pair of them had been.

Anyone who had not worked with the other two as closely as Nadeem had for years would have missed the look that Gabril threw Durzhen. It was subtle and done while Nadeem lined up her next shot, supposedly all her attention on the bullseye.

Gabril seemed to be saying, *See? I told you so.*

What really made her angry was when Durzhen nodded in agreement, just the slightest incline of her head, but enough to get her point across.

They both thought Nadeem wasn't true to them, that she was aligned with the aunts, that there was more to this assignment than they were being told.

No matter what Nadeem told them, they'd never believe her.

Nadeem threw her next knife, then blinked, surprised when it hit the center of the bullseye.

Seemed all she needed to do to be accurate was to get very angry.

She was going to have to remember that.

The sun touched the western horizon as Nadeem, Gabril, and Durzhen came through the Ladikah pass. They needed to hurry if they wanted to make it to Gaadiwala before full night had set in. They'd traveled along Knife Ridge going north as far as they could go, then bought camels for crossing the first part of the desert, going west. At the Manisal oasis, they'd sold the camels and set off across the last part of the sands on foot, heading directly toward the Kinarak mountain range.

Mint kissed the air as they walked down the rough pass. A herd of someone's goats brayed at them as they passed. Gabril and Durzhen walked behind Nadeem though the path had widened out so they could walk abreast.

They wore "town clothes" today, long skirts and loose blouses in black, with colored tunics, their headscarves equally bright. They also had wide leather belts with knives prominently displayed, sturdier sandals than most, and heavy backpacks. They'd never be mistaken for anything other than star sisters, however, given their scarred cheeks.

Durzhen kept the rear position and watched behind them as well as past Nadeem's shoulder. Gabril moved like a walking mountain, solid and steady. Despite how none of them fully trusted the other, Nadeem was still glad they were there with her. Nothing had been said on their eight-day journey to make her think that either of her two sisters had changed their minds about her—she was just glad that neither of them thought they should take it upon themselves to kill her in her sleep.

They probably already knew just how difficult it would be to surprise her, even when asleep.

Was working with distrust part of the first assignment? Yet another test of the aunts? Nadeem had finally decided that it must be. Though a star sister wasn't anything without her other sisters, perhaps each emperor's star needed to shine on her own.

Gaadiwala spread out below the them as they crested the last foothill. The buildings didn't seem organized, but set in random clusters. Was there a purpose to the sprawling town? Did every neighborhood grow up around a well? Gaadiwala didn't have a river flowing through it for houses to sprout along. There must have been a thousand souls living there.

Only one or two of the stone buildings were taller than a single story, and no wall protected the town. Pounded dirt made up the streets. Nadeem was glad it was past the rainy season: Gaadiwala must turn into a sea of mud when the rains came.

The shacks they passed at the outskirts of town had chickens in the yards, but that was their only wealth, Nadeem was sure. Only a few of the shacks had chimneys for fires to keep warm, she didn't see any rugs covering the floors and only rough, stained, and torn cloth over the doors or windows.

No one in the *kabil* of star sisters lived so poorly.

And Gaadiwala had a magician! Why didn't he do better for his people? The emperor should have done something about this man, this Atça.

Maybe that would be her next assignment, after they'd taken care of Malik.

The three of them kept to the shadows, passing a group of old men standing around a well, drawing their water together, then further into town, where the houses grew closer together. Rock walls made up all the buildings and many of the roofs. The town was stone rich, but wood poor.

Why didn't the magician encourage more trees to grow? Surely he could do that.

Nadeem considered going to the magician's house, at least walking by it. However, she already knew what she'd see: a rich palace, probably mostly made of wood, that outshone every other house around it.

It was a disgrace that Atça be allowed to live with such wealth while the rest of the town lived in such squalor.

Nadeem nodded to herself. Yes. The next time they passed through Gaadiwala. If their mission was successful. She would have words with this Atça.

F inding a tavern wasn't difficult. While there weren't many, they were all located in the same area, on side streets just off the market square.

After the three of them had looked at all the taverns that Gaadiwala held, Nadeem led them back to the tavern that seemed to have the most women working in it. It had a horseshoe embedded in the wall above the door—was that the name of the place? The Horseshoe Tavern? Or was it just for good luck? The ends of it faced down toward the ground, so it still resembled the symbol for the goddess Onnet.

The front windows of the tavern stood wide open to show the rickety tables and stained pillows covered in dust and other travelers' sweat. Would they have a courtyard behind the tavern where Nadeem and her companions could stay for the night? Could they rent a couple of tables and sleep on them?

"Come on," Durzhen said after Nadeem had stood there looking for a few long moments. Durzhen pushed past Nadeem and walked up, through the door.

Nadeem looked back at Gabril, who merely shrugged. "She is hungry," Gabril said.

Nadeem nodded.

She still hesitated.

It wasn't that she was scared. Not exactly. But it was the first time that she'd ever gone into such a place. She'd just wanted to make sure that she was making the right choice.

"All right," she said eventually. She hadn't promised the aunts that she'd look after the others. But that was her responsibility, right?

So she squared her shoulders and marched into the tavern as if she was marching into battle.

T he noise of the place reminded Nadeem of a star sister ceremony, or even the *panayirat*, when the seven star-sister *kabils* all met once a summer. There seemed to be over a dozen conversations going on all at the same time, with everyone trying to shout over each other.

The smell of the chicken and garlic soup they were serving made Nadeem's mouth water. The unleavened bread she spied seemed fresh baked that day as well.

Durzhen waved to them from a table against one of the walls. Nadeem counted nine other tables scattered across the room. They all stood only a foot or so off the ground, surrounded by pillows for guests to sit on or lean against. At least fifty people were crowded into the space. All locals—no, there were a few other travelers there.

Nadeem carefully picked her way through the crowd. Any man who looked up far enough to see her face looked away quickly.

Fools.

The women who were serving gave them quick smiles and nods. Nadeem could tell they were busy, and patiently waited until a tall, proud woman came up to serve them.

"Welcome, stranger sisters," the woman said. "I am Myrizhah. How may I help you?"

Stranger sisters? Nadeem had never been called that before. But it made sense. The traditional greeting was always "Welcome, stranger." That this woman also labeled them sisters might mean that she felt more of a kinship with them.

Nadeem spoke up before Durzhen could say something impolite, as she usually did. "Thank you, sister," she said with a smile. "We need food, if your kitchen is still serving. And someplace where we can unroll our bedrolls for the night.

"Certainly," Myrizhah said. "The courtyard is generally reserved for you and your sisters, if you'd like. The merchants have already claimed the tables." She kept her face perfectly solemn as she said that, but Nadeem could tell how little she thought of the men.

"We have at least three bowls left of the soup, as well as bread, and either beer or *igrat*." Then Myrizhah quoted a price that Nadeem was certain was at least four times what the locals paid.

Durzhen couldn't contain her snort.

Nadeem glared at her, then shrugged and sat back, indicating that Durzhen should do the bargaining for them.

One of the things that Aunt Parayat had always emphasized with Nadeem was to let others do what they were good at.

What would Nadeem be considered good at after this first assignment? Killing? Or was there more to it than that?

Myrizhah showed them the courtyard after most of the guests had left the tavern for the evening. She had dark circles under her eyes, as if she'd been awake too many hours.

And maybe she had—it was fully night, now. She had a small lamp that she used to show them where to lay their bedrolls.

"Thank you," Nadeem said, pressing a small coin into her hand as she was leaving. "Can you tell me what the horseshoe on the sign outside means?" She hadn't heard anyone calling the tavern by that name, and had remained curious all night.

Myrizhah grimaced. "It was supposed to be a sign of our good luck," she said, her bitterness evident. "Instead, it's just a reminder of broken dreams. Good night," she added, firmly turning away.

Nadeem didn't know what Myrizhah meant by that. How had a tin horseshoe represented dreams?

Gabril spoke, her words floating across the quiet dark. "It's a custom to place a horseshoe on the belly of a pregnant woman, so the channel will open and the birth will be easy."

Nadeem nodded to herself as she rolled out her blankets. She'd heard that. The star sisters didn't practice such beliefs, but she knew that the horseshoe could also represent the goddess Onnet. "Birth gone wrong?" she wondered.

"Who knows? Who cares?" Durzhen slurred. Either the girl had actually drunk all the beer they'd been served, or she was good at faking being drunk. Nadeem hadn't tried too hard to see beneath the face she wore.

The courtyard itself was paved with wide, flat stones, making it a hard but smooth surface. The smell of the ovens still lingered in the air. Above them, stars filled their sliver of the sky, what was visible between the houses all around them.

A child cried briefly, followed by a soft lullaby. An old man snored fitfully. Chickens clucked in their pen.

Nadeem was the furthest she'd ever been from her *kabil* and the oasis she'd been raised in. She had never been to such foreign lands, with so many people. She didn't understand how anyone could live with their neighbors so close, almost breathing the same air.

She suddenly understood the great hero Arzhem and why she left the corrupt city for the sparseness of the desert. Though the air here was dry and the stones as harsh as the rocks of home, it still was too closed in.

For the first time, Nadeem questioned her choice of becoming one of the emperor's stars, particularly if it meant that she'd always have to live in places like this.

The morning would bring new light. It would be up to Nadeem to find her way with it.

Nadeem, Gabril, and Durzhen were up and had left the tavern just as dawn arrived. It wasn't that far to Koruli—perhaps half a day's walk—but they needed to stop and disguise themselves before they arrived.

The wide road ambled to the north across stony foothills and brambles that supported goats and sheep better than men. At least it felt more open to Nadeem, who'd dreamed of being buried in a box under the desert, tortured with the knowledge that the open sands were just a few feet above her head.

They passed a flock of beautiful, long-haired *nadjil* sheep, the shepherd watching them carefully from the top of a small hill. They were taller than usual sheep, reaching almost up to Nadeem's waist, with white faces while the rest of their coat was black. This herd had weathered the winter well and had fat bellies and many lambs. They were rich men's sheep, valued for their straight, long hair. Nadeem had only ever been able to afford a small bit of fiber from a *nadjil* sheep once—the oils in it had left her hands soft for an entire day.

The problem with the *nadjil* sheep was that they needed better food. The more common *ivesil* sheep could eat like a goat and live on brambles and thorns. *Ivesil* sheep also had fat tails, broader than Nadeem's outstretched hand. Only a stupid farmer would trim their tails: The sheep stored water reserves there that enabled them to live through the dry season.

Their wool was coarse, though, with shorter hairs, making it harder to spin and work with than the *nadjil*.

Nadeem sighed and didn't think about what it would take to raise *nadjil* sheep where she lived. Though that might be one of the advantages to living in a town, even one as poor as Gaadiwala, if she had regular access to such wool.

Both Gabril and Durzhen noticed Nadeem's preoccupation with the sheep but they didn't comment on it—Durzhen, as far as Nadeem could tell, had no hobbies, while Gabril loved to work leather, making beautiful braided belts.

Just past the flock the road turned abruptly to the west. Up ahead, Nadeem could tell that it would turn back again, zigzagging around some border that no longer existed. To the right there appeared to be a small outcropping of rocks.

"Durzhen," Nadeem called, pointing.

Durzhen nodded and took off at a dead sprint.

She'd probably been bored with just walking.

When she got about halfway to the rocks, she turned around and gave an all clear sign.

Nadeem and Gabril followed quickly.

The rocks turned out to be just what Nadeem had hoped—a resting spot for travelers that few still used because of the way the road now turned. A merchant or caravan would have to know the rocks existed if they were traveling late at night.

But it was the perfect place for the three of them to rest and to disguise themselves.

They couldn't hide the fact that they were star sisters, or that there were three of them, though they'd debated that. Instead, they could hide their ages. Elderly women would be granted more respect and wouldn't be commented on as much as younger women.

They'd still reach Koruli by early afternoon.

But it wouldn't be the same three star sisters who'd been in Gaadiwala. Instead it would be three venerable aunts.

The rocks had at one time contained a small altar, though Nadeem wasn't sure for which god. Had it been for Enkat? The goddess of rain? That would make sense in such a dry place. Or had it been for Innis, the god of fertility? All that remained was a small cup carved out of the side of one of the walls to hold offerings.

Nadeem poured a few drops of water from one of her flagons into it, just for luck. The other walls were made from stone and falling apart. No roof covered the small temple.

"Here," Durzhen said, pointing to the foot of one of the walls. "No one from the road can see us."

"Thank you," Nadeem said as she sat. "I will go first," she added. "Then Gabril, then Durzhen. We can be the mirror for one another."

It was a practical choice. She was the strongest illusionist among them and would take the least time.

Gabril sat down facing her. "I will be your mirror."

Nadeem nodded her thanks, then held her hands out in front of her. It was always easiest for her to start with her hands, imagining the age spots that Aunt Parayat's hands now held, how veiny they looked, the thin skin, the wrinkles, the bones that stood out.

Nadeem's skin lost its youth and hardness. The callouses across her thumbs and forefingers from blade work softened and disappeared. Age took over as the veins stood up against the backs of her hands. What might have been freckles now spread and multiplied as age spots.

Old age marched on, up past her hands and her wrists, encircling her forearms. Muscles withered and wrinkled skin took over.

Then Nadeem went to work on her face. She faded the color of her eyes to a softer brown, like Aunt Parayat's. Her hair thinned and lost its glossy brown color, going gray and mousy. She felt the wrinkles forming across her broad forehead, around the edges of her mouth and the corners of her eyes. Her skin stretched and she lost youthful weight, the bones and veins now showing.

When Nadeem looked up, Gabril stared at her intently. "Ears," she said after a moment.

Nadeem nodded, shrinking her ears down a little, making them more pale as well.

"Perfect," Gabril said after another moment. Then she shook her head. "I don't see how you can change so quickly and become someone else."

"Practice," Nadeem said with a shrug. "Start with your hands, something you can see."

Gabril nodded and began.

It wasn't until much later that Nadeem realized that *practice* wasn't actually what helped.

It was her focus.

She wasn't becoming someone else.

Just a different version of herself.

CHAPTER NINE

TRULLIÇ

THE MAN WHO APPROACHED TRULLIÇ called out, "Hold, you!"

Trulliç stayed where he was, shocked and scared. Why did this man want him to stay? The man looked like one of the emperor's guards, more broad and muscled than even Muratil, Gaadiwala's blacksmith. The guard had a shaved head, meaty hands, and a bulbous nose. His dark eyes glared at Trulliç as he approached. Dark skin glistened in what little light came down to the street between the buildings.

"You need to stay here," the guard said firmly.

At least he didn't tower over Trulliç, but they did look each other directly in the eyes.

"Why?" Trulliç asked. He glanced down at Riyune. The dog looked more curious than scared. "Why do you want me to stay here?"

A crowd had already gathered around them. Trulliç's skin crawled from all the eyes staring at him, taking apart his poor sandals, his travel-stained pants, his sweaty shirt. At least his tunic was new. And kind of clean. Sort of. It was the same tunic he'd worn on his original manhood journey, so many years before. At least now it only fell to just past his waist instead of to his mid-thigh.

"Yerkoyliç has asked that you stay here until he can finish his business at the palace and come to meet you," the guard explained.

That brought a collective gasp from those around them, followed by a flurry of mutters.

Did Yerkoyliç never leave his palace? Or did he just never greet traveling magicians?

Trulliç didn't know. But if he thought about it, how many magicians would be traveling through Çandekili? Most magicians were either born near the place of their magic, or they traveled just once in their lifetime to get to their home.

He was the only magician he knew of who was homeless. No magicians had ever traveled through Gaadiwala, at least not that he was aware of.

"All right," Trulliç said, trying to be amiable. "Though it would have been my pleasure to go to the great magician instead."

The man merely grunted. He'd delivered his message. He wasn't planning on doing any more conversing.

Trulliç was fine with that. It gave him a chance to look at the people around him.

His first impression had been that the people here had a lot more money than those in the poor village of Gaadiwala. Almost everyone he saw made that apparent.

First of all, they wore clothes with colors, not the dull browns and grays of Gaadiwala, but reds, oranges, blues, and greens as well. Many of the merchants he saw had embroidered vines, leaves, and flowers on their tunics. The women, too, had similar motifs embroidered on their belts, headscarves, or blouses.

What did they think of Trulliç? They seemed to be more curious than hostile. Did they understand why he was being held? Was it just for being a magician in another magician's territory? Or was there some other law or custom that Trulliç didn't know about that he was breaking?

At least Riyune continued to be calm, sitting beside Trulliç, not touching him but close by.

Finally, a high-pitched wailing flute sounded off in the distance.

The guard turned to Trulliç and said, "Yerkoyliç comes."

Trulliç found himself standing up straighter and tugging at his tunic. He wished he could have at least washed his hands before the other magician saw him.

The crowd good-naturedly grumbled as they were moved out of the way by other guards, clearing a path. All the guards looked like the one standing near Trulliç—big-boned, with the same tunic.

That spoke of a lot of money, for someone to be able to afford to dress their guards all in the same clothes. Trulliç had never even heard of such a thing.

Finally, Yerkoyliç himself appeared.

He only came up to about Trulliç's shoulder, if that. His round face looked boyish—possibly due to how fat it was. His nose melted across the middle of round cheeks, below beady eyes. Even his chin barely stuck out, overshadowed by his flabby lips. A gold and white *chafiyek,* finely made and more for show than for actual shade from the sun, covered his head. His dark skin was lighter than Trulliç's as well, possibly from spending all his time indoors.

While the people who'd been watching Trulliç had all looked rich, the magician was obviously much, much richer. His vest was made out of the finest linen. The same embroidered vines, flowers, and bees decorated the vest, though the figures on his were outlined in gold thread that caught the sunlight. He wore fine white pants that looked as though they'd never touched the dirt. His shoes looked more like house slippers, red velvet and gold. Trulliç was surprised he'd worn them here, in the streets.

"Hello! Hello!" Yerkoyliç called as he approached. "My good magician! Welcome!"

The people still surrounding Trulliç gasped and murmured. Had no one suspected him of having magic? Had they all assumed he was some sort of criminal?

Yerkoyliç walked closer, then bowed his head to Trulliç. "What brings such a powerful magician as yourself to my humble abode?"

Trulliç bowed his own head in return. "I am Trulliç. I have been sent here to see you by the great magician Atça."

That caused even more murmurs and whispers. Three magicians, all working together! Trulliç had to admit that even in the old stories he'd never heard of such a thing.

His statement also appeared to catch Yerkoyliç off guard. But he recovered quickly, clapping his flabby hands together. "Wonderful! Wonderful!" Then he paused, nodding. "It is my honor to welcome you to Çandekili, to the city of my heart. But, tell me..." He paused, thinking.

"How may I serve you?" Trulliç asked. He could tell that Yerkoyliç wanted to ask him something. And as a guest, it was up to him to be as polite as possible in return for the warm hospitality being offered him.

"It's nothing. Just a trifle. But...did you see the wards at the city gate?" Yerkoyliç asked. He seemed confused.

"Wards?" Trulliç asked. He thought back. "I didn't see any wards, though I could tell, of course, when I crossed into your territory. Your magic is strong and sweet," he added.

That seemed to please the crowd. It was true, though. Yerkoyliç's magic did seem strong and very sweet, perfumed with flowers. Whereas if Atça's magic had a scent at all, it was smoky.

"Ah, ah, all right," Yerkoyliç said, rocking back and forth. He seemed perplexed. "You didn't see them at all?"

Trulliç shook his head. "Would you like to walk back to the gate and show them to me? So that I might see them the next time?" he asked. He really wasn't sure what Yerkoyliç wanted.

"No, no, that's too much to ask of such an honored guest, such as yourself," Yerkoyliç said.

It was clear to Trulliç that Yerkoyliç really wanted to go back to see his wards, to see what had gone wrong with them.

"Please. I insist," Trulliç said. "I would love to see your wards. You must show them to me. And your spectacular magic." That way, the next time Trulliç went to another magician's territory, he might know that magician's wards. They might be an indication of a magician's power.

"Would you?" Yerkoyliç said. He seemed very anxious. "It isn't that I would expect such paltry wards as mine to affect such a great magician as yourself. They do, however, work nicely on the star sisters, who tend to bypass Çandekili as a result."

"I see," Trulliç said, though he didn't, not really. Were these wards supposed to stop him from coming into the Çandekili? "Don't you trade with the star sisters?" He knew they brought precious spices and other goods from the desert. The merchants in Gaadiwala bought them and then moved them up along the trade routes going inland.

"No, no, we have no need," Yerkoyliç said. "Your merchants in Gaadiwala and other places keep us well stocked in spices."

He turned toward the gate and indicated that Trulliç should walk beside him. When Riyune fell into place as well, Yerkoyliç said, "I see you have a familiar as well."

Trulliç said, "He's a good companion," not accepting or denying Yerkoyliç's statement.

"Trulliç, you are a *powerful* magician, indeed," Yerkoyliç said firmly.

"No, no, you are the powerful one here," Trulliç replied truthfully. Çandekili belonged to Yerkoyliç. Every stone seemed to recognize the man. It felt as though the houses loomed in closer as he walked by. The people, too, reflected Yerkoyliç's spirit—happy, content, busy.

Trulliç wasn't sure what that said about Gaadiwala and Atça, how poor they were, how colorless, how dull they seemed.

"What causes you to travel so far from your home?" Yerkoyliç asked as they walked.

"Atça sent me," Trulliç said. "He's been my mentor and my friend." He really didn't want to admit that he was a homeless magician. Not when he finally saw the possibilities awarded to a magician who had found his home.

"Atça's also a powerful magician," Yerkoyliç said. "You are lucky to be able to count him as both friend and mentor."

"I am," Trulliç said fervently. "Though I am merely a traveler here, I hope that you might deign to show me some of your wisdom and learning as well."

Yerkoyliç gave Trulliç a large grin. "We have much to learn from each other! I am looking forward to it."

"Me too," Trulliç said.

And he found to his surprise that he was looking forward to working with the jolly magician.

He also found himself fervently hoping that Yerkoyliç's loyalties remained true.

Trulliç and Yerkoyliç reached the city gate quickly. The guards turned away the crowd who had followed them, telling them to go back about their business. Trulliç knew that he'd be the topic of all conversations for the next week: his dirty clothes and broken nails, how Yerkoyliç had greeted him, was Riyune actually a familiar or merely a dog.

Yerkoyliç stepped across the threshold of the gate. He didn't go gray like Atça did when he traveled outside of Gaadiwala. But Trulliç could tell that the fat, puffed-up man deflated slightly just outside of his city.

Would he ever go gray? Trulliç wasn't certain. Yerkoyliç's bright colors would fade the further away he got from Çandekili. However, Trulliç would bet that the other magician would always have some color to him.

Yerkoyliç turned to his right, walking a few feet to the west along the city wall, then stopped. Solid gray and brown stones, mortared together, made up the wall. None of the stones were larger than Trulliç's head. The wall itself rose up only a few feet above Trulliç. It was thick enough that a man could have walked along the top of it. However, no platform ran along the top. Dried bushes and grass grew along the base of the wall, kept short by goats and other livestock being brought to market.

No houses stood outside the wall on this side. As Trulliç had descended the road down to the city, he thought he'd seen some houses outside the wall to the north. Were those for guards? Or were those for people who couldn't afford to stay in the city?

So close to the wall, Trulliç thought he could see some of the magic there. He knew that Atça would tell him to stop being so fanciful. However, if what Trulliç was seeing was true, then the magic wasn't in the stones themselves, as he would have expected. No, the mortar held bits of magic. When Trulliç looked more carefully, he thought he could make out tiny pieces of blue, red, and green stones mixed into it.

Atça would have strengthened the rocks, made them harder. Yerkoyliç had strengthened what was in between the strong stones.

"There, do you see?" Yerkoyliç asked. He waved his hand toward the wall.

Trulliç shook his head. Because of the magic in the mortar, the wall itself appeared very smooth, the rocks perfectly aligned, almost like baked bricks. However, that was all Trulliç saw. He didn't see any words written on the wall, or some sort of magical shield.

"Hmmm," Yerkoyliç said. He thought for a moment, then stamped his foot close to the base of the wall.

Vines suddenly shot up the walls, quickly reaching waist height. Thorns dotted every branch and stem, and the green leaves looked as sharp as knives. They buzzed as though they were alive with bees, ready to attack. Flowers budded up next, then blossomed into star shapes with five petals, each looking as though merely brushing against them would cut a person to shreds.

"Are these the wards I was supposed to see?" Trulliç asked, amazed.

"Yes. Sort of," Yerkoyliç said thoughtfully. "As you approached the city, you should have seen these, or an image of them. When you got close enough, you should have triggered them. They should have sprung up on their own."

"That's impressive," Trulliç said, marveling. If he'd been walking on his own without owing a duty to Atça, would he have just walked away from Çandekili if these vines had sprung up as he'd drawn near?

Possibly. Though his mother had sometimes accused Trulliç of having more stubbornness than sense. He might have walked into Çandekili on his own anyway.

"I know it's a horrible imposition for me to ask yet another favor," Yerkoyliç said slowly.

The other magician still seemed puzzled. "No, no, not at all," Trulliç said. "What can this poor guest do to help you?"

"Try to touch one of the vines. I don't want you to actually touch it. Don't hurt yourself. But merely put your hand out," Yerkoyliç said.

The fat man stared hard at Trulliç as he slowly reached out toward one of the vines.

Nothing happened.

"See?" Trulliç said, relieved. "I'm not a powerful enough magician to warrant such defenses."

"No, that's not it at all," Yerkoyliç said, looking carefully at Trulliç. "It's because you're too strong. You overpowered them."

Trulliç shook his head, not believing Yerkoyliç. "You're mistaken," he said.

Yerkoyliç tilted his head to one side and gazed for another moment at Trulliç.

Underneath the jolly exterior, Trulliç caught a glimpse of a truly intelligent mind examining him. Atça got that same look sometimes when Trulliç performed what little magic he could under Atça's roof.

"As you say," Yerkoyliç said after a bit. He glanced from Trulliç to Riyune and back before his mask slipped back on and the jovial magician was standing in front of Trulliç again. "Come!" he said, indicating that Trulliç should walk beside him. "We shall walk along the wall of the city and contemplate the defenses. Maybe you can assist me in strengthening them."

"Gladly," Trulliç said. "Though I doubt I can help."

"No matter," Yerkoyliç said. "Let us walk."

Trulliç felt a stab of grief. What would have happened if he'd been mentored by Yerkoyliç? How would his life had been different? Would he have been able to find his home?

Then Trulliç put away his doubts. Atça had been good to him. Helped him. Taught him everything he could.

Trulliç couldn't contain his rising excitement, however, at the thought of being able to learn so much more from the happy magician beside him.

"I love my city," Yerkoyliç started out as they began walking around the outside of the city wall. "Çandekili truly is the home of my heart."

"I can see that," Trulliç said. From what little he'd seen, the city was a reflection of the man: happy, busy, a little self-indulgent.

Rich.

Trulliç didn't know what that meant about the relationship between Atça and Gaadiwala.

Then again, Atça's power had always seemed to center more around his personal home rather than the town itself. If Trulliç's fanciful imaginings could be believed.

"What does the great Atça want with such a poor magician such as I?" Yerkoyliç asked.

Trulliç knew he couldn't tell Yerkoyliç the truth. "He recognizes that you are a powerful magician, much more powerful than you claim." He held up his hand when Yerkoyliç would have protested. "I have seen it myself."

Trulliç still didn't know if Yerkoyliç was stronger than Atça or not, or if he was just that different of a magician.

"So Atça is interested in exploring a future, stronger alliance between the pair of you," Trulliç lied. He hoped this would get Yerkoyliç to talk about loyalties.

Plus, if Yerkoyliç was true, maybe Atça would be interested in such a relationship.

"To see how two such powerful magicians might better align their powers and their interests, to better their people," Trulliç continued.

"But wouldn't that be against the wishes of the emperor?" Yerkoyliç said, obviously shocked, stopping in his place. "What exactly are you proposing?"

"What do you mean?" Trulliç asked, confused. When had the emperor said that magicians couldn't form an alliance? He knew of no such decree. Otherwise, how could Atça have mentored him? Or how could any older magician teach any younger magician?

Yerkoyliç looked carefully at Trulliç. "You truly didn't know," he said quietly. "The emperor has been sending out more decrees, every month now, it seems," he added sourly.

Trulliç nodded. He'd noticed that. Atça was always receiving scrolls and messengers from the emperor, much more so now than when Trulliç had been younger.

Had Atça forgotten to mention this one to Trulliç? Or had the message arrived after Trulliç had left Gaadiwala?

"Earlier this year, the emperor let it be known that he needed to approve of any alliance between magicians," Yerkoyliç said. He looked over one shoulder, then the other, to make sure that no one had approached and was listening to them. "If one read between the lines, one could easily make the assumption that no magician was to contact another. It was part of why I was so surprised to find you here."

"I see," Trulliç said. Surely, Atça had known this. Why had he sent Trulliç to meet with Yerkoyliç? What kind of reception had he expected the other magician to give Trulliç?

Yerkoyliç nodded at Trulliç, as if coming to a decision. "You said you were mentored by Atça, correct?"

"Yes," Trulliç said slowly.

"And have you found your home? In the desert?" Yerkoyliç asked.

"How did you—" Trulliç started, then cut himself off. "No," he said softly, shaking his head. "I haven't."

"How did I know your home is in Qaenev?" Yerkoyliç said, smiling. "You smell like sand, dry and coarse. Hot winds blow around you. Even the widest street of my city hems you in."

"Yes," Trulliç whispered. He didn't ask how Yerkoyliç knew. It was the same ability that Trulliç had, the one that told him about Atça's power, Yerkoyliç's.

The ability was real. Those thoughts and feelings that Trulliç had wasn't just him being fanciful.

Atça was wrong.

"I've searched for my home," Trulliç admitted. "But it hasn't shown itself to me."

Yerkoyliç nodded. "That's too bad. I couldn't imagine being uprooted from Çandekili. It's too much a part of me."

"You were born here?" Trulliç asked.

"I was," Yerkoyliç said proudly. "By the time I was walking, the streets were bending to my will. There was already a city here, but no magician."

"I was born far to the north, in Lydae," Trulliç told him. "My mother brought me back."

"She knew you were a desert magician?" Yerkoyliç said amazed. "That's marvelous!"

Trulliç nodded. What would have happened to him had he been

raised beneath the mountains of Knassia? Where everything was green, and it snowed in the winter? He couldn't contain his shudder.

Yerkoyliç started walking again, curving around the city wall. Trulliç walked beside him. The other magician appeared to be lost in thought.

"I will be honest with you," Yerkoyliç said suddenly. "I was afraid that you might be here to challenge me. To take my city away from me."

"By Serrat's star, no," Trulliç said, horrified. "Not that it isn't a lovely city," he added hastily. "But—"

Yerkoyliç laughed. "I understand. It isn't yours. You have no interest in it at all." He paused, then added, "But I will also admit that I have a special interest in the desert."

"Really?" Trulliç asked. "Why?"

Yerkoyliç paused again. "Have you ever heard of the desert heart?"

Trulliç shook his head.

"Of course, you know the story of Forit?" Yerkoyliç asked.

"She was Innis' wife, and the fairest of the gods," Trulliç said. He found himself standing straighter, as if he was reciting for Atça. "During the great battle between the darkness and the gods, before the forming of the world, she sang such a beautiful song that the darkness revealed its heart to the gods. Innis pierced the heart with his great spear, killing the darkness. But the only way Forit could draw out the heart was by binding the heart of darkness with her own, and so she died as well."

Her body fell and became the earth. Her teeth became the mountains, her fingers became the many rivers, and the place where her heart had been became the desert.

As the gods and goddesses grieved, their tears fell on her prone body.

Her freckles, the only imperfection about her, became humanity. The darker freckles became the people of the south, the lighter blemishes became the people of the north.

"There are stories that her heart still exists in the center of the Qaenev desert," Yerkoyliç said.

Trulliç hadn't heard of such myths. He found himself biting his tongue so that he wouldn't accuse Yerkoyliç of being fanciful.

He made the decision right there and then to *never* accuse someone else of having too much imagination.

"Wouldn't her heart be infected with darkness?" Trulliç asked.

"That's what some say," Yerkoyliç admitted. "But others say that after all these years, she'd be cleansed of it. Or would have purified the darkness."

"What would you do with such a remarkable item?" Trulliç asked, wondering. That sort of power would be truly amazing.

Yerkoyliç shrugged. "What couldn't you do? But it would take more than one magician to find it."

Trulliç thought back to the start of their conversation. "Is that why the emperor doesn't want any magicians to align together? Because he's afraid that they'll find the heart?"

"Before he does, yes," Yerkoyliç said softly.

"Why would the *Padisha-i-Ghazi* want the desert heart?" Trulliç asked, bewildered. The emperor already had so much power! He controlled the lands from the northern Kingdom of Lydae to the southern tip of Tanesh, beyond the Qeanev desert. The people thanked him at all meals, now. Bells rang in the morning for him. Workmen now added his symbol, a rounded scale with a sharp tip, to every building and well.

But he was always at war with the northern barbarians who were trying to expand beyond the southern kingdom of Lydae. Did he think that he could win if he had more power?

Or did he want even more than just the barbarian lands?

"Who could say what such a one as the emperor could do with such an item?" Yerkoyliç said. "But we've strayed into such serious topics! We should talk of lighter things. Tell me of your remarkable mother, your training, your desert."

Trulliç nodded and happily changed the topic, telling Yerkoyliç of the Horseshoe Tavern, his cousins, his life.

All the while wondering just where Yerkoyliç's loyalty lay.

Trulliç waited in Yerkoyliç's outer room, as requested. Pillows in every color Trulliç had ever seen or imagined littered the floor. A silver tea service waited in one corner. A basin with a pitcher stood next to the doorway, so a guest could wash their hands when they arrived. The faint scent of flowers suffused the room—a heady odor of blossoms that Trulliç didn't recognize.

Curtains hung against the far wall—probably hiding the door to the inner rooms. Trulliç peeked behind them but didn't touch the carved wood he saw there—if he wasn't being fanciful, he'd say the doors were well warded with magic, and that Yerkoyliç would instantly know if someone entered.

Riyune had already settled in, laying in front of the door like a statue. Trulliç found he couldn't sit and instead paced the room.

His stomach still rumbled, uneasy from the great feast he'd just had. He hadn't even heard of half the dishes they'd served—like hen's tongue soup, or red lamb stew—and he wasn't used to so much fat, either.

The conversation had been stilted at dinner. Trulliç had felt shy in front of so many rich merchants. They all wore better clothes than his, rich with embroidery and fine linen. He'd felt out of place in his old tunic, the one striped gold and green like his glass horseshoe, that he'd worn for his manhood journey.

He yawned, tired from the long day, the stress of being in a strange magician's city, of trying to determine Yerkoyliç's loyalties.

The guild masters had certainly been careful about praising the emperor for his bounty. However, there was an edge to their words that Trulliç still hadn't deciphered.

"Ah, there you are, my young friend!" Yerkoyliç said, breezing into the room. He seemed full of energy, as if the night was still young.

He wore the most beautiful red vest in the style of the northern merchants—shorter, ending just at his waist, and with buttons up the front—embroidered again in gold thread, with the same repeating motif of flowers, vines, birds, and butterflies.

"Come, come!" he said, gesturing for Trulliç to follow him. "I want to show you something."

Yerkoyliç led Trulliç through the curtains, the doors opening easily for Yerkoyliç without him having to touch them. Riyune walked beside Trulliç into the room.

The inner chamber was even more grand. Tapestries showing the great palace, the walls of Çandekili, even a map of the city itself, hung there. Jewels had been woven in with the threads. Soft rugs covered the floor, all decorated in patterns of flowers and vines.

Against the far wall stood yet another gauzy curtain hiding more doors. Probably leading to Yerkoyliç's bedroom, Trulliç guessed. Beside it stood a small altar with a black-and-white cloth covering it, embroidered with a familiar zig-zag symbol—the symbol of the god Serril.

A square, sunken area made up one corner of the room, a place where guests could lounge and easily talk. In the opposite corner stood a bookshelf, similar to the ones Trulliç had seen in Atça's house. Scrolls, small statues, precious gems, and other knick-knacks covered the shelves.

The shelves caught Trulliç's attention and held it. He found himself walking toward them without asking. Riyune walked beside him.

A cleverly made wooden box maybe ten inches on a side, while slightly deeper, stood on the middle shelf. The wood at the corners interlaced, showing that two sides were made from a dark, almost blackened wood, while the other two sides were made from a wood so pale it looked white.

No top covered the box. Trulliç gasped when he looked inside.

Sand filled the box.

Not just any sand. Sand carried from Qaenev. Sand that came from the heart of the desert.

Trulliç turned to look at Yerkoyliç. "What are you doing with this?" he asked.

Was the box magical? Or had Yerkoyliç done something to make the sand, itself, magical?

"Ah, I knew you would understand the specialness of my project!" Yerkoyliç said, beaming. "I knew you were the one!"

Trulliç turned back to the box, fascinated by the sand. Memories of the desert overwhelmed him. Heat flushed through his body. Hot winds stirred his hair. He smelled baked earth and sweet palms.

Sand grated against Trulliç's fingertips as he dipped his hand into the box. He couldn't help but scoop up a handful, feel it slip easily through his fingers.

Longing filled his heart. Oh, how he needed to go back!

Riyune leaned against Trulliç's leg, returning him to the room.

Trulliç swallowed against a suddenly dry throat, stepping back, away from the seductive box.

"What *are* you doing with that?" Trulliç asked, repeating his question firmly. A regular box of sand shouldn't have affected him that way.

Yerkoyliç had done something to it. Something that had enhanced the true essence of the desert, captured it in that single cubic foot of sand.

"Searching for the desert heart," Yerkoyliç said. He took a quick step closer to Trulliç. "We *must* find it before the emperor!"

"Why?" Trulliç asked, puzzled. Wouldn't it be a good thing for the emperor, who was so powerful, to have the desert heart? To bring more glory to the Tanesh empire?

Yerkoyliç came closer still, lowering his voice to a whisper. He smelled of the sour beer he'd drunk during dinner, of faded and spoiled flowers.

"The emperor doesn't just want to conquer the northern barbarians. He wants to rule, everywhere."

Trulliç strained to hear Yerkoyliç's next words.

"He wants to become a god."

Trulliç bit back a bitter laugh. The emperor was already almost a god, never seen but always in people's minds. Just because he now had formal prayers didn't mean that people hadn't been praying to him, or using his name to curse, for a long while.

"Don't you see what that would do the empire?" Yerkoyliç asked.

Trulliç shook his head. So what if the emperor wanted to become a god?

"You think the wars with the northern barbarians are bad," Yerkoyliç said. "All the good men we're losing. What do you think will happen when the emperor declares war on the gods?"

Trulliç shivered. What happened if the gods turned their backs on the people? If they started working actively against them? How many would die? Would the empire survive? Or would the gods blast it to nothing, desolating all the land?

"We must stop him," Yerkoyliç insisted.

Calmness overcame Trulliç.

He knew where Yerkoyliç's loyalties lay.

And Atça had told him what he must do if Yerkoyliç wasn't true.

"You're wrong," Trulliç said bravely, though he wasn't sure he believed it. "The emperor will take care of us. Protect us."

Yerkoyliç gave a bitter laugh. "You are so naïve," he said. "Why do you think the prayers have changed? That the emperor's symbol is being added everywhere?"

"But the gods won't destroy us for a single madman's quest," Trulliç reasoned.

Though he didn't really believe it himself.

"I'm not willing to take that chance," Yerkoyliç said. He raised his fat chin in defiance. "Are you?"

"Yes, I am," Trulliç replied.

The flowers and vines in the rugs started to stir.

"Too bad," Yerkoyliç said. "We could really have used a desert magician."

"Yes," Trulliç said. "Too bad."

Then he attacked.

Trulliç knew he should be more afraid.

Yerkoyliç controlled everything in the room. The rugs. The walls. The tapestries.

Yet, Trulliç's heart beat strongly with excitement.

Yerkoyliç had made a huge mistake.

He'd enchanted sand from the Qaenev desert. Brought it into his inner chamber.

And sand was Trulliç's element.

Vines sprang up around Trulliç's feet, winding around his calves and holding him tightly. Riyune whined, a sound Trulliç had never heard, and bit at the vines constraining him. The cloying scent of flowers filled the air, making Trulliç gag and cough.

Without thinking, Trulliç grabbed a handful of sand with a magical fist.

Atça had never taught him such a trick. He wondered if Atça even knew it.

"Let me go!" Trulliç commanded.

Yerkoyliç sneered. "You're just a dumb errand boy. You have no idea of the stakes you're playing with."

Trulliç couldn't help but agree.

However, he was determined not to remain ignorant.

With a punching motion, Trulliç threw the sand at Yerkoyliç. It hit him squarely in the center of his fat face.

"The sand will always win," Trulliç intoned as Yerkoyliç started choking, the sand making its way down his throat. "It is mightier than all of us. It overtakes all kingdoms, all who dare to build there. It will always overcome."

Yerkoyliç fell to his knees. The plants around Trulliç's legs began to wilt. He tore himself free.

"How—why—" Yerkoyliç choked out. His face turned as red as a poppy.

Trulliç couldn't brag about Atça at that point. Couldn't even proclaim that it was Trulliç's loyalty to the emperor that drove him.

'The desert is mine," he whispered fiercely.

If anyone was to find the desert heart, it would be him.

The walls of Yerkoyliç's room faded. The tapestries on the walls dropped their gems with loud thunks. The pillows unraveled, spilling their straw onto the floor.

Riyune ran to the door of the room, then stopped and turned back, looking at Trulliç.

Though he didn't hear Riyune speak, Trulliç still knew exactly what the dog said.

Come on. We've got to get out of here.

Still, Trulliç walked back to the shelves and grabbed the box of sand. The palace would fall in on itself.

Sand—any part of the desert—should never be trapped that way.

Then Trulliç ran, ignoring the body that was already starting to rot.

Trulliç ran behind Riyune, trusting that the dog would get him out of the palace, then out of the city.

Rugs turned to dust as he ran over them. Paint spilled from wall murals as the life that bound them faded. The floor felt solid, but he wondered how long the building would last. The stench of rotten flowers made him cover his nose and mouth with his headscarf, hoping it would help him breathe.

The few people Trulliç passed in the hallway seemed dazed. One woman leaned against the wall openly weeping, reds and blues from the mural staining her arms, her face, as if she were melting, too.

A buzzing noise followed Trulliç, sounding like an angry swarm of bees. No one was behind him when he looked back.

He nearly stumbled on the mound of dried grass that suddenly sprouted in the middle of the hallway.

Was the city disintegrating? Turning back into a grassy plain? Yerkoyliç had been born in the city, to the city, and had touched every part of it, welded it tightly to himself.

Guilt struck Trulliç. He told himself that Yerkoyliç was a traitor to the emperor. The fat magician had been trying to grab the power of the emperor for himself. He'd deserved what he'd gotten, to be choked on the sands of the desert, the heat killing all his plants and flowers.

It still made Trulliç feel bad to see Yerkoyliç's people suffering.

The floor tilted suddenly. Trulliç tumbled, but he didn't drop the box of sand he'd been carrying.

He was going to lose his travel pack, his clothes and sleeping roll.

No one would notice him, though. There would be many refugees on the road.

Trulliç concentrated on running. Riyune led him down a back staircase and out into the courtyard.

From outside, Trulliç saw the damage better. The corners stayed more upright, while the center floors sagged, as if the great palace was melting.

Fire blossomed in the ovens next to the outdoor kitchen, as if angrily celebrating its freedom. Hens ran around here and there, nearly tripping Trulliç twice.

Guards stood at the gate to the palace. One recognized him. "You— magician! You can't leave!" he shouted. "You must stay! Help Çandekili!"

Trulliç paused. He knew he couldn't stay. People would eventually accuse him of killing Yerkoyliç.

However, could his magic help?

He put out his hand, fingers widespread, trying to stabilize the wall. The magic wasn't in the bricks, he remembered, but in the mortar.

Flashes of blue sparked in the wall.

For a moment, the wall stood straighter, as if it might hold.

Then the mortar turned to sand. The stones trembled.

"Run away!" Trulliç cried as the wall started to come apart.

His magic was too different than Yerkoyliç's. He couldn't help the city, or the people there.

All he could do was run, make sure he got out before the city collapsed in on itself.

<hr>

Trulliç had been right—there were many refugees on the road. No one looked twice at him or Riyune. He just seemed another homeless traveler coming from Çandekili.

His only possession was the box. He would ask Atça how Yerkoyliç had enchanted it, how he'd managed to bring the soul of the desert to such a small patch of sand.

However, Trulliç doubted that Atça knew how.

A nearby farmer had set up some fires along the edge of his fields so the refugees might at least have someplace warm to spend the night.

Trulliç avoided the fires. Someone might recognize him, identify him.

Mark him as the killer he was. Though no judge would even fine Trulliç for killing a man who'd proven himself disloyal to the emperor, he didn't want to risk the rage that Yerkoyliç's people might have against his killer.

Instead, he made himself walk further into the night, away from the groups of people wailing and mourning. He sat with his small box between his legs, Riyune curled up next to his side.

The box produced the warmth of a fire, the heat of the desert escaping out of its open top.

Though maybe that was just its reaction to Trulliç and his shivers.

He found himself reaching into the box, scooping up a bit of sand, then letting it slide out of his fingers.

Despite his fear that someone would recognize him, accuse him of Yerkoyliç's death, Trulliç found a great calm descending over him.

The desert did that to him. Calmed him. Made him feel more powerful as well.

How bright would his mage light be if he had one hand in the desert box?

Stronger than ever, he suspected, though he didn't try it just then.

Yes, he was really going to have to ask Atça how Yerkoyliç had made such a box.

And why Atça had never bothered making one for Trulliç.

CHAPTER TEN

NADEEM

NADEEM LED GIBRIL AND DURZHEN down the hill toward Koruli. She walked with a stout stick now, using it rather like a cane, as if she needed aid walking. Their pace had slowed considerably as well.

Just under the surface of her companions, Nadeem felt their impatience. Hadn't they practiced being old? Nadeem was tempted to walk even slower or to take yet another break.

However, now wasn't the time to test them. They still had secrets they hadn't told her, missions within missions.

Koruli had been built in a valley with the main part of town at the foot of the surrounding hills, though many houses dotted the slopes. Instead of tight neighborhoods like Gaadiwala with shacks crouched around each of the available wells, the buildings were more spread out.

The twisting street coming out of the hill surprised Nadeem. Had they originally been built along sheep tracks? Loose stones covered the route they followed. Nadeem wouldn't have tumbled—she was more sure footed than that—but she still went slowly. This was an unknown trail. And they were all supposed to be old.

In the center of town, a single street held the marketplace. It wasn't very long or extensive. Just a few shops. The farms here made do without buying many goods.

Then again, they had the water so they could grow more crops and animals.

Only a single inn stood at the end of the market street. A burlap cloth painted with a brimming cup was the only indication of what they served.

"Hello?" Nadeem called as she stepped out of the dusty street and into the dim room. The air stank of spilled beer and strong *igrat*. Half-a-dozen small tables littered the floor, with dissolute pillows and cushions surrounding them. Rough stones lined the floor, so at least the guests didn't have to make a choice between bug-ridden pillows or dirt.

A large fireplace stood to the right, large enough for three men to stand in, upright. It was cold now, but would probably give adequate heat during the winter months.

An older man poked his head through the door in the back of the room. He stood tall and round with a great belly. White whiskers curled around his chin, though under his nose was clean shaven. The top of his head, too, appeared clean shaven, with more white curls hanging down around the edges of his scalp.

"Ah! Good sisters!" the man called, as if he was happy to see them.

The way his eyes narrowed and his mouth turned down told a different story.

"Welcome, welcome," he said, hastily wiping his hands on a rag. "How may I help my honored guests?"

"Do you rent rooms?" Nadeem querulously inquired, sounding much like old Aunt Hareet with her quavering tones.

"I do, I do," the man said. "I am Erkiç," he added, bowing his head. "I would be happy to give you shelter for the evening."

And to take us for every coin you can, Nadeem realized.

No matter. They were here on the emperor's business in this tiny town, come to kill one of their elders.

Aunt Izmet would say there was no greater glory.

Nadeem still had her doubts.

The beds in the room were about what Nadeem had expected: straw mattresses that needed to be restuffed laying on rusting iron bedframes; stained pillows that still bore the drool marks of the former guests; a window slit that maybe a lizard could crawl through but no breeze.

At least the room was large enough that the beds didn't take up the entire space. Plus, two of the sisters could stand abreast in the aisle between the beds on the longer walls.

"Now what?" Galbril asked as she sat heavily on the bed to the right of the door. Of the three, it probably was the most defensible.

It gave a warning creak.

Galbril winced but didn't get up. Her old age mask slipped away from her, melting like dust in the rain.

Durzhen dropped her bag onto the bed against the far wall. "We wait until dark. Then we go find this Malik. And kill him." Her mask faded less quickly.

Nadeem shook her head. "You two stay here. I'm going out to scout the town first. See if I can find Malik before this evening."

"I would be the better scout," Durzhen pointed out.

"How long would it take for you to age again, dearie?" Nadeem asked, using Aunt Haleet's tones.

Durzhen pressed her lips together. "Too long," she said, gesturing toward the window. "You took too long getting here. It will be night soon."

"We needed to be believed," Nadeem said, "by all who saw us."

"Then, old mother, I wish you luck in your hunt," Durzhen said formally.

"Thank you," Nadeem said. "I'll be back before it's full night."

Quickly, she escaped the room.

What were the other two up to? What was this tension she felt between them? What were they really supposed to do?

Nadeem put all her doubts behind her. She kept her old lady mask on as she went through the main room of the tavern and out the door, back onto the dusty street.

She bowed her head to those she passed, a casual greeting, making sure she was seen as an old woman, a star sister, traveling through their town. She walked to the main well, then into one of the side streets.

When she was certain no one watched her, Nadeem *blurred* her hands, her appearance, so that no one would easily follow her.

Then she walked back into the market, needing to hear and learn all she could about this Malik.

Before she killed him.

Nadeem found an old mother sitting out on her front stoop, enjoying the last of the sun before it set between the hills. It was the last row of buildings before the start of the hills. The rock walls of the house looked sturdy and well-maintained, though the wood framing the door and windows was well-weathered. The people who lived there weren't poor, but they weren't rich, either. Chickens scratched in the yard behind a low rock fence. Not only the usual herbs and stew vegetables grew in the garden, but beautiful blue delphiniums and white daisies as well.

The old woman wore a *chafiyek* that had been carefully embroidered with vines and butterflies, once a brilliant green and red but now faded. Her brown tunic and soft blue shirt showed the same care and age, carefully mended holes done in different colored thread.

The old woman sat on a wooden bench with a large basket of fiber at her feet and two long-tined combs in her hands. She carded the wool, humming softly, arranging the fibers to be all in one direction so they could be spun.

Nadeem hadn't been able to hear any gossip about Malik at the market. She couldn't really start any conversation if no one could see her. And she had to be careful about asking about him.

Still, fiber work had always been something she enjoyed.

Before Nadeem dropped her *blur*, the old woman said, "Greetings, stranger."

Had Nadeem made some kind of unconscious noise? How had the old woman known she was there? She hadn't been able to see her. She still sat with her eyes closed, basking in the sunlight.

"Hello," Nadeem said, keeping her voice gruff and old. "What fibers are you working?"

"Ah," the old woman said, nodding. She picked up an already carded hunk from beside her on the bench. "*Nadjil,*" she said proudly.

Nadeem fingered the soft fibers. She'd rarely gotten to work with *nadjil.* It was too expensive, and those sheep couldn't survive the desert. "It's beautiful," she said honestly. "You could spin fine thread from this."

The old woman cracked a wide grin that showed gaps in her teeth. She finally opened her eyes. They were completely covered with white film.

No wonder the old woman had known Nadeem was there! She was blind and had sensed Nadeem in other ways.

"Ah, it will," she said. "Come, sit with an old woman for a while. I am Tonyal."

"Haneet," Nadeem said. She sat down with a soft sigh, still acting the part as if she was an old woman, too.

They sat for a few long moments in companionable silence, enjoying the sunshine. Scrub, green with spring, covered the hills in front of them. The bushes would turn brown as the summer gained its head. A path led from the house, up between the hills: narrow, just wide enough for a single person, probably leading to richer houses further up the valley.

Finally, Tonyal put down her combs and fished around in the pocket of her apron. She pulled out a small drop spindle, handed it to Nadeem with a chunk of fiber. "Here," she said. "I can tell you want to."

Nadeem laughed softly. She always found spinning thread so soothing.

The long shaft was made from a slender piece of wood, smoothed out through use and age. It wasn't any thicker around than her pinky finger and was about the length of her forearm. Three notches had been carved at the top to help guide the thread. The round whorl at the bottom could comfortably fit in Nadeem's palm. It was made out of baked clay, painted white and blue with a similar pattern of vines and butterflies as Toyal's headscarf.

Nadeem hadn't carried a drop spindle with her. Maybe the next trip away from the *kabil* she would.

"Thank you," Nadeem said, honored. She recognized this as Toyal's personal drop spindle, the one she'd probably carried with her since she'd been a young girl.

Then Toyal handed Nadeem a hunk of soft fiber. Not too much—just a touch, to do a small bit of spinning.

Nadeem knew that as an honored guest she could ask for more, but she wouldn't take the old woman's livelihood away. This fiber would spin into fine thread and could be sold for a lot at the marketplace.

Nadeem spun a few inches of thread from the fiber with her fingers, enough to wrap around the spindle below the whorl. She hefted the weight of the spindle—heavier than she was used to. It would spin too fast if she wasn't careful.

Carefully, Nadeem smoothed out some more of the fiber, twisting it back and forth between her fingers, before she finally let go of the spindle.

It dropped smoothly, spinning out thread from the fibers as she guided it with her fingers.

"Just lovely," Nadeem murmured after a moment. The fibers spun very nice thread. It would be strong and not break easily.

Toyal sighed. "You *are* just a traveler, then," she said sadly.

"I am," Nadeem said, surprised. "Who did you think I was?"

Toyal gave a cackling laugh. "Don't take this wrong, but you smell like the desert and death," she said. "I know that I'll be dancing in the goddess' court soon. I'd been hoping I might rate a visit from her first."

Nadeem controlled her fear. She didn't stiffen or react. "Really?" she said casually.

How could the old woman have known?

"Or maybe everything smells like death today," Toyal said sadly. "I've been away from my home for so very long."

"You weren't born here, in Koruli?" Nadeem asked, surprised. Most people rarely traveled; they were born, lived, and died all in the same place. Merchants traveled and some craftsmen and women, but that was it.

"I was born in Çandekili, west of here," Toyal told her. "Left as a young, foolish girl, following my heart. Never went back after I was married. But Narlis has been gone now going on three long years. It's time I followed him into the goddess' court. I'm surprised that I lasted this long."

"I see," Nadeem said. She wondered what it would be like to have a husband, to stay in one place, to be married and happy with a family.

She had her sisters, her *kabil*, her missions and training.

She wouldn't trade that for anything.

She dropped the spindle again, spinning fiber into fine thread.

"So tell me of your town," Nadeem said after another long moment. "What has kept you here?"

Toyal talked of her three grandchildren and four sons, how hard they worked, the large number of flocks of sheep that they kept. She mentioned many names that Nadeem didn't bother keeping track of, instead just losing herself in the flow of the story.

Nadeem perked up, though, when Toyal mentioned Malik. Something about the harvest not coming in?

"What happened?" Nadeem asked, interrupting the old woman's ramblings.

"Three? No, four years ago. When the rains didn't come. Malik helped out the famers who couldn't make the emperor's tithe," Toyal said. "Paid it himself, he did."

"Why would he do that?" Nadeem asked sourly, as if she'd heard bad things about the man.

"Malik's been as constant as the hills, helping those in need," Toyal said defensively. "Paying our debts. Never asking for more than a man can give." She lowered her voice. "Don't know as to how we would have survived without him. Koruli might have been abandoned, the town scattering, if people couldn't pay their debts."

"But the land's good here," Nadeem said. "You've got water and wells. Good scrap for sheep."

Water had always been such a concern in the desert. Any year that got less rain in the rainy season was a bad year. She remembered four years ago. It had been the summer before she'd gone into training. The star sisters planned better than most, so there hadn't been famine. But people had been hungry.

"Ah, you're from south of here, aren't you?" Toyal said cannily. "Concerned about water. All the people from the south are." She heaved a sigh. "It's true, though, what you say. We got good wells. But if we can't pay the emperor his due, we'd be slaves. People here are stubborn. They'd leave the town and go elsewhere rather than not be free."

Nadeem controlled her shiver. Was that why she was to kill Malik? To destroy the town?

There must be a good reason for it. The emperor had commanded it.

Or maybe the old woman was wrong. The people here would stay.

"The townsfolk wouldn't go to other towns, would they?" Nadeem asked, putting surprise into her voice. Most people were too settled.

"Those with a craft would," Toyal insisted. "Though the young men— always so stupid—would probably just go off to war. Thinking they could gain riches that way."

Nadeem nodded. In the *kabil*, she hadn't heard the aunts talk much about the wars. Plus, the star sisters rarely kept their sons, so didn't have to worry about sending them to be part of the emperor's troops.

"Fighting for the emperor is an honor," Nadeem said firmly. That was what she was doing. Aunt Izmet would expect such a response from her.

"Aye, it is," Toyal said. "But if everyone is off fighting, who will tend the sheep? Grow the grain? Tan the leather? Have more babes?"

Nadeem grunted, neither agreeing or disagreeing.

It was an honor to serve the emperor. To do his bidding.

Even if Aunt Parayat's voice at the back of her head was questioning even that.

Nadeem left Gabril and Durzhen at the inn, loudly complaining to the innkeeper about needing more wood for the fire, more hot water for their tea, more bread with their meal. A few locals had joined them for dinner, treating them with varying degrees of respect: On the one hand, they were old and strangers, therefore due respect. On the other hand, they were star sisters, who were never trusted because of their ability to cast illusions and trick people.

Nadeem felt confident that Gabril and Durzhen would be able to maintain the illusion that there were three of them, giving her an alibi. Not that she would need one: The assignment had been to make Malik's death look natural.

Before Nadeem left the inn she stripped off her tunic, blouse, and skirt. Underneath, she wore tight black pants that would have scandalized anyone who saw her. Women weren't supposed to wear tight clothing. However, the pants allowed her greater movement. Her shirt was sleeveless, also black, showing off her wiry muscles and dark skin. In her belt around her waist she had the traditional three knives, plus others tied to her calves. She had her blowgun attached to her left hip. The headscarf she wore was also black, and held sharp poisoned needles.

The town was dark. Very few lights shone through the windows. The community worked during sunlight hours and slept at night. It wasn't as if there were traveling storytellers who had set up for the evening in the marketplace, or even a band of players putting on shows.

And Koruli was so small that probably only happened at the height of summer, and not even every year.

For now, Nadeem waited just outside the door of the inn as her eyes adjusted. She still wouldn't be able to see much, she knew. The stars didn't shine very brightly that night, and there was only a half-moon.

Still, she felt confident that she could make it to Malik's house. The innkeeper had volunteered that information when Nadeem had exclaimed that she'd heard about some of his good deeds that afternoon, speculating that he must live in a palace in the hills.

The innkeeper had been quick to explain that Malik kept a modest house in town, and lived within his means. Particularly since his wife had died that winter.

At Nadeem's disbelief, the innkeeper had insisted on drawing her a map, using the charcoal end of one of the sticks from the fireplace, sketching on one of the smooth stones on the floor, so that in the morning Nadeem could go and see for herself.

The house was only two streets away, down to the cross street leading west off the market street, past the large garden, then up two doors on the right. From what little Nadeem could see, the houses weren't that fine. Sure, they were mostly two stories, but they weren't grand or overly large.

Chickens clucked at her from the large garden. She understood that three of the nearby families all owned the land together—all sons and daughters from a wealthy merchant who'd insisted that the land not be divided. They'd fought for a while, then finally agreed to raise chickens and grow a few vegetables there. As they all had their own houses nearby, it was a good arrangement, much more civilized than running harsh walls and dividing up the land so small that it couldn't serve any purpose.

Malik had supposedly brokered that deal as well.

Either Malik had bribed all the good people of the town into thinking he was a hero sent from the gods, or he really did have a generous heart.

Nadeem assumed it was actually a bit of each. He also provided most of the *igrat* the town consumed at its midsummer feast.

The house before Nadeem stood dark and foreboding. She made sure that she blended well into the shadows as she stepped forward.

The front window, of course, was latched from the inside. She didn't try the door, assuming that it was locked.

To the casual observer, the stones that made up the front of the house would have appeared smooth, with few cracks.

Nadeem walked close to the wall, then looked directly up.

Just out of her reach above her, the rocks stuck out a ways.

With a great leap, Nadeem grabbed hold of the ledge, her toes finding holds along the way.

The wall had been well constructed, and there weren't as many holds as she'd expected.

Still, it didn't take her long to climb up the wall, reaching a window well above the ground.

No latch held the window shut. The wooden cover swung open easily. She lifted it up above her head and held it there.

Nadeem stuck her head in the room and waited, listening, breathing in the quiet of the house.

Good pork had been cooked that night, a rich man's feast with sweet carrots and fennel. The house itself was still. She didn't hear any steps or breathing.

It was too dark to see much. There appeared to be hunks of furniture in the room, maybe a desk under the window. An office, perhaps, where Malik conducted his trade.

Nadeem pulled herself up and through the window. She didn't want to put a foot on the desk—it might not be strong enough to take her weight, even as slight as she was—so she jumped into what she believed was an open space, landing on her hands and summersaulting gracefully.

Then she stopped again, listening. Had anyone heard her? Suspected that their castle had just been violated?

But she didn't hear anything besides the muffled sounds of the night.

Nadeem walked quickly across the room for the door in the corner. She opened it an inch and peeked out.

The hallway was well lit, which surprised her. Was Malik still up? Entertaining guests, perhaps?

Nadeem waited, but she still didn't hear anything. Didn't smell anything beyond rich leather polish and perfumed pillows.

Nadeem stuck her head out a bit further.

The office she'd climbed into had been at the end of the hall, built out of the corner. To her right stood an open doorway, as well as a closed one further down. To her left the staircase opened up.

Malik would be up here, in his bed. Hopefully alone. Which room, though?

Nadeem *blurred* herself. She couldn't turn herself invisible, unfortunately. And there weren't many shadows to blend into in this brightly lit hallway. She still made it as difficult as she could for the eye to track her.

The floor was made of dark wood, scarred and old. Nadeem walked silently along it. She only had leather strips wrapped around the balls of her feet to give her traction.

Just before the open doorway, Nadeem paused again.

She didn't hear anything inside the room.

She took another step forward.

Peeked inside.

Just inside the door an older man sat on the floor, leaning against pillows.

"I don't see you," the man said carefully. "But I know you're there. I've been expecting you."

Nadeem stiffened, surprised. How did he know she was there?

The man nodded to himself. He pushed himself up slowly, using a solid cane, showing his age. He had long white hair that he wore in the northern style, cut around his shoulders and curled under. His large bulbous nose proclaimed him from the north as well, though his thin, long face and darker skin spoke of southern origin as well. Perhaps his mother had been from this south, while his father from here.

No one had mentioned that during their praises of the man.

"Please, won't you come join me?" he asked, turning his back and walking further into the room.

Nadeem didn't bother asking if he was Malik. She assumed he was. A servant or someone playing the part of the rich merchant wouldn't have this confidence.

She cut the thread of illusion surrounding herself. It didn't really matter if he knew she was there, if he saw her.

He'd be dead before too long.

And she had too many questions.

"Why did you expect me?" Nadeem asked as she stepped into the room, stepping around the pillows.

Malik poured himself a large mug of water, then did the same for Nadeem. "I've dreamed of three stars streaming across the sky," he said, "coming from the far east. After they passed over my house, it burst into flames."

"What do you think the dream means?" Nadeem asked, freezing.

"Three star sisters came into town this afternoon," Malik explained. "We haven't seen your kind in a decade or more. And you arrived from the east. So I assumed that you are the three stars I saw crossing the sky. As for my house burning—I figured that meant that you were here to kill me."

He peered at her closely, at her black sleeveless shirt that allowed her free movement, the tight black pants that others would consider indecent. The knives tucked into her belt, her blowgun and darts attached to her hip.

"A stranger coming as you did, crawling up the wall of my house and in through a window, isn't here to share dinner and break bread," he added.

Nadeem nodded. She should have known that such a great death, ordered by the emperor, would trigger a warning dream.

Next time, she would be more prepared.

Or at least that was what she promised herself.

That there would be a next time.

That she couldn't fail at this.

———

Nadeem took the glass of water Malik had poured for her, then toasted the man when he raised his cup. However, she'd learned over the past three years how to fake drinking, so didn't bother to actually take a sip.

The room had no bed in it. It appeared to be another study. A small bookshelf sat against the far wall. Had this at one point been the room for one or more of his children? A painted wooden doll still sat on the shelf between the scrolls and small boxes sitting there.

Under the window stood a low writing desk, for kneeling behind. Rich pillows leaned against the other walls. This was a more intimate meeting room, where deals could be struck informally. A different kind of office than the one Nadeem had come through.

Bright clay lamps, hung from the ceiling, lit the room well. A single glass lamp stood on the writing desk. Expensive but practical.

Malik lowered himself back down to the ground, leaning heavily on his cane. It was made from a solid piece of black wood, with a silver head in the shape of a snake.

Strange symbol for a man of such power. None of the gods were represented by a snake.

Nadeem glanced around the room again before she sank down gracefully, showing off her youth and agility. No altar was tucked away in any of the corners.

Stranger and stranger.

"I was born here, in Koruli," Malik started. "My mother came from the north."

Nadeem nodded. She'd assumed that was the case.

"Things were different, then," he said.

Nadeem didn't roll her eyes, but she wanted to. He was starting to sound like Aunt Haneet and the others, who constantly complained that children didn't understand, that things had been so much better when they'd been young.

"The emperor had less power, then," Malik continued.

That made Nadeem sit up a bit straighter.

Maybe Malik really was a traitor. Maybe she could kill him without guilt.

"The people don't resent the prayers that have been added," Malik said softly. "Or that his symbol is now added to all buildings."

Nadeem nodded. Of course the people shouldn't resent such things. The emperor had been good to them. The years, fruitful.

"Only some of us ask about the meaning of such symbols," Malik said. He picked up his cane and held it toward her.

The snake head was finely made, of course. The skin was covered in tight scales, carved out of silver.

Each scale looked like the emperor's symbol.

"Where did you get this?" Nadeem asked. She reached out and touched the cold silver, running a finger along the bumps.

There wasn't anything magical about the head of the cane.

It still made her shiver. There was something…off about it. Something unnatural. She'd never seen such a thing before. Were any of the *kabil* aware of this sort of thing? Something that was, but was not, magical?

"From the emperor, himself," Malik said. "To thank me for helping the town."

"I see," Nadeem said. "And now, as your repayment for such kindness, you incite the people of Koruli against him?" she asked archly.

"No, no," Malik said, shaking his head. He gave her a rueful grin. "I exhort them to follow his edicts. To pray to their gods. To do their duty. And this watches me, makes sure I do."

Nadeem shook her head. "It isn't magical," she told him. "I don't sense any magic in it at all."

Malik blinked, obviously surprised. "Really?" he said.

He picked the cane back up and examined it briefly.

Then he shoved it at her.

Nadeem blocked the cane automatically.

Malik smirked at her. "You wouldn't defend yourself so violently if there was nothing about this cane that unsettled you."

Nadeem shrugged. "I might have. You moved quickly. I'm trained to defend myself."

"As all the star sisters are," Malik said, nodding. He paused, then added, "I know you've probably taken a blood oath to take my life."

"I have," Nadeem told him gravely. "You will not leave this room alive," she added.

She didn't see any reason why she shouldn't be honest with him. "If there is something you need to tell me, some confession you must make, I would make it now," she said. She didn't know where this conversation was going. She didn't like the edges of it, though.

Malik nodded. "I've made my peace with Enkat and Xannil," he said.

That surprised Nadeem. That he followed the goddess of rain and the god of the sun, as opposed to Innis, the god of fertility, whom most merchants followed.

"Did you know that Xannil is portrayed as a happy god in the north?" Malik said casually.

Nadeem shook her head. She hadn't heard of that before. Xannil was an angry god, sullen, often jealous of his wife Enkat, hiding her so no rain came.

"You should travel to the north sometime," Malik told her. "Listen to the people there, to the priests and their gods. See how the emperor is viewed." He held up his cane again. "The snake god that's slithering his way into their hearts."

Was Malik implying that the *Padisha-i-Ghazi* was becoming a snake?

Then she remembered his symbol. It looked like the scale of a snake. And the great cloak that the emperor wore, composed of scales made from the afterbirths of all the magicians and illusionist.

What kind of power did that cloak give him?

He'd already lived a long, long time. Longer than any man. Almost two hundred years, if the scholars were to be believed.

Was he immortal?

Was he like a god? Growing more godlike every year?

Nadeem opened her mouth to ask another question when she noticed Malik had grown pale, suddenly.

His mouth gaped, hanging open like a dead fish's.

Then he slowly tumbled to his side.

Nadeem leaped to her feet, turning toward the door.

Gabril and Durzhen entered silently.

"What have you done?" Nadeem asked angrily.

They looked at each other, then back at her.

"We've completed the assignment, as we swore to do," Durzhen said, putting away her blowgun.

"The question is, what were you doing?" Gabril asked.

Nadeem looked over at the body, then back again.

The poison had already killed Malik. It would putrefy his body next.

"Learn all you can about your enemy," Nadeem instructed them. "Wasn't that one of the first things we were taught?"

"No," Durzhen said, shaking her head. "Do your duty. That always came first."

Nadeem swallowed back any more words she might have said.

Silently, she cursed Aunt Parayat's voice, that questioning tone she heard at the back of her head.

Aunt Izmet had taught obedience first.

Unquestioning obedience.

Nadeem had never learned not to question.

Now, she had to learn how to keep asking questions, but at the same time, stay alive.

———

"You know, his death was supposed to look natural," Nadeem told the other two sourly. "There's no way to hide that he's been poisoned."

At least Durzhen looked guilty for a moment.

Gabril spoke up. "You were supposed to smother him in his sleep. Not talk him to death," she said.

Nadeem had always assumed that her team was as curious as she was about everything.

Now, she realized how little they questioned her direction.

They'd never thought for themselves, though she'd always tried to get them to. Instead, they just followed her.

Blindly.

She cursed silently. She'd always considered herself a good leader.

She knew better than to blame Malik for stripping that away from her as well.

"He was expecting me," Nadeem said quietly after a few moments. "I couldn't have surprised him. Couldn't have smothered him in his sleep." She paused, then added, "What would you have done?"

"Strangled him the moment I walked into the room," Durzhen said firmly.

"But he'd had a dream about us coming," Nadeem said.

"So?" Durzhen said hotly.

Nadeem sighed. "A command from the emperor to kill a man is an important event," she explained gently. "Big enough that someone may dream of it. If I hadn't stopped and asked and talked with Malik about that, I wouldn't have that useful bit of information for the next assignment."

"Oh," Durzhen said. She pushed her lips together as if she wanted to dispute what Nadeem said.

Nadeem held her peace and didn't say anything more. She knew she was right.

"All right," Duzhen said stubbornly. "I guess that's useful. For the next time."

"But what are we going to do with the body now?" Gabril asked.

Nadeem nodded. She was the one responsible for their training.

Or their lack of it.

"We burn the place down," she said.

Malik had said that the stars had left his house ablaze.

<hr>

Everyone had gathered at the inn that morning, before Nadeem and the others had made their way back down to the main room.

Seemed there had been a terrible fire at Malik's house.

Luckily, the walls had been thick enough to contain the fire, and it hadn't spread beyond the house.

It appeared he'd been drinking his own *igrat*, which people knew he did from time to time.

Since his wife had died, he had been drinking a bit more.

But this time, he'd drunk too much. Had been careless with one of his fancy oil lights.

Or at least that was the story people were telling each other.

"It's a shame," Nadeem said truthfully.

Malik had been a good man.

But the emperor's will had to be done.

And Nadeem, still wearing the appearance of an old woman, had a better, more stout stick to walk with as well. A cane with a silver snake head.

CHAPTER ELEVEN

TRULLIÇ

TRULLIÇ CARRIED THE BOX ALL the way back to Gaadiwala. Though the box was small, just a little bigger than his outstretched palms, the sand in it made it heavy. He found early on that he didn't have to take the full weight of the box, that he could magically float it and just appear to be carrying it. He tried once to have it floating just behind him. While he could do that, he didn't want other people to see it, for them to realize he was a magician. He didn't want to run into refugees from Çandekili and have them remember him, or accuse him of killing Yerkoyliç.

Gaadiwala looked dim in the late afternoon light. Trulliç missed the colors of Çandekili, the colors of the hillsides with rain. It all seemed gray to him.

He decided that while his people would not be as gaudily dressed as those in Çandekili, they would still wear colors. The houses would be more colored, too. Not just rocks and bare dirt.

He could almost see it in his mind's eye, this town on the edge of the desert, with golden-sand colored buildings and flags flying everywhere, palm trees and tall *meslit* thorns growing along twisting streets.

Was that his home? Or was he just being fanciful?

No. He'd made the decision to not call anyone else fanciful.

He wasn't being fanciful either.

Those square towers. Those gold and green striped flags. Those sweet smelling dates.

Those were real.

He would make it so.

Was it too late to go directly to Atça's house?

Trulliç decided he didn't care.

Atça needed to explain too many things.

Riyune followed eagerly behind. Trulliç could tell the dog seemed… happy, perhaps. Not smugly satisfied, but content.

He didn't feel any of the guilt Trulliç felt about killing Yerkoyliç.

Trulliç wasn't certain the dog could feel guilt about anything.

He assumed that anyone who saw him in town and recognized him would tell his mother that he'd come back.

He would go to the tavern next.

Atça's house also seemed gray, cast in shadows. It still looked grander than all the houses around it, three stories of finely milled stones, set beautifully together.

Trulliç had once thought it was the finest building he'd ever seen.

Now, he wondered if even poorest slums of Çandekili had been better.

He knocked on Atça's door and waited.

The old magician came quickly. He seemed surprised to see Trulliç. "My boy! Welcome!" he said. He peered at Trulliç, at the box he carried, then glanced quickly at Riyune and away again. He wore a tunic striped black and blue, the colors of Barzhat. It hung loosely on him, unbelted, going down to the start of his thighs, with a blue pair of baggy pants and an off-white shirt.

"Do you know what this is?" Trulliç demanded, hefting the box toward Atça.

Atça gave him a cold smile. "Of course. That is a land box."

"Why didn't you make one for me?" Trulliç asked. He couldn't help the pleading note in his voice.

"My dear boy, the emperor outlawed those decades ago," Atça said smugly. "I take it you took this one from Yerkoyliç?"

Trulliç nodded mutely.

"I suppose that he might have claimed that he wasn't breaking the law, since he made a land box for land that wasn't his," Atça said, speculating. "However, if any of the emperor's guards find *you* with it, they're likely to kill you outright."

"Oh," was all that Trulliç could say.

The box *was* powerful. It did make his magic more powerful. He didn't feel as strong as he usually did when he stepped across the border into the desert. It still increased his power dramatically.

"Why does the emperor want magicians to be weak?" he asked. But he knew the answer already.

The emperor didn't want any of the magicians to challenge him.

A group of magicians, all with land boxes…they might be strong enough.

Or they might not be.

Not if the emperor became a god.

"Has anyone seen you with the box?" Atça asked archly.

Trulliç shrugged. "Just the people here," he said. "But none of them would know what it is. What it means." Plus, they were his people, the people of Gaadiwala. They wouldn't report him to the emperor's guards when they came through.

Would they?

"Maybe. Maybe not," Atça said with a shrug. "You can't keep it here, in Gaadiwala."

Trulliç sighed and nodded. What was he going to do with the box? He didn't want to give it up. Couldn't just leave it someplace.

Was he going to have to take it back to the true desert? To release the sands there?

Atça seemed to consider for a moment, before saying, "You can come in. But you must cover the box. And you should never use it here, in Gaadiwala."

Trulliç turned to Riyune to see his reaction to Atça's request.

The dog nodded once, as if agreeing.

"All right," Trulliç agreed.

He stepped across the threshold of Atça's house.

He felt Atça's magic immediately. He'd sensed threads of it after he'd crossed the border into Gaadiwala, the stirring of Atça's power. But the house was the center of it.

While Yerkoyliç was all flowers and bees, Atça was stone and dirt. Hearty in ways Yerkoyliç wasn't.

They were both strong.

But Trulliç had killed Yerkoyliç, had proven himself stronger.

Was it possible that Trulliç was also stronger than Atça?

That remained to be seen.

Trulliç relinquished the box to put on house slippers. His power immediately faded. He took his tunic off and covered the top of the box with it before he picked it back up, wrapping the cloth around it fully.

He couldn't help his sigh of relief, how happy he was with desert power flowing back over him.

Atça made a sour face at him. It was obvious that he'd been hoping that Trulliç would ask for something to cover the box with, something that Atça could have then used to control the box somehow.

Trulliç shivered when he considered that Atça might have tried to poison the sands.

No. Atça could never touch the box or the sands inside.

T rulliç followed Atça into the study. Atça had obviously been working there. Scrolls lay out on the writing desk. A half-full cup of tea sat beside it. The lights all flared brightly as Atça stepped into the room, making it seem as bright as day.

Atça poured Trulliç a cup from his own tea service, then indicated that Trulliç should join him, leaning against the best guest pillows done in red and gold.

Trulliç remembered Yerkoyliç's patterns. How everyone who could afford to had vines, flowers, and butterflies embroidered on their clothing. What were Atça's patterns or motif? Did he have any?

Trulliç sipped his tea and looked around the room. Riyune had taken up his usual place by the door, sitting as still as a statue.

There. Patterns of stripes.

Now that Trulliç thought about it, he realized that very few people he'd seen on the road wore stripes. It wasn't uncommon. However, it wasn't as common elsewhere as it was in Gaadiwala. Almost everyone in the town wore some sort of stripes, generally a striped tunic, though some of the richer merchants also had striped shirts. Many of the women wore striped headscarves.

Pleased, Trulliç looked back at Atça, who stared at the covered land box.

"What was Yerkoyliç doing with a desert land box?" he asked.

Trulliç didn't see any reason not to tell Atça. "He was looking for the desert heart."

"Really?"

Trulliç didn't like the satisfied, smug smile that Atça gave him.

"What did he tell you about it?" his mentor asked. He tried to sound casual, but he failed miserably. He was very curious about what Trulliç knew.

"That it was Forit's heart, still alive in the desert," Trulliç told him honestly. "That the emperor is also searching for it, to become a god. That the other magicians—and he was part of a group—wanted to find it first."

"So they could use it themselves, I imagine," Atça said sourly. He gave a dramatic sigh. "Those fools! They could have been working *for* the emperor, instead of against him."

"What do you mean?" Trulliç asked, surprised.

"Don't you see? If the emperor is searching for the heart, that means it must exist," Atça said.

He almost seemed excited. It was very strange.

"We should find it first. So we can present it to him, as a gift," Atça continued.

Trulliç stiffened. He bit his lips together so he didn't automatically disagree.

It sounded like a bad idea, either way. Either the emperor would use it to become a god and throw all of the empire into war with the rest of the gods, or the heart would still be corrupted with darkness. Releasing such a plague on the world would also be a bad idea.

"Just think of the reward the emperor would give for such a prize!" Atça continued.

"Maybe," Trulliç said. If such a thing existed, it would need a strong magician to hold it. Right?

Or maybe they just needed to find it. Then the emperor could come and claim it.

"As a desert magician, I would think you should consider it your duty to find the desert heart for the emperor," Atça said in his lecture tones.

Trulliç shook his head. He didn't agree.

"Does it even exist?" Trulliç asked. "Haven't magicians been searching for it for years? And wouldn't the emperor have found it already?" He didn't think this was a good idea at all.

Atça pursed his lips and thought for a moment. "You're right, it is a very old legend, that the heart still exists." He paused, then added, "But it is also part of the story that the old kings knew of the existence of the heart and hid it for millennia."

"That doesn't mean it exists," Trulliç said. "That's just another excuse for why people never found it." For all of Atça's flaws, he always had tried to get Trulliç to think and not just accept whatever was presented to him.

Atça nodded. "That's a possibility. Or it could be that their magic is finally draining out of the world and the heart can finally be found."

"And you want me to go looking for it," Trulliç said dryly.

Atça gave him a wintery smile. "Oh, I doubt that you'll be able to find it. It has been lost all these many ages. And you can't even find your own home!" He chuckled.

Trulliç took a deep breath. That hurt. Despite how true it was.

"I do need to go back into the desert," Trulliç said slowly. "I need to release the sands in the land box."

Atça looked at him curiously. "Can't you just break the box?"

Trulliç studied the small box sitting beside him for a moment. Despite being covered, he still felt the sands there, calling to him.

The box itself wasn't magical. The sands had been enchanted, though.

"No," he said. "That would just spill the sands out, have them uncontained. They wouldn't lose their magic. Not for a while."

He'd been surprised that the sands had maintained their magical abilities after Yerkoyliç had died, since his city had fallen with his death. Trulliç had assumed that all of the magician's works would die with him.

"You might seek a guide, you know," Atça said. "To help lead you through the desert. Maybe one of the star sisters who frequent that tavern of your family's."

Trulliç blinked. "That's a good idea," he said seriously. "Thank you." Then he grimaced. "I have no way to pay such a guide, though."

"When you find one, send them to me," Atça said. "I will pay their fee. That way, I can honestly tell the emperor's guards that I helped destroy the land box."

"Thank you," Trulliç said.

It wasn't until much later that evening that he wondered what else Atça might tell the emperor's guards.

Particularly if Trulliç didn't do exactly as Atça requested and go looking for the desert heart.

Trulliç wasn't surprised to find his mother waiting for him in the small shack they shared. He knew enough people in Gaadiwala had seen him arrive that afternoon and that they'd tell her.

"Well?" she asked as he came through the door.

Trulliç nodded. "Hello, Mother," he said. He walked over to his sleeping roll at the back of the one-room shack and put down the box. Riyune came in after him and settled down next to the box.

"Where's your pack?" Mother asked.

"It was destroyed when Çandekili collapsed," Trulliç said honestly. "I had to get out of the palace alive. Leave it behind."

Mother stared hard at him. "Was it really that close?" she asked, disbelieving.

"The floors were starting to disintegrate under my feet," Trulliç told her. "The murals on the walls were melting."

Would Gaadiwala survive Atça's death? Probably. Atça wasn't as involved with all the parts of the town, hadn't formed it in his image, not like Yerkoyliç had fashioned Çandekili.

Mother nodded, as if she agreed with where Trulliç's thoughts had gone. "And what's this?" she asked.

Trulliç uncovered the box, taking his tunic and tossing it to the side. Then he lifted the box with his magic and flew it over to where his mother stood.

Mother stood very still. She didn't take a step back, as Trulliç had expected her to. She didn't seem startled, either. She looked at him, then looked inside the box.

"Sand?" she asked.

Before he could stop her, Mother reached her hand into the box and drew out a handful of sand. It slid evenly through her fingers back into the box.

Trulliç knew his mother didn't have any magic. The sand didn't react to her as it did to him.

It still recognized her.

Trulliç wouldn't be surprised if the sand, the desert, didn't claim his mother as one of hers, a child of the sand. He knew that Myrizhah had made trips to the desert, that she'd walked the desert every year, like he did, though at different times of the year from him.

"What is it?" Mother asked again.

"A land box, according to Atça," Trulliç said. He sighed. "The sand has been enchanted. It's as if the desert, or the spirit of the desert, lives still in this sand."

Mother nodded. "I can feel it. It soothes my heart, my aching bones."

Trulliç blinked. He'd never really thought about his mother having aches and pains like an old person.

But his mother wasn't young anymore. Gray streaks ran through her long black hair. Wrinkles gathered around her eyes. Her knuckles were obvious, the skin seemingly thinner now across the backs of her hands, showing blue veins as well.

"Where did you get this? Did Atça make it for you?" Mother asked.

Trulliç shook his head. "Yerkoyliç, the magician in Çandekili, had made it." He grimaced. "You can't tell anyone about the box," he warned. "The emperor has forbidden them."

"Ah," Mother said, nodding. "What do you intend to do with it?"

"I must release the sands in the desert," Trulliç said. "To just break the box and dump them out anywhere else would be foolish."

Mother nodded. "What happens when you place your glass horseshoe in the box?"

Trulliç blinked, surprised. "I never thought of doing that."

"Try it," Mother said.

Slowly, Trulliç undid the glass horseshoe that always hung from his belt. The glass felt cool and smooth in his hand as always.

Gingerly, Trulliç reached into the box, laying the horseshoe down on the sand.

Nothing happened.

Trulliç looked up at Mother. "Nothing," he told her.

Her face fell.

Trulliç bit his lips together. He couldn't help being such a poor magician, such a disappointing son.

Then Trulliç reached back into the box, grasping the horseshoe again.

He gasped.

There, just at the corner of his vision, he could see that same town he'd seen earlier that day. With desert all around it, though it wasn't centered in the desert. The desert ended nearby.

Tall, square pillars made up the corners of the town's walls. Many of the buildings were square as well. Golden sand-colored stones made up the walls. Flags and banners flew from the top of every roof, in every color imaginable. Finely paved streets ran between the houses and through the markets, not straight but as curved as the desert winds, with dates and figs growing in the gardens. Great statues of dogs guarded the gates.

"What is it?" Mother asked.

"I think I know where my home is," Trulliç said eagerly. He described what he saw.

Mother shook her head and gave a bitter laugh, then she quoted:

"In Osmerli you will die—in front of buildings of colored sand
From each roof banners fly—like wings of birds sailing from a
mighty hand."

Trulliç put his hand over his mouth. "No," he whispered, shocked. But she was right.

The poem was from the times of the old kings. When their greatest warriors went to battle against the emperor. When had Mother learned it?

The emperor had laid waste to the entire area, causing a sandstorm to swallow the grand city whole, calling rock out of the earth to choke off the Pirazizil River that fed the oasis.

The city had been located at the southern tip of the Qaenev desert. The emperor had crossed the entire desert in a day to battle the old kings.

"But I see it," Trulliç told her. He grasped the glass horseshoe tighter in his hand. "I know where it is." That was probably why he'd never found his home. He'd needed to travel much, much further across the sands.

Mother nodded. "Do you believe this to be your home?" she asked quietly.

Trulliç answered her honestly. "I don't know. I've seen the city now, twice. But I've seen so many places in the desert." So many secret spots that also called to his heart.

"You should go to Osmerli, then," she told him.

"Will the emperor let me raise the city again?" Trulliç asked.

Mother gave him a tight smile. "His blood hound enabled your birth. I think he would have you make your city."

Trulliç didn't know how to answer that. Didn't know how to respond when she added, "And I will join you there."

Though Trulliç had a better idea where his home in the desert might be, he still thought that Atça's idea of finding a guide was a good one.

The Qaenev desert was huge. Though the emperor crossed it in a day, it would take them most of an entire season. And luck would have to be on their side, with good water and no storms.

How could Trulliç prepare for such a journey? Would he have to cross over the top of the Qaenev desert first, to the far east, then down the ridge of mountains there, keeping to the coast, and then cross over again into the desert when he got to the far south? It was the only way that he knew would work. Though the mountains to the east of Qaenev weren't small or easy to cross, the ones to the west and along the coast there, were known as being particularly foreboding.

It would take a long, long while to get there. But Trulliç was determined to at least have a guide for the first part of the journey, across the wide top of the desert. Then he'd find a second one after he'd made his way to the tip of the continent.

It hurt that he no longer had a decent pack. That he'd lost his sheepskin and sleeping roll.

But if he was going to be gone for a very long while, he could just take everything from his home.

He didn't know how he'd pay for such a long journey. But maybe he could work with one of the caravans that traveled the coast, from north to south.

As long as he managed to stay away from the slave ships that ran there.

Trulliç walked with his mother into the Horseshoe Tavern early that morning. He left the land box in the shack, trusting that no one would bother it. Though his mother had some sort of affinity for the box, he didn't believe anyone else in all of Gaadiwala would take a second look at it.

Not unless Atça told them of it.

As Trulliç would at least tell his mentor that he was searching for the desert heart, he didn't think Atça would turn on him. Would report him to the emperor's guards for holding contraband.

At least, not yet.

Trulliç's cousins seemed happy to see him, demanding to know of his adventures along the road. They'd all heard the news about Çandekili, and Yerkoyliç.

The speculation was that the emperor had had the magician assassinated, that one of the blood hounds had done it. Strange dogs had been seen roaming the palace just before the magician's death.

Trulliç managed to contain himself and not look at Riyune.

The dog maintained an innocent air that Trulliç didn't quite believe.

Trulliç spent the day working at the tavern, cleaning the old attic and carting barrels with his cousin Bekbel.

It wasn't until later that night, after supper, that Trulliç saw her.

It wasn't uncommon for star sisters to stay at the Horseshoe Tavern. Generally they traveled as a group, in twos and threes, but it wasn't uncommon for one to be traveling by herself.

The star sister who sat alone appeared to be about his age. She had a small nose, thin lips, and dark brown eyes. Her hair was short, shorter than most—cut far above her neck. She didn't bother wearing a headscarf inside, though it sat bunched up on the table next to her, a lovely dark green color with gold thread running through it. She wore a tunic similar to his own, dyed a light, golden-sand color with dark stripes of black and blue running through it. It was done in the southern style, open all the way down the front, merely tied together at the waist with a brown leather belt as wide as his outstretched hand.

She had knives in her belt, of course. And probably other places as well.

Trulliç could tell she was a powerful illusionist. She practically glowed with power.

And with dark rage.

He nearly didn't go up to talk with her. She had a thunderous air that warned off most. The other diners at the tavern sat away from her, farther along the rough benches, giving her a wide space.

"Can I get you anything?" Trulliç asked as he came up.

Stormy eyes glared at him. She considered him for a moment, blinking. "No, magician," she said slowly. "But you are not the town's magician, are you?" she said after another moment.

"I am not," Trulliç said. He took that as good enough of an invitation as any and sat down directly opposite her. "My home is in the desert. Far to the south."

She nodded. "Then what are you doing here?"

Trulliç grimaced. "My family is here. That's my mother," he said, pointing her out. "I'm saying goodbye," he added, realizing that it was true. This was probably one of the last nights that he'd be here. "I'm looking for a guide."

"Guide?" the woman asked, puzzled.

"Someone to lead me across the top of the desert," Trulliç said. "The sands…they tend to confuse me," he admitted.

"I see," the woman said, nodding, though she still looked perplexed.

"I know the star sisters sometimes guide the caravans across the sands," Trulliç added.

She gave him a tight smile. "And you'd like to hire me?"

Trulliç nodded and held his breath.

The star sister's anger flared for a moment, then damped right back down again. She quoted him a price.

Trulliç swallowed. That was a lot of coin.

But he didn't have to agree to the price. He'd let Atça bargain with her. All he did was say, "Let me take you to my mentor. He'll be the one paying."

She nodded once at him. Held her hands out, palms open, the way the desert people greeted each other.

"I am Nadeem."

It surprised Trulliç how tall Nadeem was when she stood beside him. She'd seemed shorter when she'd been sitting. Then again, she'd been hunched over her tea, as if she was one of his aunts trying to keep warm during the winter.

Nadeem stopped when she saw Riyune come up next to Trulliç. She looked for a moment at the dog, then at Trulliç, then back again. "What is that?" she asked.

"He's my familiar," Trulliç said.

"No, he isn't," Nadeem said.

Trulliç blinked, surprised. "How do you know?" he asked.

Nadeem looked between them again. "There's no connection between you," she said after a bit. "If he was your familiar, I should be able to see some sort of ties or something. But there's nothing."

"So he just looks like a normal dog?" Trulliç asked, curious. Yerkoyliç had certainly believed him when he'd said that Riyune was his familiar.

Nadeem shook her head. "That isn't a normal dog."

"Do you see him as magical?" Trulliç asked. Maybe Atça was wrong!

"No, not really," Nadeem said. "He casts a strong shadow," she eventually added.

Trulliç didn't understand what that meant.

"He sits there, like a regular dog," Nadeem told him. "But the shadow he casts is extra strong. And long."

Trulliç vowed to look carefully at Riyune's shadow the next day in the bright sunlight. He'd never noticed such a thing.

He didn't know what that meant.

"So what oasis are you from?" Trulliç asked as they left the tavern together.

Nadeem looked at him strangely. "Why do you think I grew up at an oasis?" she asked.

Trulliç bit down his apology. He was *not* being fanciful. He knew it. Instead, he shrugged. "You have that look. That feel," he said. "Of a desert person."

Nadeem nodded. "So do you," she said. "I grew up in Lhadara, to the east."

Trulliç knew she lied. The Lhadara oasis was too small to support a *kabil* of star sisters.

He didn't question her, though.

He had enough secrets of his own. Like the land box that sat beside his sleeping pallet covered with blankets in the shack he shared with his mother. He could *feel* it. Not as loudly as the desert when he stayed near her. But loud enough that he no longer worried about someone taking the box. Even if it was stolen, he'd still know where to find it.

He did wonder, though, if she'd grown up in the Kardeş oasis. It was rumored that a large *kabil* of star sisters lived there and kept it permanently hidden.

He'd dreamed of it once, which was the only way he'd known about it.

Twilight was just starting, casting a purple hue to the sky. Stars had started to come out to the east. The moon was already halfway through its journey, just a sliver, almost new.

People in Gaadiwala looked strangely at Trulliç and Nadeem. Then again, they always did. He could just imagine the gossip already starting back at the tavern. Though if anyone was stupid enough to say anything to his mother, well, they deserved what they got.

"I grew up here," Trulliç told Nadeem. "In Gaadiwala."

"How do you like it?" Nadeem asked him. She seemed actually curious, not just being polite.

"It's difficult," Trulliç admitted, "as a magician, to live in the town of another magician."

Nadeem nodded. "He's not very strong," she said.

Trulliç didn't defend his mentor. "But he's always here," he said instead.

"That makes sense," she said. "And he's the one who will pay my fee?"

"Yes," Trulliç said.

"Determined to get rid of you?" she asked.

Was she teasing him? That sure sounded like something one of his cousins would say.

"You know how it is with mentors," Trulliç said lightly. "Always disappointed no matter how hard you work." He hadn't meant the words to come out as bitter as they'd sounded.

"My mentor..." Nadeem paused for a long moment. "I think she'd be proud of me. But it's complicated."

To that, Trulliç couldn't add anything more.

Atça opened the door wide when Trulliç knocked. He wore one of his striped tunics, gold and red, with a gleaming white shirt and black pants. He looked at Trulliç, then at Nadeem, one eyebrow arching.

"Atça," Trulliç started. "I have found a guide who has agreed to take me through the desert." He didn't bother spilling out the rest of his plan to his mentor.

He would tell Atça later all of what his journey would entail.

Maybe.

"Nadeem, may I introduce Atça, the magician of Gaadiwala," Trulliç said formally. "He is my mentor and has volunteered to pay your fee."

Trulliç didn't bother mentioning any amount. The pair of them could haggle about it.

He wasn't sure which of them would get the better deal.

"Ah, thank you, my son," Atça said. "It is truly an honor to meet one of the star sisters," he said, addressing Nadeem.

"The honor is mine," she murmured.

Trulliç felt himself bristle at her words. She'd used the proper form and the words sounded correct, but they had an edge to them that didn't sound right.

Like she was actually mocking the old man or something.

Atça didn't reply but merely nodded. "Come in, come in," he said, holding the door open wider.

Trulliç let Nadeem enter first.

When he would have followed, Atça held up his hand, stopping Trulliç.

"No," Atça said. "This bargaining should take place without you here. Trust me that she and I will come to a mutual agreement."

With that, Atça shut the door in Trulliç's face.

Trulliç rocked back on his heels. Anger washed over him.

How dare he? It was *his* journey. *His* path across the desert.

But Atça was paying. It was his money.

With a sigh, Trulliç turned away.

Riyune sat in his path for a moment, as if questioning why Trulliç was leaving.

"Come on," Trulliç told the dog. "I'm sure Nadeem will tell us all about it."

Riyune gave Trulliç a classic dog eye-roll, but trotted beside Trulliç as they made their way back to the tavern.

Trulliç knew that Nadeem wouldn't tell him anything that she didn't think was appropriate. The star sisters were very strict about their oaths.

Hopefully, there was nothing about this bargain that she would keep from him.

CHAPTER TWELVE

NADEEM DEPARTED FROM HER SISTERS just before they reached Gaadiwala.

They'd spent the morning walking north from Korbul to maintain their story of three elderly star sisters on a training journey. When they cut back south, they lost their disguises and gave the town a wide berth before finding the trail south again.

Nadeem had kept an illusion around Malik's cane so it appeared to be a stout stick tied to her bag. Though the cane wasn't magical, not in a sense that she understood, it still took to the disguise well. She had to maintain the tiniest thread to hold it in place.

The late afternoon sun warmed her *chafiyek*. She was glad for the scarf's length, protecting her neck. She wore one of her favorite tunics. She'd dyed all the thread to be used before one of the aunts had woven it together: the light, golden-sand color coming from *meslit* bark, the black from the nut of the logwood tree, and the blue from desert crickets.

It wasn't solid in the front but split, held together with her wide belt. She wore a gauzy blouse underneath, thick enough to protect her from the sun but cool enough to let breezes in, as well as a pair of loose, baggy pants instead of a long skirt.

The three of them had been quiet all during their walk. Nadeem led, wondering how she could teach the others to question, if that was even possible. She'd had the advantage of Aunt Parayat her entire life. The others hadn't.

How else had she failed her team?

Would she even to be allowed back into the training camp?

"Nadeem," Gabril called from behind as she neared the crossroads. Just before Gaadiwala the trail split, going roughly in all four directions.

Nadeem stopped and turned back.

Gabril and Durzhen stood shoulder to shoulder just a little ways down the hill.

Would she ever be able to stand like that with them again? Or had she lost her team as well?

"We go on our next assignment from here," Gabril told her.

Nadeem nodded. "I see," she said, though she didn't. Not really.

They'd been given another assignment? More tasks for them to do, before going back to the training camp? Or sent back to their own *kabils*?

Why hadn't she been given another assignment? Aunt Izmet had actually told her to take her time returning. Nadeem had assumed that the others had been told the same thing, that they'd travel together, slowly retracing their footsteps, maybe going off and having an adventure or two along the way.

Instead, the other two were leaving her. She'd have to travel on her own.

It wasn't uncommon for star sisters to travel alone. Still, Nadeem felt as though a sharp blade had severed the ties between them.

Nadeem swallowed down the hurt.

She'd failed them.

She willed away the shock and pain that probably was plainly showing on her face.

"I wish you well, my sisters," Nadeem said, bowing her head low. And she did.

"Much success in your journey, too," Gabril said, also bowing.

"Until we meet at the golden halls, or before," Durzhen added.

So. It was a final goodbye. The last wasn't generally said casually— only when someone was going on a long journey and possibly wouldn't be returning.

"Until then," Nadeem said. She gave them one last bow then deliberately turned her back on them and continued up the hill toward Gaadiwala.

If they were going to attack her they should have done it earlier, before they'd given her any warning.

Now, she'd never trust them again.

Nadeem studied the young man standing in front of her. He was obviously the son of the woman who had served her. He had the same long chin and thin face. But his bulbous nose came from a father from the north, and his eyes weren't as dark as his mother's or his cousin's.

He had power. She'd marked him from the moment she'd stepped into the tavern. She'd never met a magician before.

But this wasn't his home. He seemed rootless. Like a storm billowing and blowing, just looking for a place to strike.

He was as tall as she was, though a bit younger. He might grow taller still.

She was surprised when he invited himself to her table and sat down. She'd deliberately given off an air of *don't touch*. It had been remarkably effective.

But he also had power and so wasn't automatically scared of hers.

It puzzled her that he was looking for a guide. When he said that he was from the desert, that his home was in the desert, everything came together. That storm he carried. The dry winds.

Why would he get lost in the desert? It didn't make any sense. How could it overwhelm someone who was a native? Even if he'd been raised in the town? Surely it was close enough that he'd visited. Why had he never found his feet?

The dog, Riyune, didn't make sense either. He was like the cane she carried, tied to her pack. Not quite what he seemed.

He wasn't a familiar. Though Nadeem had never met another magician or seen a familiar, Riyune didn't belong to anyone other than himself.

His shadow was as strong as he was. Even in the dim light of the evening, it walked beside him. Nadeem didn't understand how or why, but just told Trulliç honestly what she saw.

Trulliç led her to the house of the town's magician, Atça.

The old man had a miserly soul, more grasping than Aunt Haneet.

This had been the man who'd raised Trulliç. Responsible for teaching him. Mentoring him.

Suddenly, Trulliç's inability to find his own feet in the desert made a lot more sense.

———

Nadeem took off her sandals as requested by the old man. He wore a striped tunic similar to her own, though his stripes were wider, and the colors of the goddess Barzhat, blue and black.

She looked around the front hallway. She'd never seen so much wood in one place before.

Instead of impressing her, it made her question why more trees didn't grow in Gaadiwala. Couldn't they get the water? But surely Atça should have been able to raise it.

The hallway leading to the back of the house made Nadeem put a hand on her knife at her waist. Spiders lived there in the corners of the ceiling, spiders she couldn't see but felt, nonetheless.

The formal sitting room that Atça led Nadeem to had more wood, of course. Shelves covered in scrolls that she wished she could ask about. This miser would collect fascinating things, of that she was certain.

Atça directed Nadeem to sit in the place of honor. Nadeem took it without the usual dance of initially refusing.

It wasn't that she was in a hurry to get out of this place. But a way of indicating to Atça that yes, she was that much further above him. Her rank was indeed that much higher, that she should naturally take the place of honor.

"Have you been enjoying your time in my town?" Atça asked after he served what Nadeem had to admit was a fine cup of tea. His tea service was made from polished silver, ornate and obviously not from the region.

"I'm just passing through," Nadeem told him. She'd really only seen the tavern, as well as walking in and out of the town. She remembered her initial impressions of Gaadiwala, how poor it seemed despite the fact that they had a magician.

Her opinion hadn't changed.

"Trulliç asked for me to be a guide for him across the desert," Nadeem said after a moment. She knew that she should spend more time inquiring after her host's health.

She didn't have the patience for that.

But Atça just nodded. "Yes," he said slowly. "Tell me, what do you think of that poor boy?"

Nadeem opened her mouth and shut it again. It was one thing to tweak the town magician's nose.

It was another to tell him to his face just how poorly she thought of him and his teaching.

"He's lost," she said honestly. "Still searching for himself."

"I agree," Atça said. "And dangerous, too," he added. "Did you hear about Çandekili? There's a rumor that Trulliç actually killed the magician there."

"Ah," Nadeem said, nodding as if she had, though she hadn't.

She was pretty certain that the rumor had started with Atça, and that he would spread it far and wide.

"I'm worried about the boy," Atça confessed.

Nadeem merely smiled at him, encouraging him, instead of snorting in laughter.

Of course Atça was worried about Trulliç.

Trulliç was a more powerful magician than Atça, though the boy didn't know it, and Atça wasn't ever going to admit it. This "mentor" had probably told the boy often enough that he was a pitiful excuse for a magician, specifically so he'd never find his true power.

"He's a danger, not just to himself but to others as well," Atça said.

Reluctantly, Nadeem agreed. Trulliç was a storm waiting to happen, lightning looking for a post to strike.

"You know, it might be better if Trulliç didn't return from the desert," Atça said.

Nadeem blinked, surprised. "And what would you suggest I do?" she asked.

A vague hint about death was never enough, not for a star sister. If she was to take another assignment, another blood oath, then it needed to be spelled out. And then judged whether the death would be right or not.

"I'm sure you can take care of it," Atça said breezily with a wave of his hand.

"If there's something you actually want me to do, you need to tell me outright," Nadeem said. "Otherwise…there's too much room for misinterpretation."

Atça paled and swallowed hard.

Nadeem retained the silence. Either let the fool say what needed to be said or this job would pass, too.

"Trulliç needs to die," the old man finally whispered.

There it was.

Nadeem nodded, thinking it through. Aunt Parayat had told her that others would approach her, asking her to enact their petty vengeance.

She did not have to fulfill any request someone made, particularly when it came to taking a life. It was always up to her whether or not to do such a deed.

Did she agree with Atça that Trulliç needed to die? Was he that much of a danger?

She'd seen the wild look in his eyes. How tightly wound his power was. That strange dog whose eyes were the color of the sky.

Trulliç had been raised by a bitter old man who hadn't taught him to think, hadn't taught him grace, hadn't taught him anything but grasping control.

An old man who probably gave out punishment before teaching the moral of any lesson.

Yes, Trulliç would explode one day if he never found his feet.

"What if he finds his home?" Nadeem asked. That would probably settle Trulliç down, though she didn't know. She'd never dealt with magicians before.

Atça gave a dramatic shudder. "That would be worse."

"Why?" Nadeem asked.

"I only raised him for this long because I thought I could help him," Atça whined. "But he's gotten headstrong recently. Independent. Started listening to trouble makers." Atça leaned over and said urgently. "He's no longer loyal to the emperor."

Nadeem blinked, surprised. Trulliç didn't strike her as the type of young man who would lead a rebellion.

"He's going to find the desert heart," Atça continued. At Nadeem's questioning look, Atça added, "A very powerful artifact. I was the one who told him the legends of it, thinking that he could gift it to the emperor. But he's determined to use that power all on his own. It's why he wants to go to the tip of the desert. He claims his home is there, but he'll never find that either."

Atça seemed pleased that Trulliç wouldn't find his home, of course. He would never wish for another to be happy or productive. That wasn't his way.

"These are grave charges," Nadeem said. "I cannot just take your word on it. Not when a life hangs in the balance." Though she might have failed her first assignment, that didn't mean she'd take another, an easy job, without question.

That seemed to throw Atça off. "But you must!" he insisted. "The boy needs to be dealt with."

Nadeem believed that. Atça wanted the boy out of the way. And Trulliç might truly become a danger someday.

"All right," Nadeem said slowly. "If I determine that Trulliç is false, then he shall die by my hand."

Nadeem pulled out the knife in the sheath at the center of her back. It had an obsidian blade that was brittle and would break or chip easily against bones or a hard blow.

But it was also her sharpest knife, and the one traditionally used in a blood oath.

Nadeem held out her right hand, the knife steady in her left.

Slowly, Atça held his own right hand out.

Nadeem didn't smile at him. It wasn't necessary for her to take his blood as part of the oath. However, most outsiders didn't know that.

And this was a serious enough matter, the taking of a life, that Nadeem felt Atça's blood should be on the line as well.

Nadeem drew a swift line across Atça's palm. The blood beaded up immediately. Then she cut her own hand.

Before Atça could draw back, Nadeem intertwined their fingers and pressed their bleeding palms together.

"As our blood mingles, so shall our will and our words," Nadeem said formally. "I swear by the blood that this shall be done."

Atça stayed perfectly still for a long moment before he finally nodded.

"So shall it be," he intoned.

"Good," Nadeem said. She released Atça's hand and licked off her palm, just to watch the look of disgust cross his face while he struggled to be polite.

"Now, let's talk price," Nadeem told him as she picked up her tea.

Nadeem's blood oath weighed heavily on her soul. Had she just committed to foolishness?

Atça could now claim a blood oath with all the star sisters. He couldn't twist the words of the oath—there was power in the blood. If he claimed the oath, going to another star sister to get her to fulfill it, they would know exactly what she had promised to do.

Of course, Atça didn't realize that. He would claim that she promised something else.

Anyone he went to would straighten him out immediately, however, so Nadeem wasn't worried.

She spent the evening at the tavern watching Trulliç. Surely Atça was twisting the truth when he talked about Trulliç being a rebel, no longer loyal to the emperor.

Yet, when the evening prayer was said before the meal thanking the emperor for his bounty, Trulliç grimaced and didn't even bother to mouth the words, while the others spoke fervently around him.

They were to leave the next morning. It was obvious to Nadeem that Trulliç was saying goodbye to people that he didn't expect he'd see again.

His cousins, aunts, and uncles, however, didn't appear to have the same understanding. They all thought he was just taking another short trip into the desert.

Trulliç arranged with Nadeem to meet her in the early morning at the tavern. He arrived before the dawn when the world was still gray and indistinct. The cool air wouldn't last. They'd get to the Ladikah pass by noon and would stay there for the rest of the day, not traveling down the far side of the Kinarak mountains until the next morning.

They would camp on the far side of the mountains overnight and wait there through much of the day as well, not traveling across the desert until it was cooler in the evening.

They could, of course, just stick to the border and not cross desert sands at all. That would take much more time, however. And though Atça had paid Nadeem generously—much more money than he'd wanted to— he hadn't paid for her to take an extra month of travel.

Trulliç carried a strange box, each side a little bigger than his large, outstretched hands. It was wooden, well made, and enchanted.

When Nadeem looked at it, then up at him, he shook his head mutely.

After they'd left Gaadiwala, Trulliç said, "It's a land box. It was made by Yerkoyliç, the magician from Çandekili."

"What's it for?" Nadeem asked. She'd never heard of a land box before.

Trulliç stopped and turned, floating the box over to her.

Nadeem stiffened. She'd never seen Trulliç do magic. Yet it came effortlessly to him.

It made sense that his magic was more powerful out of Gaadiwala, where it no longer was overshadowed by Atça's.

And they were closer to the desert as well.

Inside the box lay sand. Desert sand.

How did the box hold essence of the desert? Nadeem marveled and reached in.

Though the morning was still cool, the sand held in the heat of baked sands.

"Yerkoyliç created it so he could look for the desert heart," Trulliç said casually.

"You took it from him," Nadeem said, looking back up at Trulliç to watch his face.

"I did," Trulliç said gravely.

Nadeem blinked, surprised.

It seemed Atça was correct.

Trulliç had killed Yerkoyliç. But why?

"And now you're looking for the desert heart?" she asked.

Trulliç grimaced at that. He still responded, "I am."

"Tell me about it," Nadeem said as Trulliç gathered the box back to himself.

Trulliç nodded and turned, walking again. As he walked he recited one of the great poems about the birth of the world, Forit's death, the tears of the gods creating all people.

Nadeem fell into an easy step behind him. He had a good voice for telling stories, a nice rhythm, and was interesting to listen to.

After he finished the poem, he told her of the legends, of how Forit's heart still existed in the desert, purified of the darkness. Of how the emperor wanted this heart. Of how the magicians were also trying to find it.

"And you?" Nadeem asked after a moment. "What would you do if you found this heart?"

Trulliç gave a bitter laugh. "I don't know," he said softly. "Leave it where it is, if I can."

Nadeem nodded and didn't ask any more.

Possibly Atça was correct about that as well—that Trulliç was no longer one hundred percent loyal to the emperor either.

She watched Trulliç stop on the border between the foothills of the Kinarak mountains and the true desert.

Deep purple sky spread out over the dark sands. The heat from the day still rose from the baked earth. Stars peeked out at them, the moon just new.

"Why are you stopping?" Nadeem asked Trulliç.

"This is the border, here, between the scrub and the sand," he said.

Nadeem came to stand beside him. They'd had a good travel day. They'd learned many of the same epic poems and battles. Nadeem's favorite story was also Lyons, the one who'd raised a stone eagle from the stone egg. She'd gotten the inspiration for her favorite illusionary fighter from him.

She looked carefully at the earth where Trulliç pointed. She didn't see the difference between the two lands. It wasn't fully sand, it wasn't merely scrub, but a combination of the two.

A lizard popped up nearby, then scurried and dove for another hole in the ground when it realized it wasn't alone.

"Here?" she asked, stepping across the border.

Trulliç nodded mournfully.

"You can come across," Nadeem told him.

He looked like an addict, hungering for his next drink. She'd seen a few—aunts who needed their nightly *igrat*. They didn't tend to live long once they'd reached that stage.

"It will be all right," Nadeem said softly, though she didn't know for certain what would happen once Trulliç stepped onto the sands.

She put her hand on her right hip, wrapping her fingers around the hilt of the knife there.

He wouldn't attack her, would he?

He'd be surprised at just how fast she could move if he did.

With a shuddering sigh, Trulliç stepped across the border.

Nadeem saw the change immediately.

Trulliç had always been about her height. She now realized that he constantly hunched his shoulders. Suddenly, he stood up straight and tall, and probably had at least two inches on her.

His shoulders broadened as well. Instead of a boy, a man now stood in front of her.

A powerful man.

His dog, too, transformed, though the change was more subtle. He grew more spindle-legged and gaunt, like a feral dog. All his features grew sharper as well, his nose longer and more angular, his ears more pointed, his tail thinner and shaped like a blade.

Trulliç looked at Nadeem and smiled. "You glow like the moon," he said softly, "though with more colors. Light blue and pink. Luminous."

Nadeem wondered if the aura he saw had come from the *ağrikat* shells.

"This way," Trulliç said, turning and walking east.

The box now floated behind him, tagging along like a lonely, dark cloud. The magic from it had spiked as well.

Trulliç's feet barely touched the sand as he glided along. When he looked down, he stopped, making an effort to walk normally. But as soon as he lost focus, he glided again, like a desert wind. Nadeem would have to run to keep up with him if he didn't slow down.

He'd be able to go miles and miles at that pace and never tire. He looked as though the very sands fed him.

Nadeem shook her head, confused at the change. It was obvious to her that he belonged here.

Then she thought for a moment.

Atça.

Trulliç had asked Atça about his true home.

And Atça had lied to him.

"Wait," Nadeem finally said as Trulliç raced ahead.

He looked back. Even in the dim light she saw his guilt.

"I just…wander when I get here," he said as he came back. "That's why I needed you for a guide."

Nadeem shook her head. "Tell me the real reason why you're looking for the desert heart," she said.

Trulliç blinked, surprised.

"If it's here, if it exists, it belongs here," he said plainly.

"Even if the emperor is looking for it? Even if he wants it?" she pressed.

Trulliç bit his lips together and looked away for a moment, then looked directly back at her, his eyes boring into hers.

"He can't have it," Trulliç said. "It's mine." Then he gave a bitter laugh. "It isn't as though I'll be able to find it," he added. "I can't even find my true home."

Nadeem shook her head.

She didn't have to tell him. She shouldn't. She'd sworn a blood oath to end his life if he was not loyal to the emperor.

But the emperor had had her destroy a town. Probably to create slaves of its people.

He wanted an army of fanatics like Aunt Izmet.

Not questioning thinkers like Aunt Parayat.

"What is it?" Trulliç asked.

It was so obvious. Anyone would be able to see it.

Anyone but a student of Atça's.

Riyune stared hard at Nadeem. It also seemed that he, too, wanted her to say something.

If the dog could have spoken, he would have said something.

Nadeem beckoned Trulliç closer. She held out her right hand to him.

Puzzled, Trulliç held out his hand in return. It felt hard and hot in hers, like a rough rock baked long in the sun.

"Don't you see?" Nadeem asked, gesturing in front of her, at the sand, the wide open space before them, the stars spilling across the heavens, the sand reflecting the faint glow.

"See what?" Trulliç asked.

"This is your home," Nadeem told him.

Trulliç automatically shook his head. "No," he said. "Atça said—"

"Atça hired me to kill you," Nadeem told him. She kept their fingers intertwined, but opened up the palms, so he could see the cut that had nearly healed. "He wanted you dead before you figured out that your home is the entire Qaenev desert."

"No," Trulliç said. He sounded heartbroken. "It can't be! How could I live here? What is there to eat?"

"Are you hungry?" Nadeem asked seriously.

"No?" Trulliç asked, sounding uncertain. "But surely I still need water."

"What direction is the closest water?" Nadeem asked.

Trulliç automatically pointed.

"You see?" she said.

"But—" Trulliç stopped when Riyune came up and butted his head against his other hand. He shivered, hard.

The land box thumped, falling to the ground.

"The desert *is* my home," Trulliç whispered. "It's always been my home."

"Your home is the entire desert," Nadeem told him again. "All of this."

Trulliç nodded, his eyes still staring off into the distance. "I can feel it. All of it. The borders. The sands." He paused and turned to her. "The Kardeş oasis of the star sisters."

Nadeem stiffened. How did he know of that?

Of course. Her home was now part of his property, the area he controlled.

No wonder Atça wanted Trulliç killed. Particularly if he was no longer loyal to the emperor.

"My city is in the south," Trulliç said. His voice still sounded as though he talked in a dream. "Osmerli," he added.

The city of the old kings. Before the coming of the emperor, over two hundred years before.

"Go," Nadeem said, releasing his hand.

"But—" Trulliç turned back to her, though she could tell it was already calling him, his body listing to the south.

"Go," Nadeem told him gently. "I'll be here when you return," she lied.

She knew that if she placed a single foot on the sand, he would be able to find her. She would have to leave the desert, and soon, if she wanted to hide from him.

Trulliç turned away, then turned back. He took both of her hands in his and kissed the fingertips softly. "Thank you," he said. "If you hadn't told me…if you hadn't insisted on it, I might never have figured it out."

She nodded. Of course he wouldn't have been able to figure it out. She hadn't spent that much time in the presence of men, but it seemed to her that most couldn't see beyond the tip of their noses.

"Thank you," he said again. Then he disappeared, his dog a white blur behind him.

Nadeem stood alone in the desert, just the land box beside her.

She knew that he ran to the south to raise his great city. It would be a marvelous sight, the pillars rising out of the sand. That soon caravans would make it a regular stop. The star sisters, too, would come to pay homage.

Before the emperor attacked.

In the meanwhile, Nadeem had her own work to do.

Nadeem paused, blade in her hand. The moon lifted its face high above the desert, though it didn't shed much light. She knelt comfortably, admitting that she'd not be able to do this standing, not by herself.

If she was truly brave enough, she'd take her own life. She'd betrayed the emperor, failed at her first assignment, then broken a blood oath to take the life of one who would oppose the emperor. She'd failed her sisterhood, failed in her dreams.

She could no longer call herself a star sister.

But she wasn't ready to dance in Barzhat's golden court. Not yet.

Plus, she had too many questions that Aunt Parayat had to answer.

Nadeem kissed the tip of the blade, then put it against her left cheek. With a steady hand, she sliced open the star that her aunt had cut there. Her greatest pride. Her mark of sisterhood.

Nadeem didn't know how many cuts she needed. She couldn't cut the star out of her cheek. That, too, would be against the wishes of the emperor.

But she could scar it. Make it hard to identify. Destroy the symmetry of it, the delicate lines, until all that was left was a mess of lines.

Tears streamed down Nadeem's face as she cut away her identity.

Finally, when her hand shook with the pain and effort, she reached down and grabbed a handful of sand from the land box. Then she pushed the hard grains against her burning cheek.

The first time her cheek had been cut, the magic of the *ağrikat* shells had been pushed in.

Now, she took on the magic of the desert.

The world exploded as the sand sank into her blood.

And Nadeem dreamed.

GODS AND GODDESSES

The goddess of death lives beneath the great inner sea of the Tanesh empire. She sits in judgment of the dead on her throne encrusted with pearls and shells. In front of her is a huge golden court, full of souls dancing.

Every bad deed a person commits while they are living is weighed by Barzhat after they die. She creates a black vest covered with golden weights, each shaped like a teardrop. You must dance before Barzhat until all the weights fall from the vest. Only then will Barzhat give you the final kiss of true death, cleansing your soul for rebirth.

A common curse: May you dance forever in the goddess' court.

The star sister Manisat picked up an *ağrikat* shell on the shore of the Barzhat Sea. When she raised the shell to her ear, she heard the sad sighs of the goddess Barzhat and realized how lonely the goddess was. Manisat had made her way to the goddess' golden court while she'd still been alive and had promised the goddess that the star sisters wouldn't merely venerate her, but love her. They would welcome the goddess at all their feasts, big and small. A bowl was always left empty at every meal, a welcome place for the goddess.

Barzhat tests the sisters sometimes, coming for dinner as a stranger. They must show her hospitality or she will make them dance. However, in return for a star sister's devotion, Barzhat will grant her a single boon during her lifetime, if her need is great enough.

Though cutting across the Barzhat Sea would make travel from one end of the empire to the other faster, no one sails across it regularly. Men can only travel on the waters at her indulgence. Sailors must always be on the lookout when in her territory. If the waters are clear and blue, they can travel freely. If the waters turn black, they run. Otherwise, the goddess takes them down into her golden court where they must dance for centuries.

The goddess is always depicted with two faces, one blue and one black. The blue face is used for judgment. The black face is used for death. She is often called fickle, and is temperamental, as are all artists. She is often shown with four dancing legs and twelve arms, each holding a different weapon.

Symbol: Feet. Also represented by a single line toward the bottom of the space, ____

Colors: Blue and Black.

Innis

The god of fertility lives in the court of the gods. He is forever mourning his beautiful wife, Forist, whom he killed in the great battle with the darkness, and from whom all humanity came. He is known as a dark, somber god. Brining a new life into the world isn't to be done lightly.

Symbol: The spear. Represented by a single horizontal line —

Colors: Red

Serrat/Serril

The goddess/god of desolate places lives in the desert.

Like Barzhat, Serrat/Serril has two faces, a female and a male face. The male aspect (Serril) is worshiped by the land magicians, while the female aspect (Serrat) is honored by the star sisters.

Serrat/Serril is known as a trickster god. He/she leads men and caravans astray in the desert by creating fake oases. He/she also tricks sailors by making Barzhat's waters seem calm.

Yet, Serrat/Serril just wants to be loved.

Originally, Serrat/Serril lived in the court of the gods. However, the gods banished the god/goddess after he brought magic to man. Serril, in his male form, made a bet with the goddess Onnet, that a mighty human hunter could out shoot the goddess and her bow. In order for the hunter to win, Serril gave the human magic.

As Serrat, the goddess has a birthmark in the form of a star on her left cheek, which is why the star sisters carve one in theirs. However, she isn't much loved by them. (They love Berzhat instead.)

Symbol: Z

Colors: White (for Serrat) and black (for Serril)

Enkat

The goddess of rain lives in the court of the gods. She dances for the gods and goddess until the sweat pours from her and drips down from her hair to the earth as rain.

In the desert lands, Enkat is often portrayed as a female form with no face, just hair streaming down everywhere.

Symbol: Represented by three vertical lines. | | |

Colors: Brown and green

Xannil

The god of the sun lives in the court of the gods. In the north, Xannil is often portrayed as a fair-haired, happy god. In the south, he's shown as a darker, sullen, sadistic god. He is married to Enket. Stories tell of how jealous he gets. When he's in a rage, he hides her or sends her away so there's no rain. In addition, Xannil is also jealous of Enket's brother, Innis, the god of fertility. They are forever trying to best each other in drinking contests and wrestling matches, often with disastrous results. Serrat/Serril is usually called to come and fix whatever has been broken.

Symbol: Three horizontal lines.

Color: Yellow

Onnet

The goddess of childbirth and the hunt lives in the court of the gods, though she is often away, traveling, hunting.

Onnet is often portrayed as a crone, though she can take the form of a golden goddess as well. She aids women in childbirth and through their pregnancy. She has a magical bow and can shoot down any prey, no matter how far away. She also uses her bow and magical arrows to bring couples together. There are many stories of young men and women who are great hunters and shoot an arrow into the air, vowing to marry the person who finds it, who after many trials does turn out to be their one true love.

Symbol: Omega. Often represented by a horseshoe.

Color: Orange and green

Creation Myth

In the beginning, there were just the gods and goddesses and no light. Darkness reached everywhere. The gods and goddesses fought with each other all the time just to bring some sort of activity to their endless nights.

So Xannil, the god of the sun, created the first light, which the darkness stole away. He created a second light, which the darkness stole again.

After the third light had been stolen, the gods declared war against the darkness. The darkness divided itself into many beings to fight the gods. The battles raged across the heavens for eons.

Forit, Innis' wife and the fairest of the gods, sang such a beautiful song that the darkness revealed its heart. Innis pierced the heart with his great spear, killing the darkness.

However, the only way Forit could draw out the heart of the darkness was by binding it with her own. When Innis killed the heart of the darkness, he killed his own wife as well.

Forit's body fell from the court of the gods and became the earth. Her teeth became the mountains, her fingers became the many rivers, and the place where her heart had been became the desert.

As the gods and goddesses grieved the loss of the fairest of them all, their tears fell on her prone body.

Forit's freckles, the only imperfection about her, became humanity. The darker freckles became the people of the south, the lighter blemishes became the people of the north.

There are some myths that her heart, still bound with the heart of darkness, lives in the center of the desert.

ABOUT THE AUTHOR

Leah Cutter writes page-turning, wildly imaginative fiction in exotic locations, such as a magical New Orleans, the ancient Orient, Hungary, the Oregon coast, rural Kentucky, Seattle, Minneapolis, and many others.

She writes literary, fantasy, mystery, science fiction, and horror fiction. Her short fiction has been published in magazines like Alfred Hitchcock's Mystery Magazine and Talebones, anthologies like Fiction River, and on the web. Her long fiction has been published both by New York publishers as well as small presses.

Find Leah's books here.

Follow her blog at www.LeahCutter.com.

Never miss a release!

If you'd like to be notified of new releases, sign up for my newsletter.

I only send out newsletters once a quarter, will never spam you, or use your email for nefarious purposes. You can also unsubscribe at any time.

http://www.leahcutter.com/newsletter/

Reviews

It's true. Reviews help me sell more books. If you've enjoyed this story, please consider leaving a review of it on your favorite site.

ABOUT KNOTTED ROAD PRESS

Knotted Road Press fiction specializes in dynamic writing set in mysterious, exotic locations.

Knotted Road Press non-fiction publishes autobiographies, business books, cookbooks, and how-to books with unique voices.

Knotted Road Press creates DRM-free ebooks as well as high-quality print books for readers around the world.

With authors in a variety of genres including literary, poetry, mystery, fantasy, and science fiction, Knotted Road Press has something for everyone.

Knotted Road Press
www.KnottedRoadPress.com